MONSTROUS SOULS

REBECCA KELLY

AGORA BOOKS

ABOUT THE AUTHOR

Rebecca Kelly was brought up with books but denied the pleasure of a television. Although she hated this at the time, she now considers it to have contributed to a life-long passion for reading and writing.

After a misspent education, Rebecca had a variety of jobs. She's spent the last years raising her children but has lately returned to her first love — writing.

Rebecca lives in the UK with her husband and youngest son and an over-enthusiastic black Labrador, who gives her writing tips.

🐦 twitter.com/RKellyAuthor1

debut novel is one well worth reading!' — Anita Frank, author of *The Lost Ones*

'*Monstrous Souls* will suck you in and not let go until you've dashed to the end.' — Marianne Holmes, author of *A Little Bird Told Me*

'I'm surprised that this is a debut as Kelly is pitch-perfect in the genre, and this book will sit very comfortably alongside the big name thriller writers. In tone, perhaps there is something of Ann Cleeves (only snappier) and Anne Perry (only more subtly realistic). The writing, pacing, and characters are definitely up there with the best in the business.' — Clare Rhoden, author of *The Chronicles of the Pale*

'A literary crime novel that packs a punch!' — Jane Isaac, author of *Before It's Too Late*

'Kelly's prose is gorgeous, and her subject matter is as dark as hell. You won't regret taking a twisted journey with her to get to the truth.' — Laura Pearson, author of *I Wanted You To Know*

'An assured debut: tense and chilling, the author's wonderful turn of phrase sets the scene for a heart-breaking story of regret and friendship lost.' — Louisa de Lange, author of *The Dream Wife*

'*Monstrous Souls* is an excellent, pacy thriller that grabs hold of you from the very first page and doesn't let go until it's thrilling end. I devoured it in one sitting. Rebecca Kelly has certainly found herself a new fan!' — Caz Finlay, author of *The Boss*

MONSTROUS SOULS

SOULS

REBECCA KELLY

First published in Great Britain in 2020 by Agora Books

Agora Books is a division of Peters Fraser + Dunlop Ltd

55 New Oxford Street, London WC1A 1BS

ISBN 978-1-913099-55-8

Printed and bound in Great Britain by Clays Ltd, Elcograf S.p.A.

For my husband, Hugh, who has believed in my writing from the beginning and to my beautiful sons, Thomas and James.

It's the sort of day that you dream of: a blue sky, a hot fist of sun and the sound of bees in clover, yet the air vibrates with unnatural tension. By late afternoon, the blue has a dense, uneasy quality, and wind sighs restlessly through the grasses. In the distance, a gathering of cloud hovers at the edge of the horizon.

It begins to rain, flattening ash on to the scorched grass. Nina lies, one leg bent at the knee — a dancer poised for flight. Her hand, palm up, is curled inward like an upended crab.

As a last curl of smoke dissolves, the sky clears and the blood in Nina's veins thickens, and, it is as if the world, momentarily paused, begins to move on.

2001

DENISE

It's early evening, and Denise is conscious of the rap of her heels against the hospital tiles. The sun, blood red, has stained the walls a dirty pink, and her stomach flutters at the prospect of visiting Heidi. She is tired, and her neck and shoulders throb with tension. The shift had begun at 2 pm, and, because she had been in the area, she was asked to assist at a road traffic inci-dent where she had knelt at the kerbside supporting the upper body of a female driver as the door and roof were removed. The woman had not been injured, but the impact of the acci-dent or sheer opportunistic salesmanship had prompted her to try to sell Denise a new range of make-up designed for black skin, guaranteeing to keep the ravages of age away forever. Because Denise was holding her head and could not justify putting her hand over the woman's mouth, she had effectively been held hostage to the sales pitch for over an hour. Later, she had returned to the squad room to find someone had spilt coffee over the notes she'd spent the previous day compiling. The call to visit Heidi has come late in the afternoon.

Walking beside her is Brenda Carver. Brenda has been a serving officer for over twenty years and will conduct the interview, such as it will be, because the doctors have already advised them that Heidi is still mute. Whenever Heidi's case is mentioned, Denise feels a peculiar sense of inadequacy. This is the first time it has fallen upon Denise to meet Heidi face to face, though she has been involved behind the scenes from the beginning.

At times, she's aware that she has been so engrossed in following leads and going over witness statements that she has lost sight of the victims altogether. But here, in the hospital, with the evening leaking in through the windows, and the peroxide scent barely masking the undernotes of shit and pain and illness, she is filled with the horror of it all. This is worth fighting for, even if the leads seem to be going nowhere, and their only witness is lying injured and without words in a hospital bed.

This case, more than any other, has challenged her general goodwill towards her fellow man. And even though the perpetrator has remained anonymous, she has, over the months, grown to hate him with a passion. She can understand better how it is possible for a member of the police force to mete out punishment behind the locked door of a cell. For weeks she has lived, dreamt, and absorbed the case until, at times, it is all that seems real.

A porter hurries past, pushing a vast trolley piled with hospital supplies, and the wheels rattle and echo like distant thunder. Brenda turns to her, raises her eyebrows wearily, and they wait for the lift doors to open with a clang before arriving on Level Four. Here, they negotiate yet another maze of corridors, hers and Brenda's feet tapping out their individual rhythms, never quite in sync, like amateur tap dancers, until finally, they reach Martindale Ward. Denise feels a swell of anxiety.

"God, you could lose serious weight working here." With a wetted finger, Brenda rubs at a pale spot on her uniform jacket and sighs. She seems unaffected by the forthcoming meeting.

"Is Heidi's mum well enough to attend the interview?" Denise asks.

Brenda shakes her head. "We had to appoint an appropriate adult. Hopefully, she'll be there already."

"Is there no other relative?"

"Not a one. Heidi is quite alone."

The nurse at reception takes them to one side. "There's someone waiting for you over there." She nods to a row of plastic chairs. "I'll call Dr Andrews."

A woman rises from one of the seats, smoothing her skirt.

The ward is quiet. Somewhere a bed creaks and there is the distant ring of a phone. Eventually, a tall, heavyset man emerges from an office beyond and beckons them in.

"You're here to see Heidi Bevan?" The name tag, hanging at an angle, reads *Hilary Andrews*.

"We thought we would try again," Brenda says, reaching for her police identification and then abandoning it with a listless hand.

Dr Andrews frowns. "There's no change, as I explained on the phone, and I think it's highly unlikely that you'll be able to interview her." His face is grim.

"Does she remember anything?"

"If she does, she's not disclosed it. As far as we believe, she has little or no recollection of what happened."

"We have to keep trying."

He shrugs.

"Have you determined yet how bad the brain damage is?" Brenda asks.

Denise gets a sudden, horrifying image of Heidi's battered skull.

Dr Andrews clasps his great hands in front of him. "It's difficult to tell exactly until she's more communicative. There's certainly considerable physical damage, but her virtual muteness makes diagnosis difficult. The psychiatrist believes the emotional trauma could account in a large measure for her reluctance to talk, but, frankly, it's too early to say where physical damage ends and emotional trauma begins. Any progress finding the sister?"

Brenda shakes her head. The ward is warm. A fly buzzes lethargically on the ceiling, hitting the plastic shade of a yellowed strip light as though attempting a slow, repetitive suicide. Sweat trickles inside Denise's shirt and stiff collar.

"Very well." The doctor gets up from his chair.

"How is she in herself?" Denise asks and then feels foolish. She sees Brenda's quizzical look and flushes. "I mean, I know she's..."

Dr Andrew picks up a pen and twiddles it in his thick fingers. "Considering what happened to her, I would say fair. She's strong and has youth and good health on her side. The physical injuries are healing well enough, although it will take a long, long time, and she will need skin grafts. It's a pity her mother's not able to visit. I think it would make a great difference. I'll take you to her."

He leads them through the ward where a clutch of beds support a motley group of patients attached to a variety of equipment. Past here, the corridor reveals several plain white doors.

"Does she know yet about Nina? Has anyone told her?" Denise asks Brenda.

"I don't think so. For now, we are keeping questions to a minimum. I don't think telling her that her best friend died at the scene will help her."

"Nor that her sister is missing," Denise adds, biting down on a spasm of pity.

The doctor pushes one of the white doors open with a squeak, and Denise gets her first glimpse of Heidi. *Jesus Christ*, she thinks.

The small body is swamped by the hospital bed. Above, the part of her face that is not bandaged appears to belong to someone much younger than thirteen. A purplish, angry scar bisects the left temple where the red hair has been shaved and is making patchy attempts at growing back.

With difficulty, Denise swallows her dual reactions of pity and horror. The room is deathly still. A drip is taped to Heidi's wrist, and monitors flicker and tick on the wall behind. On a bedside table, a plastic jug of water sits beside a disposable cup and straw. There are no flowers.

"Hello, Heidi." Dr Andrews gives her a warm smile. Heidi's eyes focus on him, but her small mouth remains firmly closed. "These two policewomen want to talk to you."

Heidi's gaze skims them and then returns to the wall behind.

Brenda sits, tugging her chair closer to the bed. "Hello," her tone is hopeful, "DI Brenda Carver, I came to see you before, remember? And this is DC Denise Gilzeen. As Dr Andrews told you, we're police officers. We're still doing everything we can to find the person who did this to you." For a moment, it looks as if Brenda is going to put out her hand and touch Heidi's arm, but, at the last instant, she withdraws it and tucks it away.

Brenda continues with a series of gentle question, but it's clear that Heidi is not going to respond, and Denise realises that Brenda never really expected her to — that they are just ticking boxes, covering their bases. The silence deepens, and Denise begins to feel uncomfortable — the sight of Heidi's small and damaged face against the white pillow, the heat and dryness of the air, and Brenda's professional distance. It's easier, Denise realises, to chase the villains than to witness their victims. Something squeezes at her heart.

"Heidi, can you look at me?" Brenda asks finally, but Heidi's gaze remains obstinately fixed at some point behind them and at last, Brenda rises, gives a barely audible sigh and stands beside the bed. Denise and Brenda exchange glances.

"We'll say goodbye for now," Brenda says cheerfully, "but we'll come again when you're feeling a bit better. Try not to worry. You're safe now." There is more left unsaid than said.

"Goodbye." Denise's voice sounds rusty, and, just briefly, Heidi's gaze flicks over, appraising her, and Denise catches a flicker of intelligence, like a light suddenly illuminated beneath murky water. It gives her a strange sense that Heidi is conscious of more than she is revealing, but as quickly as she sees it, it's gone, and Denise is left wondering if it had been there at all.

2001

HEIDI

Beneath the branches, the ground is a sea of shifting sun and shadow. My breath clouds against the icy, January air. I have stopped running because a stitch is biting into the side of my belly, but I have easily beaten Nina — not that it was a race. We each have a bag of sweets and fizzy drinks. The bag is heavy and has knocked against my knee, which is now sore with the uncomfortable beginnings of a bruise. We're nearly at the top of the hill where the slightest of breezes catches the heads of damp grass and rustles in the oak boughs above. In the distance are the cheers and shouts from the football teams in the park, though we left them behind a long time ago.

We're alone. Only the most determined walkers venture this far up the hill. Behind us, the wood is dense, and the area grows wild with bramble and fern. Dog walkers tend to stick to the well-travelled paths further down the incline.

I stand and turn, hearing rather than seeing Nina's approach. From here, there's a clear view of the valley with the blue thread of the Thames and the grey edifice of the Water Tower in the distance. Nina groans as she reaches me.

"God, I'm too hot." Her cheeks are red. With a thump, she plonks herself down on a trunk and unwinds her scarf. I sit beside her. Birds sing in the branches around us, and I reach into the bag and pull out a can of Coke. I remove the lid, hearing the satisfying fizz as foam bubbles over and colonises in the dip at the top. Taking a gulp, I pass it to Nina. The winter sunshine is thin on my skin, and if we stay idle for long, I will get cold.

"I wish the bunker wasn't so far," Nina moans.

"I suppose." But I like it up here, so far from town — the silence, the secrecy.

"Come on," I urge, and she gets to her feet, and we make our way to the top of the hill where the trees rattle above us like whispers. It is colder now and a crow caws from the branches before lifting off into the white sky. And I'm filled suddenly with a rush of joy — to be out here, away from the world, school, Mum's nagging, and Anna's annoying presence. Just me and Nina. I turn and catch her with a grin.

The bunker is hidden behind a mass of bramble that we've spent the previous year turning into a den. It is only us that uses it, as far as I know, but there must have been a time when others were here. Nina and I had to empty it of lager cans, cigarette butts, the discoloured film of food wrapping, and, in the corner, a pile of old takeaway boxes.

I push the briar aside and see that the plastic sheeting we've been using to try to shield the entrance has failed in its task entirely — again.

"Shit."

Nina pulls it away, and we examine the damage. The towels and bed linen we have on the ground are beginning to mould, and a dank and unpleasant smell is becoming increasingly familiar.

"It's not too bad inside," I say.

13

Nina crawls to the middle where she lifts a towel and retrieves our treasure box from a cavity in the floor. We make sure it is always stocked with cigarettes and sweets. She takes out the candles and begins laying them out and lighting them. Flame flickers on the brick. The sheeting snaps in the wind, but, apart from that, it's quiet. Nina hands me a cigarette, and an illicit thrill runs through me. It's chilly and I zip my coat high against my neck and fish in my pocket to give Nina three pound coins to add to our supplies.

On one wall, where the brick has crumbled, we have placed a picture of a cat in a silver frame, something we found in one of the charity shops. I pull my magazine from the bag and begin flicking through it. It starts to rain, a soft thud, and I smell the wet greenness of the woods.

Nina cups her hand around the lighter and takes a drag on the cigarette. She glances up at me through her thick lashes. She has strange eyes, I think, dark and feline. A quick smile reveals her white teeth. Over last summer, we both developed spots, and my gaze strays to her chin that is red and bumpy.

She smokes quickly, pulling hard at the end with her lips. The shadows fall across her face, and I get the sense of her as a stranger. In the past months, things seem to have changed. I feel that we've been growing apart, and I don't quite know how it's happened. I've always followed in Nina's wake — she is the funny one, the popular one, always ahead in the fashion game. Being Nina's best friend is like earning a badge of approval.

"You seem quiet," I say.

"I'm just tired."

"Is it something I've done?" I've searched my memory over and over looking for anything that might have caused offence.

"No, stop being so paranoid."

"Okay," I flick through the magazine and begin to read.

We've only been here for ten minutes and already my toes are beginning to numb. When I look up, Nina is leaning back against the wall, the magazine unread on her legs. She is staring out into the rain. I watch her profile for a while, then she turns — her dark eyes are unfathomable.

"Would you come with me if I wanted to run away?"

I laugh, but her expression doesn't change. She means it.

"We could go when it's warmer, once winter is over. We could camp somewhere."

I'm not sure if she's joking or not. Nina is always full of ideas, but I don't want to run away. I'm happy at home.

"We don't have any money."

"Turn away." Her voice has a strange intensity.

I look out at the woods but can half-see Nina from the corner of my eye.

She crawls to the back of the bunker. At first, I think she's going to retrieve the box again, but instead she crouches halfway along the wall, takes a penknife from her pocket, and begins levering at a brick.

I watch her surreptitiously. The brick comes loose, and she places it on the ground, then puts her arm inside the hole, bringing out a scrunched-up carrier bag. "Here," she says triumphantly, handing me the package.

The parcel is in fact several bags wrapped over themselves many times. Cautiously, I take it in my hands, and dirt runs off the surface and on to my knee. I open the bag and am astonished to see that it contains a fortune in money.

I stare blankly at her. "Oh my God, this must be hundreds. Whose is it?"

"Mine, stupid. It's nearly £1,000. We could buy a tent and food and a stove. We could really do it — go somewhere where nobody could find us." Her eyes gleam in the darkness.

But I'm too surprised by the fact that she has produced so

much money to respond to this proposition. "£1,000? Where did you get it from?" It's more money than I can ever imagine having.

"I've been saving."

"You never told me." Hurt prickles in my chest.

"So, will you come with me?"

And I'm grateful that at least she asked. "Why didn't you tell me?" I press.

She takes another cigarette and lights it. She passes one to me, and I do the same. The smoke fills my mouth, both bitter and familiar. It makes me cough.

"Noob," she says.

Leaning against the cool wall, I try to make sense of my feelings. The idea of running away holds no appeal for me, and I don't understand why it might for her. She is quiet for a while, tracing her fingers along the cement of a brick and smoking. I feel the stillness of secrets. When she looks at me again, she seems suddenly afraid.

"Did you steal it?" I say. We have both stolen from the corner shop and once in town, but £1,000 is a vast sum of money. More than her mum and Ken have.

"I told you, I've been saving."

"Well I don't know why it's such a secret. I tell you everything."

She opens her bag and pulls out a packet of sweets, rips it open and starts popping them into her mouth.

"If you don't come with me, that's fine. I'll go on my own." She spits the words out. "I don't care." And she stuffs the money back into the bag and closes it, wrapping the notes tightly back into the carrier.

Outside, the rain falls more heavily and begins to drip into the bunker. Droplets hang on the brick, waiting to fall. I'm unsettled by the outburst, and, for the first time, I really study her and wonder at the changes. We stare into each other's eyes for a while. She's the first to look away.

2016

DENISE

As Denise crosses the bridge, she turns up the heater in the car. Fingers of mist hover over the black ribbon of the Thames, and although it's late, Heidi's unexpected request to see her has filled her with a sense of urgency. She has made an effort to keep in touch with Heidi since the attack — and, in recent years, she likes to believe that the relationship has evolved into a sort of guardianship. There are times now when, for a while, Denise forgets altogether what Heidi has been through, but then she'll catch the scarring of Heidi's hand or remember Anna and Nina.

At the beginning, Denise and the rest of the team had lived in hope that Heidi might begin to recall something — something that they could act upon, but it never happened. And as time passed it became less and less likely.

And then she had received Heidi's text, asking if Denise could visit. There was something Heidi wanted to tell her. She examines her feelings and is surprised at her reaction. Instead of the thrill of curiosity, something darker moves through her,

18

and she experiences a strange twinge of anxiety. The lights turn green and Denise presses ahead.

She reaches Heidi's street and parks. Wind scrapes in the branches and a silky moon passes behind clouds. When Denise walks, her shoes echo on the paving stones.

Heidi welcomes her into the tiny maisonette where Denise takes off her coat and scarf. Heidi's cat looks up briefly from her basket and then stretches and disappears through the cat flap. The room is tidy but sparse and always reminds her of somewhere temporary rather than a home. A bit like Heidi herself — as if she has never quite come to fully inhabit her own body.

They make small talk as Heidi prepares coffee, and then Heidi takes a seat and falls into a reflective silence. Denise watches her curiously.

"I've never asked about what happened that day in detail. I only Googled it once, but I couldn't read it. It made me feel..." Her voice is flecked with uncertainty. "But I think I'm ready now." She puts the cup down. "The press doesn't always tell the truth — could you tell me?"

Denise folds her hands inside each other, playing for time. It's been at least 13 years since Denise has worked the case. She's not sure she remembers all the facts. "Are you sure?"

"I'm sure."

"Okay." For a moment, Denise's mind is filled with those early scenes: the tents and white suited Scenes of Crime Officers, the lurid green of grass caught in moving lights of police helicopters, sirens screaming, and the terrible knowledge of what lay beside the bunker. Denise can almost smell the horror that hovered in the warm evening air.

"Your mum reported you missing." Initially, when the call came through, the response had been lacklustre; three girls, late home on a summer's evening — nothing alarming about it at all.

"Your mum knew you had a den in the park and that it was at the top of the hill." It had been a policewoman who had eventually discovered them — not on an illicit camp-out, as they had assumed, but a devastating scene of death.

"Nina had been strangled?"

Denise nods.

"But I wasn't?"

"The perpetrator—" Denise hesitates "—used a brick to assault you. Afterwards, the crime scene was set on fire, but it didn't take. We never found a trace of Anna."

Heidi doesn't react, not visibly. "And then?"

"You were flown straight to hospital, and the investigation began."

Heidi stays silent for a moment. "Why weren't we attacked in the same way?"

"You raise an interesting point, which actually led to a number of theories. The general consensus was that Nina was killed first, and you were attacked in a moment of panic. The injuries you received are more consistent with an unplanned assault, and, although we can't rule it out, we had no reason to suspect two perpetrators. Maybe you arrived after Nina was killed or perhaps you were hiding in the bunker."

"So Nina was the target?"

"It's possible, but we don't know."

"And the fire," Heidi touches her hand, "did it destroy everything?"

"The evidence we recovered wasn't significant, sadly. Your injuries were so severe that we believe the perpetrator must have thought you were dead, too, and then set the fire to compromise the scene. If there had been evidence on Nina's body, it was almost certainly destroyed."

"So the fire worked?"

"To a degree, but forensic science only gets results when you have something to use it against — for example, if you find hair or blood that doesn't belong to the victim, you can test it against a suspect for comparison. Although we did get a number of samples from the scene, we weren't able to match them to anyone, and, of course, it isn't a certainty that what we recovered actually came from a suspect at all. The bunker had been well used for some years, and both you and Nina would have brought hair and fibres from your lives at home to the scene."

Heidi leans back against the sofa.

"Are you okay?" Denise asks.

"Yes, it's…" Heidi sighs. "You must think I'm strange. Sometimes I feel so detached. After it happened, when I woke up in hospital, it was as if it had happened to someone else. I felt so far away. And then there were so many things I couldn't remember — about home, school, Mum, and Anna." She closes her eyes. "I read somewhere recently that in really traumatic events, the victims can leave their body altogether and it's like it's happening to someone else. Do you know what I mean?"

Denise nods. "Yes. Is that what you think happened to you?"

"No, I don't think that happened exactly, but losing so much of my past is a bit like that, I guess. Whoever I was before disappeared."

"You're still the same person inside, Heidi, even if you've lost all the landmarks. He didn't take it all."

"He took a lot." Anger blooms in her eyes. "He took too much. And he took Anna."

"Anna," Denise echoes. The press photo they used flicks into her mind. The gap in Anna's small teeth, the wide-set eyes, and the graze on her knee where a sticking plaster has come loose.

"Do you recall much about her?" Denise asks.

"Not much. But it's odd, although I struggle to remember, I still have this... this love there, you know, for them both, for Mum and Anna." She touches her fist to her chest.

Denise remembers Lynn. She had fought for some weeks to hold herself together but losing Anna and nearly losing Heidi was too great a trauma. The Family Liaison Officer had arrived only just in time. An hour later and Lynn would have been dead. After her stomach had been pumped, she had been moved to a psychiatric hospital. She has never left.

They sit in silence, Heidi's loss and grief claiming the room. There are no words of comfort that can bridge the divide.

"Sometimes," Heidi gathers herself, "I go and sit in our storage area at the warehouse."

"Where all your things are?"

Heidi nods. "I go through them, hoping to remember, hoping it will bring something back. For years, it's meant nothing, or very little, but last time, a few weeks ago..." again she pauses, "...I felt a new connection to my past."

Denise experiences a trickle of surprise. She would never have guessed at this secret pilgrimage.

"And I can't help wondering if there's any chance that Anna could be alive?"

Denise knows the likelihood of this is remote. Within a week of the investigation, the police were tacitly acknowledging that they were probably looking for another dead body. Even if Anna had run away from the scene to hide and then got lost, a seven-year-old cannot survive for long without help. Most likely, she had been abducted and was dead within the first 48 hours.

"Nobody can know for sure, but it's unlikely. I'm sorry," Denise says.

Heidi twists her hands in her lap. "I know in my head that this is probably true, but there's always, always just a little spark of hope, isn't there?"

"There's always a small chance, Heidi."

Heidi takes a breath. "And what happened next, after you found us?"

"It was a very high-profile crime. Everything was thrown at it: a massive police search was conducted, roadblocks were set up, cars were checked, and door-to-door enquiries carried out extensively. There were a few leads, but nothing that threw any light on Anna's whereabouts, and nothing that led to us discovering who did this to you or to Nina."

"Why didn't they kill Anna when they attacked Nina and me?"

"There's no way of knowing. Anna may have been the original target, or she may have been with you when you met the perpetrator."

Heidi begins to speak, but then pauses and catches Denise in her gaze. Her cheeks flush. "Where were we exactly when you found us? I mean Nina and I. Were we lying together?"

Denise is thrown momentarily by the strangeness of the question. "You were outside the entrance of the bunker, lying side by side when we found you. Why do you ask?"

Heidi's eyes shift warily. "What colour were Anna's shoes?"

Denise scrabbles at her memory. "Red, I think. I can check for you. Why?"

"I saw her being taken," Heidi whispers. "Before you ask, I don't remember an attacker or anything useful. I just remember being there — lying beside Nina — and I see Anna being taken."

For a moment, Denise is stilled by this revelation.

She leans forward. She can see the amber flecks in Heidi's irises. "You actually saw her being taken? Can you tell me more?"

"It was hardly anything. I just saw her legs, her red sandals." Heidi gets up and collects the cups. "It was barely a second." She turns, and light glances along her pale skin, accentuating her fragility. "I knew that Nina was dead."

When she speaks again, her voice is hoarse. "It's beginning to come back, isn't it?"

24

2016

HEIDI

Denise has left, and I sit motionless for a while in the stillness of the room. A chill grows from somewhere in my middle. Had I doubted my memory? Not entirely. I try to visualise Nina and I laid out together, side by side. Did I see Nina being strangled? Did whoever it was just want Anna? I would have fought to save her, wouldn't I? Is that why we were attacked?

But there is only a gap, a river of nothingness. The fragment I picked out of the fog has been of little use. It confirms only what has been assumed from the beginning — that Anna was there. And the fact that I see her carried away — does that give weight to the theory that she was the target? And then, the most terrible thought occurs to me, and I search that sliver of memory for proof or disproof — could she already have been dead?

Closing my eyes, I see her legs, her red sandals, one strap undone or broken and hanging loose across the top of her foot. Her legs are still. If she had been alive, surely, she would have been struggling. My heart contracts.

I imagine the crime scene, being found, police and ambulances, the fervour. There are enough police dramas on television for me to visualise the flapping blue tape, the ominous tent, uniformed bodies, and urgent radio messages. And then later, search parties prodding the ground with sticks, moving forward in straight lines like a battalion.

There's only one early memory I retain. I'm lying on a hospital trolley, and, above, a light comes and goes in my vision. The walls swim. I see a blue uniform and feel the rhythm of wheels reverberate through my body. Someone says, "Nearly there. It's okay. It will all be over soon." A sharp, unpleasant smell is in my nostrils, and one of my eyes is shut. Beside me, a rattle of feet and a pale, small hand on my arm — my mother's? I'm certain this memory comes from very soon after the attack, perhaps even from the same day. I reflect on the sensation of lying beside Nina. I don't see her, but I am sure of her presence and the faint touch of her skin against mine.

Pain swells inside my ribcage like a fist. I catch my reflection in the screen of the television, a white face with the smudge of shadow where worry lines darken my forehead. Pushing the feelings away has become second nature, a habit. And I'm aware of my profound loneliness — I'm not just a stranger to myself, but to others, too. Getting too close is a risk.

I move to the bedroom and unearth the suitcase I brought with me from residential care. It's stuffed at the bottom of the wardrobe, gathering dust and fallen clothes. It recalls my time there, my room with the yellow walls and the mural of a sun that was beginning to chip away at the edges — the emptiness I felt, the lack of connection. I still couldn't quite grasp that it was all real, particularly in those first months, wrenched away from the hospital and from the attentiveness of nurses and doctors and the rhythm of hospital life.

The hospital structure had felt safe: the nurses' check at six am; breakfast at seven of juice and toast, sometimes sausages and eggs; the doctors' rounds, the nurse changeover; then lunch. I think, at that stage, I was still expecting my mother to come, to tell me that it was going to be all right now and that I could go home. But even home was a vague concept. Instead of a house, I saw a blur, out of which strange and unexpected images would emerge like beasts lumbering from a patch of mist: the new, white fridge with silver piping, and the freezer compartment at the top where Mum had filled ice cube trays for summer days and a packet of ice pops that were strictly rationed to one each after school. I could see clearly the rack where Anna and I put our shoes — two pairs of black flats and then our home shoes — a banister with coats, cardigans, and Mum's scarf trailing off and spilling on to the stair carpet.

In my mind, I tried so many times to climb those stairs, to open a bedroom door or walk into the bathroom and peer out of windows on to the back garden, but it made my head hurt, and I would erupt with anger and frustration. There were times when I hated the nurses and doctors. I remember being rude and churlish on days like that, refusing food and refusing to talk. And where was mum? She stopped visiting.

I heave the case on to the bed. It must be more than eight years since I opened it last, and I fumble with the stiff metal clasp. Inside, on top of old schoolbooks and cuddly toys, is an album. The plastic cover is cool and bumpy to the touch. On the first page, someone has inscribed my name. Whoever wrote this writes with a slight forward slant and has a lighter touch than me. The ink is blurred.

Slowly, I turn and begin to look. The photographs are all stored behind yellowing, transparent covers. There is one of my mother sitting on the arm of a chair. Her hair sticks out more on one side than the other, as if she'd just run her hand through it. A tea towel dangles limply across one wrist. One of Anna. Her face is slightly different to the one that I remember. The hair is more gold than white. She is sitting on the swing we had in the back garden.

Seeing it, I remember the blast of creosote that hung around the damaged fence between our and Nina's house and the scrubby grass. It is a narrow plot with a shed at the back on which Nina and I used to climb. In the picture, Anna's wearing shorts and a tee shirt. Her small tanned feet are bare, and there is a dull sheen on her toenails. Her hair is caught up on top of her head, a few tendrils have escaped and brush the oval face. Gazing at her now, I acknowledge her prettiness. This, perhaps, is how she will always be.

There's one with my father that elicits strange emotions. He's tall and slim, and the leather jacket he's wearing looks new. He seems too young for fatherhood and yet, here he is, holding me in his arms, one pink fist curled around the collar of his coat. It can't be long after this that the motorbike accident took his life.

In another, I'm cross-legged, opening parcels on the sitting room floor with a crooked line of cards on the mantelpiece behind me. I'm holding up a pair of roller blades, and I look young and happy, unrecognisable. I yearn to feel this memory, for it to saturate my skin, to plump out my heart and fill the gaps that my mind has erased.

The next — a beach — brings a deeper stirring of emotion, something oddly uncomfortable. There is no landmark for this picture, and I have no idea if it was a holiday or a day trip. The beach is crowded and to the right of the scene a flowered parasol looms. The photograph has been taken so that our backs are to the sea and the outline of a head and upheld arms — the photographer — casts a shadow on to the sand in front of us. I wonder if this is my mother. Nina's wiry body in the bikini looks tanned next to the whiteness of mine. In the picture, I'm grinning and looking proud as we display our sandcastle — a sprawling city of humps and bridges topped by a castle decorated with shells. Nina, too, is smiling, but the parasol casts a shadow over the angles of her face, obscuring the light in her dark eyes.

I remember Nina now, her foxy grin, her bad temper. Frowning, other memories flood in: she and I swiping sweets from the newsagents, stealing jewellery from the department store in town, how she liked to smoke. At the time, I'd considered her grown up, sophisticated, and daring. Now, looking at the girl in front of me, I feel otherwise. As I gaze at her image, the realisation comes to me in a flash — she had been deeply unhappy. In the attitude of her head and shoulders, I begin to interpret all her misery. Her smile is barely a shadow of mine, and her eyes hold on to something other than joy.

Shocked, I place the photo down. The idyll that I had imagined our childhood to be is altered. I am confused. Summoning all my mental strength, I try to remember Nina and her life, but it is blank, and an idea slyly worms its way into my mind, and my heart beats a little faster. Nina and I were neighbours. If Nina's mother is still there, it would be easy enough to visit, to see the house where Nina lived, to hear what her family have to say.

I put the pictures away and consider. Would they want to see me? In all the years since Nina's murder, they have not attempted to contact me. But seeing them might dislodge other memories, and if that happens, the image I glimpsed of Anna could break open more, and maybe I could see beyond the hands of her abductor to a face.

Rain spatters on the window and I huddle into my jumper. In the phone book, I trace down all the Carpenters, and then I find it: *C Carpenter, 12 Hobin Road*. My skin prickles. Unconsciously, I realise I've already made the decision, but when I attempt to visualise Nina's mother, I'm presented with yet another gap. Frustrated, I turn to the photo again and notice other things — in the background, to the left, a little girl wearing a striped swimsuit. She has dark hair that is caught up in two untidy bunches. A man stands over her, smoking a cigarette. He's tall and thin with dark hair swept back from his face. Even from the photograph, I can see that his skin is pockmarked. He's not smiling, but his uneven teeth are visible through the smoke of a cigarette. A pool of dislike settles inside me. I know him and the girl, but I can't think how or why.

In the final photograph, I guess I must be about 12. Maybe this is the last to be taken before the attack. In it, I'm wearing jeans with embroidery along the hem. Something nudges at my memory, and I think I remember the jeans — a little bird with iridescent wings, yellow butterflies, a green palm tree, and I'm touching them, running my finger over the thread. The image is gone as quickly as it came. Nostalgia and longing grow until I feel my body can't contain it, and I put the album down with the intention of closing it. As I move to fold the cover across, I notice at the corner of the picture, barely visible, a tiny foot and the tip of a red sandal.

Suddenly, I am overwhelmed. I stretch out on the sofa. The room is warm, and I hear the comforting sound of a chair being pulled out from the flat above. I close my eyes, and, just as I am drifting to sleep, it comes to me. The girl is Danielle, Nina's little sister and Anna's best friend. And the man — Ken — that was his name. He was Nina's stepfather.

When I wake later, I smell ash and burning meat in the air. The skin on my body is hot and damp with sweat. I can't breathe. My heart thumps. It doesn't feel like my body anymore. There's a numbness in my legs. From my throat, small animal-like noises escape, over which I have no control. I try to sit up, panic clawing at my chest, and I sense something cool and soft against the skin of my arm.

Opening my mouth, I gasp for air and manage to raise myself to sitting. Looking down, I expect to see earth and blood and ash, but am faced only by the plain white bed cover. The door is ajar and light from the kitchen seeps from the hall and into the room. It's silent. Although the dream is passing, I still feel the memory of Nina's dead fingers on my arm, and the smell of blood mixed with the fumes of our rancid, burning flesh. I lean over the bed and am violently sick.

We're in the back of Ken's car. The heater pumps out a steady flow of warm air. I like being a passenger with the gentle vibrations of the engine and the sense of rushing through the world at speed. Finally, he slows and then stops at a pair of ornate gates. A fancy lettered sign reads *The Castle*. I watch Ken press a button and lean forward into the intercom. Like magic, the gates slide open.

"Wow," I mouth at Nina. The winding drive cuts through expansive, well-kept gardens.

Ken turns in the driving seat. "Pretty classy, right."

We park in front of a sprawling manor house. A gold car and several sporty-looking vehicles stand idle on the forecourt.

"Why are we here?" Nina sounds angry.

"I won't be long. Wait here." A look passes between them.

Ken steps out of the Nissan, grabs a case from the boot and leaves us in the back seats. I gaze with astonishment at the house with its vast windows and pillared door. Nina watches him with pursed lips.

I study her face, see the dislike for her stepfather sour her expression.

"Who lives here?" I ask.

"Some rich, old bastard."

"Is he a friend of Ken's?"

Nina snorts. "No." She is emphatic.

"How is he so rich?"

"He's got loads of businesses and stuff. Garages, I think." But she's not interested.

It's only as I hear a slam that I realise I've missed the sight of whoever lives here altogether. Nina wriggles across the top of the front seat until she can reach into the glovebox and takes two cigarettes from Ken's packet.

We get out of the car and crouch behind it, out of sight. Smoking's still quite new for me, so I watch Nina's proficient sucking and blowing and copy as best I can without coughing too much.

"Who is he then? Who lives here?"

"He's this man called Brandon. Ken sort of knows him."

"You've been here before?"

She flicks ash from her jeans and pulls her hoodie closer. The grey sky looks full of rain.

"What's he like?"

Nina shrugs as though bored.

"Did you see inside? Is it really posh?"

"I guess so."

The car is still warm from the journey, and the smell of oil drifts up from the undercarriage. Standing up, I stamp my feet which are beginning to feel chilled. I look down at the lawns leading to a pond, where a discoloured cherub spouts water. Neatly trimmed hedges and borders edge the gardens. "I really want to see inside," I say, burying the butt in the gravel. "Come on."

"Leave it, Heidi. Ken'll be out in a minute."

"I'm just going to look in the windows."

We creep by the car, our feet shifting on the stone chips, and make our way to the house. There are French windows, and I edge along the wall towards them. I can't hear any voices. When we are right beside the windows, I peer in. There isn't much to see. The room is dark, and I get only a vague impression of sofas and tables, a swathe of curtain.

"Can I say I need a wee?"

Nina looks cross.

"I do need a wee." And just saying the words makes me conscious of the press of my bladder.

"For fuck's sake," Nina hisses, her brows drawn. "Just go and find a bush."

"It's freezing. I'm sure he won't mind, right? And it's too cold to wee outside."

"Honestly, Heidi, you're better off going in the garden somewhere."

"Why?" I say. "What's the problem?"

"You wouldn't understand."

"I would. And I do actually need to go now." I nag her until finally she turns and starts to make her way back to the car.

"Not everyone is lovely, Heidi. Sometimes you're so immature. If you want to go in, then do it." Nina watches me, her black hair lifting in the breeze, something unreadable in her eyes. "Go on — ring the bloody bell."

"Come with me," I whisper.

"No way."

Bravado makes me walk up the steps and to the front door where I ring the bell. The sound echoes slightly in the hall beyond. Nina is back at the car and out of sight. For a moment, the sun dips behind the roof and the shadows deepen around me. I wait, secretly glad that nobody has answered. And then, I hear footsteps, soft as though slippered, and the door opens. *Not everyone is lovely*, she had said, and suddenly, I am afraid.

The man who stands there towers above me and is nothing like I expected — he is just a man in ordinary clothes.

"Sorry, can I use your toilet?"

He smiles, showing white teeth, but his eyes are searching beyond me. "Where's Nina?" His voice is haughty. "You better come in."

The hall is square and there are fancy pots on tables and paintings and all the things I expected. The temperature is cool. Smoke, not from cigarettes but something richer, hovers in the passageway. We pass a room and I see Ken in one of the chairs, a glass in hand. On the table are packages. As I look in, he reaches forward and slips something under one of the packets, out of sight.

"Hello, Carrots," he calls, and I flush, disappointed to have this man hear my childish nickname.

The bathroom is at the end of the corridor and is boringly ordinary — no gold taps for me to gloat about at school. I wash my hands with one of the soaps and then use the moisturiser.

I leave, and as I pass the room again, they are deep in hushed conversation.

"Just see yourself out."

I walk slowly, studying the pictures and ornaments. It would be easy to steal something, I think.

Nina is in the car, her face dark. "Well?"

"It was boring."

She seems pleased. I see that she has tucked another cigarette behind her ear, and I wonder if Ken will notice, although I have a feeling he doesn't care. Sometimes he gets Nina to light them for him.

We drive back in silence, past the green woods and the flat fields. As we near Riverbridge, he starts to hum.

"Just one more stop, girls," he says, turning in the seat to grin at us, and Nina raises her eyebrows in annoyance.

We pull up to the kerb, where he reaches into the glovebox and pulls out one of the packages. I watch him disappear up the path. Once more, Nina leans over the seat and opens the glovebox. She pulls the remaining packet out, giving me a sly look. It's white and oblong. Opening the top, I gasp.

"How much is that?" It's filled with money.

"Less than before," and she tugs out two twenty-pound notes. As she does so, she dislodges a small square photograph. I lean down and pick it up.

"Who's that?" I look down at the girl in the picture. She's about Anna's age, with blonde hair and freckles, too.

Nina takes it in her hands and gazes hard at it. Flicking a glance at the house, she returns it hurriedly to the parcel and then puts it back just before Ken emerges from the front door.

"Is that where you got your money from?" I ask.

"Maybe."

"Doesn't he know? Did you steal it all from Ken? How come he has so much?"

"Shut up, Heidi."

Ken is back. "All right, girls? I'll drop you off at the park now."

Nina leans her cheek against the window and stares out at the passing countryside. She doesn't talk. Occasionally, I look her way and see her face reflected in the glass. She looks angry, her mouth turned down at the corners, but, as the journey progresses, I decide it's something else altogether. It's not anger I see, but sadness.

The pub is filled with the noise of lunchtime drinkers.

"I can always trust you to be thorough." The older man leans forward and captures the younger in the blue of his eyes. Rather than diminishing him, age has made him more vigorous, more distinguished. Outside, the traffic passes in a steady flow. "It could mean trouble for us all," The Chief smiles, letting his eyes linger a little, "if Heidi remembers. But I know I can trust you."

"Always." It does not need consideration. This is the way it is. The way it has always been. He never doubts it. "But why are you so sure she will remember anything?"

The Chief runs a long-fingered hand through his hair. "I have ears and eyes in many places, and there's a rumour that her memory is returning. Nothing as yet to concern us, but I don't like it." He pauses. "And there's a detective, Gilzeen, who has the bit between her teeth, as usual. A dog with something to prove. She won't let it go." He sighs. "It's better to be safe than sorry, as they say."

"How much did Heidi know back then?" he asks.

"We don't know how much she knew, but there are things that are best left as they are. And, of course, we know that Heidi was there and probably witnessed what happened, or some of it, before she lost consciousness."

The younger man fixes him with a look. "You think Heidi knows?"

He shrugs his broad shoulders. "Who can say? Those girls were close enough that Nina may have confided in her. If she starts to remember..." He leaves the sentence unfinished.

"What do you want me to do?"

"For now, I want you to keep your eyes on things, on her. See who her friends are, who she talks to, and what her routines are. Let me know if you think she's going to be trouble. Deal with it if necessary. You're good at that." A smile passes between them.

"Okay."

"You need to be better than Gilzeen. I doubt people will talk, but it's possible that, after all this time, someone might be prepared to open up."

"Do you think that's likely?"

The Chief's laugh is easy. "People are stupid. When you're older, that will become more and more apparent to you — they think a few years down the line that they're safe. They forget. They forget who they're dealing with."

The younger man frowns. "They'll be harder to trace though."

"You think people move on? People stay the same, same habits, same places. Some will have died, a few may live somewhere else. It's only the few of us who have a higher vision, have the flexibility to adapt and grow," he leans forward, traces the features opposite him carefully, "as you have." He smiles again, chains his fingers behind his head. "You'll know what to do. Just keep an eye. Just in case."

The younger man nods and gazes at the face he knows so well. The face he has come to trust. "I'll do my best."

"Of course you will. I don't doubt you, not at all." The dying sun is reflected in his eyes, twin satellites. They are not easy to read, but he has no qualms about his task, and somewhere tugging at his insides is the thrill of excitement.

2016

HEIDI

As I walk, I keep looking down at my boots, and the closer I get to my old home, the more anxious I feel. But I've become obsessed with seeing Nina's mother and wondering if memories might be prompted by visiting her.

Turning on to Hobin Road, I am assailed by an avalanche of recollections, cameos of the life we lived here: Mum ironing our uniforms, the smell of starch, Anna and I rolling marbles along the hallway. For a moment, I have to pause and master the wave of loss that hits me. I have only vague impressions of Nina and her family — a vague sense of Danielle and older brothers, noise.

And now I am outside. Our house is changed — the windows and doors have been replaced with shiny PVC. In my day, the metre of front garden had been laid with brick, and Nina and I would pick the fat, white-headed dandelions that grew between the stones. "He loves me, he loves me not," we would chant watching as the seeds floated into the air, full of promise. The front is now paved with slabs and a hedge borders the path between our house and theirs.

My home has been repainted into something unrecognisable. There is nothing of us left here — maybe some other child is bedded down where Anna once slept. I turn my face away to look at the adjoining house.

In one of the upstairs windows, a curtain blows furiously from the gap where the sash has been raised. I pause only for a moment, then walk up the path and ring the bell. Sounds from inside filter out — the rise and fall of television laughter, the banging of a door, and finally the footsteps of an approaching figure.

And then she's standing before me and her face dislodges a wave of memories. "Carol," I say.

She puts her head to one side, her eyes narrowed, and then she realises who I am.

"Heidi. Heidi Bevan." She stands back, her lined mouth falling open in shock. Surprise is replaced by something else. My heart flutters in my chest.

"What are you doing here?"

I'm not sure what I read in her voice, anger, hostility, curiosity, or perhaps something of all of them. "I'm sorry, I should have rung first."

She's put on weight, and her once dark hair is now entirely grey.

"I was passing," I lie.

Her eyes run me up and down, and then she stands back. "Do you want to come in?"

I follow her through to the sitting room, identical in shape to ours next door. There are two white sofas and a huge television. A young woman sits on the arm of one of the chairs, feeding a baby in a highchair. The boy thumps his little fists on the tray and gives me a small-toothed grin.

"It's Heidi Bevan," Carol says. There is stale alcohol on her breath. When the girl turns, I see it's Danielle, and an image of her as a child with messy bunches returns to me. Danielle is now tall and heavyset, with beautiful hair that falls in waves around her shoulders.

I think I see a flurry of alarm, and her hands tighten on the spoon, but her gaze examines me minutely. She flushes and glances awkwardly at her mother.

"You better sit down," Carol urges, and I take one of the sofas. Carol reaches across and presses the remote control for the television and suddenly the room is silent. One wall is entirely dominated by a framed photo of Nina, and I want to look and look again at that thin face. But I am aware of the pressing interest of Carol and Danielle. Carol's lips are set hard in her unhappy mouth.

"So, long time no see," she says eventually.

I wonder if she's disappointed that I haven't visited before, or perhaps she blames me. I redden. How do I explain? "I've thought a lot about Nina recently. I don't remember her, not properly. Today, I had an urge to see where I used to live, and then I wondered if you still lived next door."

Carol's face tightens with some emotion, and I feel clumsy and thoughtless, barging in on their grief.

"Do you want a coffee?" Danielle asks.

"Please."

"Get us a lager, will you, love?" Danielle hesitates for a moment and then leaves the room. Carol now turns to me. "We didn't know how you were — you know, whether, you were all right or..." Her eyes scan me for signs of injury, lingering over the scars on my hand. I crush myself to the back of the chair and think of the scars that she can't see, the ones hidden by clothes, and then the deeper ones, ones that not even I can observe. "How long were you in hospital?"

"Six months or so," I say. "The attack caused a lot of damage."

Danielle hands me a coffee and puts a can by Carol. She takes the baby and jiggles him in her arms.

"So how are you now? Are you okay?" Carol asks.

"I have a lot of problems with my memory, but physically I'm fine."

There is no warmth in her face. "It's fifteen years now, since we lost Nina."

"I know. It's hard to believe." Sitting here, the smells of the house conjure the friendship I had with Nina, and I want to close my eyes and relive it, just for a moment.

"Do you remember anything about the attack?" Carol asks, leaning forward.

I push away the sensation of Nina's hand against my arm. "Nothing, I'm afraid."

"He's still out there." Her bitterness spills into the air, and in her face. I read the years of loss, rage, and despair. "I can't sleep for thinking about that. He could be anyone. It's a pity you don't remember." There's a thread of accusation in her tone.

"I wish I could."

Carol takes a well-practised sip of her beer. "And still nothing on Anna?"

I have to tell her no.

Her body seems to shrivel, and she considers me more kindly. "Poor Anna. No wonder your mum broke down. They thought you might end up brain damaged, so she nearly lost you both." She reflects on this, and when she speaks again, her tone is gentler, "How is she? Lynn?"

"Not great. She's still in Fair Mile."

Carol fumbles in her pocket and takes out a packet of cigarettes, "Get us an ashtray will you, Danny? I'm going to have this inside." She nods at Danielle and lights one. "I don't usually smoke inside, not with Robby, the little 'un." She takes

43

a drag. "I should've visited Lynn, but, you know... we were friendly once." She sighs deeply. "But life goes on. Danny tells me all the time, don't you? I can't live in the past." She takes another puff and her eyes screw with grief. "But until you lose a baby like that, until..." Her breath is caught momentarily in her throat, and I turn away, disarmed by the depth of her pain. "Anyway," she reins her emotion back, "I'm a granny now — I have little Robby."

"How old is he?" I ask.

"He's eight months and bright as a button. A chip off the old block, eh?"

"Have you got someone?" Danielle asks me.

I shake my head.

Just then, I hear the rattle of the front door and footsteps. Carol gets up and goes to the hall to meet whoever is there. Their whispered voices are impossible to understand. A tall man with darkish hair and angular features enters the room.

"This is Scott, one of my boys. You must remember him?"

His high cheekbones and pointed chin are only a little like Nina, but he has her eyes, dark and thickly lashed. For an instant, he is a stranger and then, I recall him, leaning against one of the kitchen counters in a pair of skinny jeans and black tee-shirt and how my heart had thumped. Nina had been crouched, searching the cupboards for something to eat and I had turned and gone upstairs to her room to hide the blush on my cheeks.

"Hi," he smiles, but there's a wary look on his face, and I get the sense again that I am not entirely welcome. "Mum was saying you still can't remember anything."

"That's right."

Their disappointment is evident. The baby begins waving his arms about and gurgling. Scott picks him up and bounces him against his shoulder.

"So you never had an idea, either, of who did this to us?" I ask, feeling brave.

"If we knew, he wouldn't be around. You can bet your life on that. So, if you do remember, let me know first. The police are useless, and prison is too good for bastards like that." His expression is suddenly cut with anger.

There are more photos of Nina in frames on the mantlepiece above a gas fire. I point. "May I look?"

Danielle brings them over. In most of the pictures, Nina is wearing a school uniform, and I recall fragments of those lost days: the smell of the science lab and the red covers on our French textbooks, Nina resting against the wall of some corridor, a rucksack slung over a shoulder and an insolent look. I trace her features with a mixture of recognition and sadness. There is no older Nina with whom I can reconcile her face; she will never grow old.

There is a little mole at the corner of her lips. Other than that, her clever eyes and sly grin are all familiar to me. I see no unhappiness here and wonder again at my earlier impression. They watch me carefully as I study each photo, balancing her image in my hands.

I hand them back. "Thanks." There is a slight break in my voice.

"I found one my mum had of us all on a beach somewhere. Ken was there."

Something passes between Carol and her daughter, and Scott gives me a sharp look.

"I remember," Danielle says, "We went by train for the day to Southampton. You remember? It started to rain in the afternoon, and you got stung by a wasp when you bit a sandwich."

Carol shakes her head. Her eyes are red and swollen. She holds the photos of Nina listlessly in her fingers, somehow lost.

"I don't recall it," I say to Danielle. "Who was there?"

"Me, Nina, Mum, and Ken, and then you, Anna, and Lynn."

"Did we really go to the beach?" Carol asks Danielle.

"Yeah, there was a fair, too. We had candyfloss and hot dogs."

The baby spits his dummy out and begins to wail.

The frisson that passed between Carol and her children when I mentioned Nina's stepfather is marked, and I recall the thin man in the photograph, his black hair lying greasily against his head.

"Are you still married to Ken?" I ask.

Carol laughs bitterly. "No, he took a hike years ago, fucking bastard. Good riddance to bad rubbish." She looks down, squeezing the can between her reddened fingers. Scott hands Robby back to Danielle. They both watch Carol. There is a tense silence. I wait, but she says no more. Feeling awkward now, I stand and begin to button my coat.

"Thanks, but I ought to get going."

Nobody protests. Carol accompanies me to the door, and I know that she won't welcome seeing me again.

After the door has closed, I walk slowly up the street, keeping my eyes averted from my own house. My chest feels tight, as if I've been running. Nina's face haunts me, and I feel the pressing of memory, the memory of her. I am so deep in thought that it's only as Danielle catches my arm that I realise she is there at all. She is breathing heavily. Her cheeks are flushed.

"Come and see me, if you can. I go to the toddler group on Prospect Street on Saturday mornings. Meet me at the café. It's in St Martin's precinct, you know? Mum doesn't like talking about Nina." Her eyes are wide and pleading. "Please? I remember Anna. I remember you."

My heart flutters. "What time?"

"Twelve. I'll be there anyway." And then she's racing back to the house, her hair swinging darkly along her back.

2016

He watches her in her smart black coat and office skirt. The chill has painted colour on to her white cheeks. She has a particular way of walking — hesitant, slightly apologetic, perhaps. If she meets someone coming her way, she is the first to move, as if she has less right to the pavement than everyone else. And yet, he also senses something resolute, something firm and solid about her, as if she could not be shaken from her skin.

He tries to imagine the inside of her skull. Is there physical scarring that can still be seen through a scanner? It gives him a curious buzz. This is the sort of task that he is good at. He's pleased that he has been asked.

Some insecurity, that is always distantly present, is temporarily eased. Once again, he has become important to him. The Chief will think about him, wonder what he has discovered, and that thought is profoundly comforting — like coming home.

He is good at being invisible, at waiting and watching. His brain is often empty; time can pass and, later, he has no recollection of what filled those minutes. Heidi will give him something to focus on, something to think of, before he goes to sleep. He watches as Heidi unzips the handbag on her shoulder and takes out a phone.

The sun comes out, briefly showing her hair is more red than brown and, even though she is 29, she could pass for someone much younger. Heidi flicks down the screen and then puts it in her pocket. She walks more briskly, and he slips a few people behind to follow. He decides that, like him, there is something almost invisible about her too. She keeps her head down as though deep in thought.

Heidi stands at the bus stop now, fiddling with her purse. A gust of wind blows across the street, and she lifts a hand to push the hair back from her cheek. She checks her watch, then looks up at the grey sky that is heavy with cloud. Her mouth is sad.

A man moves into the shelter beside her, and she shifts away, just a little. It is such a subtle movement that he doubts anyone else would notice it, but he does. Raindrops begin to fall.

The queue has grown now, but Heidi seems somehow apart from the others, and again he thinks they must be alike in some ways. Both of them on the outside, looking in. He's not sure how that makes him feel.

The bus rumbles down the street towards her, and, for a moment, he steps out of the shop doorway. His heart beats a little harder in his chest, but now the bus is between them and, when it moves off, it leaves the shelter empty. His pulse settles. The rain gets heavier, and the drops begin to slide into the collar of his jacket. Umbrellas are hurriedly raised like a garden sprouting its first blooms. He gazes for a long time into the space she has left and experiences those strange sensations that her face elicits.

2001

HEIDI

Anna is standing by the small front wall at the front of the house, flopping Boo, her favourite soft toy along the bricks. "Mum's car is broken, and I can't go to swimming."

I see now that she has her pink kit bag beside her. Mum is bent over the front of the car, looking in the engine.

"What's the matter with it?" I ask.

She looks up. "I can't get it to start."

"Can you mend it?" The car is expensive, but I cannot imagine our life without it.

She sighs. "I'm just checking the obvious. Ugh," she looks down at her wrist, "Anna, I'm sorry, you'll have to miss swimming today. There's not time to get the bus now."

"Hurray!" Anna jumps down from the wall.

Ken's car turns into the road and comes to park alongside us. "Hello, hello," he says and gives us a wink. "Need a lift?"

Anna and I are sitting in the back seat of Ken's car, as he tows mum to the garage.

"It's going to fall off. It's going to fall off." Anna's eyes are round with the drama.

"Keep still, stupid. It's not going to fall off." But though I have no intention of voicing my thoughts, I, too, keep thinking that the towing rope is going to break.

"Here we are," Ken brings the car to a stop underneath the arches of the railway bridges. A large sign announces that we have arrived at Castle Garages Ltd.

The forecourt is filled with vehicles and beyond that is a large building with metal doors. Two mechanics in dirty overalls are working inside. We get out and stand on the concrete. Overhead, a train rumbles across the tracks, and the vibrations tickle my feet.

"There's somewhere you can sit over there, if you like." Ken points Anna and I to a mobile unit.

It's warm inside and most surfaces are covered with paperwork. Dirty mugs and ash trays cluster on the desk. A piece of faded green tinsel hangs from one of the grubby windows. Anna wrinkles her nose. "It's yucky in here."

For once I can't argue. "Yeah."

"I don't want to be a car person when I grow up."

"Neither do I."

I take the office chair, and Anna sits on one of the plastic ones. Putting my hand on the desk, I manage to swing myself round. Through the window, I see Ken and a mechanic bent over the car and mum stamping her boots in the way she does when she is cold. She looks up and waves. When I turn to say something to Anna, she has gone.

"Fuck's sake," I mutter under my breath.

Outside, the sky is white, icy enough for snow. Anna isn't with Mum, so I cross the yard and walk behind the units to where the canal threads along the waterbank. Sometimes, in summer, we go for walks here and cross the weir. I always pause then, and look down, imagine what it would be like to be caught in the black torrent, no handhold to keep you from being pummelled to the riverbed.

There's a wire fence at the back, rubbish blown into its netting, and a dirty scrabble of grass. No Anna. Another train thunders over the bridge, and I walk back to the garage entrance. The two mechanics have gone. The van they were working on is raised on a platform and the air smells of oil and cigarettes.

"Anna!" My voice echoes.

Ahead, I see a light through the filthy glass of an office. A man is standing there, his arms folded behind his back. As I get closer, I realise it is the posh man with the big house, Brandon. I move out of sight and stare. There are footsteps now, and Ken walks in but does not see me. There is a squeak as the office door opens and the sound of a radio. Ken says something to Brandon, and they begin to laugh.

I turn and see Anna. She's standing next to Mum, looking at the car.

"Where did you go, idiot?" I ask her.

"Heidi!" Mum frowns. "The car needs a new battery. We're going to have to wait a while."

"I'm not going in that yucky office again," Anna moans.

"Are you calling the boss's property yucky?" Suddenly, Brandon is standing there, and I recall what Nina said about his owning garages. "Hello again," he says to me and then he crouches down, meeting Anna at eye level. "And what would your name be Miss Yucky Office?"

Ken looks over and catches Brandon's eye. Something passes between them, but it's hard to read. Mum's face is flushed, and when I look again at Brandon, he's smiling at her. I think of the big house and the cars on the drive.

"Come on," Ken grabs Anna's hand, "there's a coffee place

over the road. Let's get something to drink. Ring me when it's done. Thanks, mate."

We walk past the arched bridge and to the road where Anna presses the button at the crossing. I glance back. Brandon is standing in his dark, wool coat, the collar turned up on his neck against the chill. He's still smiling. His hand is held high, and he lowers it. I think perhaps he was waving at us, but then I see the glint of a screen. Something squeezes at my insides. He was taking a photo, I'm sure of it.

2016

DENISE

The air conditioning in the basement filters the smell of paper and dust, yet fails to dispel the airlessness. Crystal is sipping a cup of tea and twisting a strand of hair around her finger as she sorts through a pile of documents. Denise can smell mint.

"Hey, stranger," she says when she sees Denise.

"Hello, love."

"How's the body business?"

"Ha bloody ha."

"You're here to check out Anna Bevan's files?" Crystal raises one neatly plucked eyebrow. "It's all round the station. Come on, spill the beans."

"There's not much to tell. Heidi remembered seeing Anna abducted that day. I wanted to check out a few facts before rumours went awry."

"That ship has already sailed." Crystal puts down the tea. Her long nails are cerise pink.

The entire basement is partitioned with ceiling-high shelves and metal cupboards. Staff jokingly call it The Morgue. And there is something disquieting about the knowledge of what is contained within these walls: crime scene and pathologist photographs, folder after folder recounting details of death and violence. Added to this is the fact that the cellars are the oldest part of the building, originally designed as cells, and the whitewashed walls seem to cling to some faint spectre of the men and women held here. If there were ghosts, it's here that they would congregate.

In contrast, Crystal is a peacock in her finery. Today, a pink blouse matches the glossy nails, and trailing around her neck is an orange and blue scarf.

Denise follows her through the maze of storage units to an offshoot room, which is redolent with the smell of damp. Crystal scans the shelves until she comes to the Bevan archive. Denise can see the names, dates, and case numbers inscribed on the boxes.

"Thanks, hun," Denise finds the ones she needs. She puts them on to a trolley, which she pushes to an adjoining room. The wheels click on each revolution.

As she closes the office door behind her, the light splutters uneasily into life, giving off a harsh but faltering glow. Denise waits until the room is fully illuminated before making her way to the desk. With the door shut, it is utterly silent. She picks up the top file and places it in front of her.

Lynn Bevan had made a statement about what Anna had been wearing on the day she vanished. Making careful notes, Denise copies down Lynn's description: blue T-shirt with yellow dots and blue denim shorts, white socks, and there, in black and white, red shoes with a strap across the top. Denise shivers. Reading on, she learns Anna had also been wearing a cheap necklace that had been attached to the comic she had bought that morning with her pocket money. Going over the material, she begins to recall the details. Some time in the early afternoon, Anna had said that she was going out to see how Danielle, next door, was. The last time Lynn saw Anna was through the front window of the house. Anna had been sitting on the wall separating the front garden from the pavement. She had been holding Boo, a knitted rabbit that had once been cream but was then discoloured and missing an eye.

Turning the page, she reads other statements where the clothes are described in more detail. A picture of Anna wearing the distinctive T-shirt is pinned to the top, along with a photograph of the necklace she had been wearing at the time.

Putting down her pen, Denise stares at the streaked walls — her disquiet humming in the air. With growing discomfort, she reads on. The details are familiar, and she recalls the taut energy of the team. Nobody expected the investigation to lead to a dead end, but that's what happened. So many channels of investigation shrinking to nothing. Anna disappeared leaving no witness — no witness but Heidi and the perpetrator. She thinks about Heidi and what the opening up of that memory could mean.

Sometimes, Denise wakes in the early hours and remembers — remembers the bunker, remembers Nina, but most of all she thinks of Anna. And where is Anna now? Heidi's memory confirms what they all believed: that Anna did not run voluntarily from the scene. She was taken. Denise doesn't want to consider what sort of death she suffered, because, surely, she is dead. And somewhere, there is a grave that may lie forever undiscovered.

In another folder, she discovers pictures of the crime scene, and, again, Heidi's recollection is correct: the two girls lie side by side, Nina's body slightly curled to the left with one leg bent at the knee. One of her hands rests on Heidi's arm. Their clothes are charred. It had been some sort of miracle that the fire had gone out before it killed Heidi.

Above, the light flickers, and she feels sealed in and far from the world outside. She gazes down at the photograph, into the blue of Anna's eyes, and at the gap between the front teeth. Lynn had kept her baby teeth in a box in her bedside drawer. Closing the file, she pushes back the metal chair, and the screech against the floor cuts through the silence like a scream.

HEIDI

The day is heavy with the portent of rain, and I pace briskly, my face muffled in a scarf. Riverbridge is full of people browsing the shops, umbrellas at the ready. Three teenagers in jeans and beanies skateboard along the pavement, leaving tram lines on the paviours.

The café is situated between a butcher and an optician. I push open the door and enter, grateful for the warmth. Inside are plastic tables and the aromas of bacon and fried bread. I order a cup of tea and choose a place near the entrance, so I can watch for Danielle's approach.

Condensation runs on the window, and, with the corner of my jumper, I rub a square of glass and look out on the precinct. I am stirring sugar into my cup when I see her — her hair is loose today, and the damp has made dark waves of it around her face. She is pushing the buggy, with Robby invisible beneath a rain cover. I get up and hold the door open as she reverses in. She smells of coffee and baking.

"Sorry I'm late," she gasps.

"Would you like a tea, something to eat?"

She smiles, showing even teeth. "Tea, thanks."

Parking the buggy in a space by the door, she lifts Robby out of his seat, his body entombed in a swaddle of clothing. At the counter, I order a pot of tea and some cakes. It feels strange to be meeting someone with whom I shared a childhood but can barely recall. The image of her on the beach in her bathing suit has failed to elicit other memories.

When I return, Robbie is unwrapped and sitting in a high chair, a dummy in his mouth. I take the seat opposite. "Thanks for asking to meet me." I fish in my bag and bring out the present I bought.

"What's this?"

"It's nothing, just a small gift for Robby."

"Thank you, that's really kind." She pulls off the paper to reveal the xylophone.

"I hope it won't drive you mad." I remember his fists banging on the tray of the highchair.

"He'll love it." She pauses. "Sorry about Mum. She finds it really hard — I mean we all do, but especially Mum."

"I understand that, and I'm sorry. I should have warned you that I wanted to come. At least then I would have given her the opportunity to say no." At close quarters, I am able to study her face. It's round, but her cheeks are flat. Her dark eyes are lined with kohl, and she wears large, hooped earrings. For a moment, her features merge with Nina's, and I have the unworldly sensation that I am sitting not with Danielle but with an older Nina. Swallowing, I turn away.

"I remember you really well," she blushes. "I used to love it at your house."

I digest this information. "Did you come over a lot?"

"Yeah, after school and also at weekends. Anna and I played together all the time."

"Did Anna come to yours much? Did I?"

She puts her head to one side in concentration. "I think I mainly went to yours, Nina, too. Our house was too crowded with Scott and Jason and…" She gives me a quick glance, but the answer feels unfinished. "It must've been really hard for you since it all, you know…"

I nod. "I barely had any memories straight afterwards, and I spent a long time in hospital. It's difficult to explain."

"I know you said you couldn't remember anything of what happened, but have other things come back?"

"Yes, definitely, but sometimes it's hard to know if it's something I forgot or just something that was there that I didn't think about. I do certainly remember a lot more than I did when I was first in hospital."

"I still miss Anna and Nina." Her voice is suddenly soft, and the resemblance to her sister is evident again, something about the angle of her brows and the shape of her mouth. I catch my breath.

"What do you remember about Nina?" I lean forward.

Danielle rubs her chin on Robby's head. "She was pretty wild, I suppose. And badly behaved." She frowns. "She argued with everyone, but she was really funny as well."

"That rings a bell," I say.

The waitress comes over with a pot of tea and cakes. When she's gone, Danielle pours tea into her mug.

"I have vague impressions of Nina. Looking back, I sometimes think she was unhappy." My heart gives a little jolt at the impertinence of the statement.

Danielle continues stirring her tea. I feel that she wants to tell me something, and my skin tingles. Instead, the silence stretches. "Things were hard at home," she says finally.

I give her a questioning look.

"Mum was a bit of a mess then, and Scott was always in

trouble and…" She changes her mind about what she was planning to say next.

"It must have been devastating for you all when it happened."

"Pretty much."

"What happened afterwards?" I ask.

"It all got a lot worse. I only remember bits now. Mum completely lost it, but Jason was 16 or 17 then, and he kind of took over. I think if it hadn't been for him, I would have ended up in care. You were in care?"

"Yes."

"Was it awful?"

I try to remember, but it seems so distant now — the smell of the kitchen with its endless fried fare, the laundry room where the constant activity of the washing machines vibrated in the hall, rattling the table when it went into the drying spin. And, on racks, our uniforms hung like absent people — rows and rows of white school shirts, black trousers, and skirts. I recall the echoing bathroom with its tiled walls, and the bedroom that always felt borrowed.

By then, I had withdrawn into my own world — a protection against the reality of my changed circumstances, and also in response to the stares and whispers that my injuries elicited. Even recalling that time sends a damp chill through my blood.

"It was all right," I lie. "Your mum said she kicked Ken out?"

She looks at me for a long time. There is something she is not saying. Deep in her eyes, I see fear. Robby has fallen asleep.

"Looks like the baby group tired him out."

She grins.

"You say you remember Anna?" I ask.

"She was a year younger, but still my best friend. To be

honest, it's awful to say, but I missed her more than Nina — I mean, in a different way. Nina, it was terrible, still is — but I thought about Anna the most."

"Can you remember her well?"

"She was fun." Her face is full of animation. "We used to play hide and seek at your house and also this spies game. That was my favourite."

"Spies?"

"Yeah, we were like really into you and Nina. You seemed all grown up, and so we used to spy on you and follow you." She laughs. "We even used to try on your clothes." She gives me a penitent look.

"Did you spy on us that day?"

Danielle looks pained. "I had an upset stomach and spent most of the day in bed or downstairs on the settee."

"So you didn't see Anna that day?"

"I did," she pauses, remembering. "She knocked for me in the morning, but Mum sent her away." She sees the disappointment on my face. "But she sneaked in the back way later. We did that a lot. Your mum and mine never locked the back doors, and there was that gap in the fence at the back, you remember? She came in, brought me a puzzle she had. You know, the ones with ball bearings where you have to get them in the holes. I still have it."

I try to imagine them — Anna and Danielle. "Do you remember if she said what she would do if she couldn't play with you?" I realise I'm leaning forward.

Danielle shakes her head. "I'm sorry. The police asked me that again and again. She did say she would try and sneak in again with some biscuits, but she never did. Then later..." But she reddens and looks away. "Sorry, it's so long ago."

"What else do you remember about Anna?" I ask.

"She liked pretending she was a fairy."

And suddenly, I get a glimpse of Anna, in our sitting room, wearing a pair of gauzy wings, stained and slightly torn, and a knot of grief swells in my throat. "Did you ever come up to the bunker? I keep wondering why she was there."

"A few times, but you didn't want us going there. It was your den. You two got really pissed off if we followed you. You were secretive." Her voice is hushed.

My fingers grip the table edge. "How do you mean?"

"I…" She looks down, places her hand on the baby's head. She looks anxious, and I wonder if she had intended to tell me so much. "Nina had secrets."

There is a strange sensation in my belly, something dark and tapping, and suddenly, I am afraid.

Danielle's face shows a mixture of strain and curiosity, and I know this matters to her as much as it does to me. The same hand of fate has blighted us both.

"Secrets?" I whisper.

"I haven't ever really been able to explain," she frowns. "But, before it happened, something changed. Nina changed."

"Did the police know this? Did they find out?"

"I can't really remember." But her explanation sounds inadequate.

"What do you think it was that was different?"

Danielle's expression is impenetrable now, yet I feel the weight of something behind it.

My heart is pounding. "Do you think I knew?" I ask. "Did I know, too?"

Danielle leans towards me, there is sugar on her breath. "It wasn't just Nina, Heidi. It was both of you. You changed, too. If anything," her eyes slide away from my face, "you were worse."

Her words snatch my breath away. I see Nina, tears

streaming from her eyes, her cheeks flushed with anger. My head is tight, as if it can't bear the mass of what is inside.

"Are you okay? What is it?" Danielle's voice is urgent.

I shake my head, but I know she's right. There was something. Even at this distance, I feel a profound thread of unease, as if my body is recalling some burden that my mind has erased.

Robby stirs and begins to moan.

"He's hungry," she says apologetically. "Look, Jason asked if you would meet him. He was closest to Nina out of all of us. Would you?"

I barely remember Nina's oldest brother. That snippet of recollection about Scott returns again, the soft brown of his eyes and the way he made me feel then. But most of that is not just passed but lost. I bite down hard on my lip. I have stayed single and alone. Always alone.

She fishes in her handbag and scribbles his number on a piece of paper, which she pushes towards me. "Jason's done really well for himself.

"Okay," I say.

At the door we look at each other and the tenuous thread of our loss crosses the distance, beyond words. I put my arms round her. I don't want to watch her go, so tell her I need to use the bathroom.

In the loo, I shut the door, sit down, and put my head in my hands. I see Anna again, the wings hanging at an angle from her back and shut off the memory. The grief can wait till later.

The past weeks have been like that — holding back and letting go. I feel like two different people, two brand new but entirely different people. And the secrets that Danielle hinted at. I sense their truth.

I wait until she has gone and leave the cafe, a film of sweat and cooking on my skin. It's frosty outside. In the distance, I catch a final glimpse of her as she turns off the street, her dark hair curling behind her. One of Robby's arms, in its stiff blue coat, is visible, emerging from the pushchair.

Turning, I cross back towards the river, needing fresh air to assemble my thoughts. A sudden mist has risen from the Thames, amorphous and white, obscuring the distant trees and giving the illusion that the pedestrian bridge finishes halfway across and disappears into nothingness.

It isn't anything particular that happens, no footsteps behind me or the pressing gaze of a passing stranger, but, without warning, my senses switch to alert. I turn and peer into the wall of cloud behind me. There is nobody, at least nobody I can see. The mist thickens and closes around me, and I feel suddenly alone, sealed in a world apart. Again, I search around me and then, out of nowhere, I see the shape emerge. He is matching my pace. I lurch forwards, nearly stumbling with fright.

I reach the bridge at a run and leap up the metal steps. As I get to the brick concourse, I tell myself I'm being stupid and paranoid. But then I hear the dull ring of his soles on the risers behind me. With a cry, I rush forwards towards two women in Puffa jackets. As I pass them, more people are crossing, and, when I get to the other side and am disgorged into the busy street, he has gone. There is a small coffee shop, and I turn into it and wait, half hidden by the door but able to look out on the street. I wait and wait, but, if he passes, I don't recognise him.

2001

HEIDI

The sky is grey, but I barely notice as rain begins to fall. I hear the ring of Nina's bell in the house beyond and voices. The sound of heavy feet. I tuck my hair behind my ear, straighten my shirt, and wish that my cheeks had not grown suddenly hot. But it's not Scott who answers, it's Jason. His hair is wet with gel and a hoodie hangs loose on his thin frame.

"Nina," he shouts. I follow him through the narrow hall and put my head into the sitting room where Danielle is sitting on the sofa, knees drawn up, watching television.

"Hi," I say. She glances at me briefly and gives a shy smile. Carol is in the kitchen, and I smell bacon and toast. No Scott, so I head upstairs to where Nina is lying on her stomach, listening to music, and eating a packet of crisps.

But she doesn't want to talk, her replies to my chatter fall flat. I swallow my uncertainty and view the familiar walls, grease marks left by Blu Tack, and a montage of photos of Nina when she was younger. After a while, I turn and study her — the wiry frame, the way her hair curls at the back of her neck. Everything seems to have changed, but so slowly that I hardly know how we have got to here. I remember the day that she had asked me to run away, it marks the moment in time when I first acknowledged the differences in her, but how long before that had she been different? How long since the withdrawal of secrets shared, the sudden bursts of anger and at school, where Nina had once been keen to keep her top position, she now barely bothers. Instead of being the first to put her hand up, she answers back and plays the teachers for laughs. Anxiety flutters in the pit of my belly. Perhaps, soon, she will move on from me and find another best friend. She finishes the crisps and licks her fingers.

"So, do you want to go into town or something?" I ask. "Or we can go to the bunker or to the park?" She looks up at me then, her expression flat. Crumpling the packet, she sits up, swings her legs to the floor and shrugs. "I don't care where we go but I don't want to hang about here."

We trail listlessly through Riverbridge, pausing only to buy some chocolate, and then we're sitting on a bench overlooking the Thames. Water slaps against the banks. Beneath the trees, the shadows are lengthening. Nina is far away, and I'm cold and bored. She's barely uttered a word.

"Nina."

"Mmm?" She shoves her hands into her pockets.

"That money."

She gives a groan of irritation. "I told you I didn't steal it."

"Except the bit from Ken's envelope."

Her cheeks are pink with the chill. "I was just showing off. I put it back, and even if I did, who gives a fuck anyway? Ken's a dickhead. I hate him." Her eyes narrow. "And while we're talking about it, I notice that you haven't said you'd definitely run away with me."

"Mum would be so upset."

"Well you could leave a note, duh! Tell her you'll be fine. It's not like you'll be on your own."

I swallow, trying to dislodge the lies that sit in my throat. To tell Nina that I don't want to go with her is too hard to admit. "Why do you want to go?" I ask. "Your mum and Ken aren't that bad, are they?"

Something shoots across her face. "Fuck you!" She gets up and starts to walk away.

"Nina?" I don't understand her reaction and race after her, putting out a hand to enclose her wrist. "What is it? Please, I'm sorry. I'll come okay." I imagine we wouldn't last for long without being found. And it will be ages until it gets warm enough to camp, and by then she will have changed her mind.

"Really?" She flings her arms around my neck.

I smell the stale smoke and perfume in her hair. "I knew I could trust you," she pulls away to look into my eyes. "Thank God for you, Heidi."

Suddenly, I am warm inside. It will be okay. We're still best friends.

A man with two dogs walks past and gives us a smile. I smile back, but Nina turns on him. "What the fuck are you looking at?" she screams. I start back in shock and embarrassment.

The man turns red and walks away at speed.

"What did he do?" I ask.

"All men are creeps." She puts her hand to her mouth, showing the chipped varnish of her nails. Wind lifts her hair, and her face is suddenly so sad that I move towards her, place an arm across her shoulders and pull her into me.

"What's the matter, Nina? I know something's the matter."

She begins to weep, and it's as if she's never cried before and has been holding on for too long. The tears are excavated from a place so deep and so raw that I feel powerless to comfort her. When she's finished, she looks at me. There's a smudge of mascara on her cheek and she shivers.

"What is it? What is it, Nina?"

"Let's get out of here." From her school bag she extracts her make up case and begins to dab her eyes, applying more kohl and rubbing away the mascara stain.

We walk to the park and make our way to the bunker. The sky is overcast, and shadows stretch and grow between the trees. Nina pauses to retie her trainers, and behind us, further down the hill, a flock of crows suddenly lift into the sky with harsh caws. I stop dead and my heart thumps. For a moment there had been someone there, half hidden.

"Come on then," Nina says. "Hurry." I open my mouth to say something but imagine Nina's sarcastic response and shut it again. As we walk, I turn frequently, straining my neck, and, though I do not see the figure again, I feel watched.

Rain begins to fall, and I glance at Nina, something tight and nervous in the pit of my belly. Whatever she wants to tell me, I have some strange sense that I do not want to hear it. Once we're there, we light cigarettes and Nina bites her lip, twists her brow, and her anxiety filters through my skin and into my heart.

"What's wrong?" My voice is pinched.

She takes a deep breath, looks down, scratches at a mud stain on her foot. "Ken and his friends," she cannot look at me, "they make me do things, you know."

And I know. I don't know how — but I know. Waves of horror roll through me. Now she turns and searches my face for a reaction.

"Oh my God." I can't find words to convey my feelings. "Does your mum know?"

She shakes her head.

"Tell her!" I say. "Tell her what he's like. She'll boot him out."

"I can't."

I think of Ken and a day when he gave me a pound to buy sweets. "Aren't you going to give us a kiss to say thank you?" he had demanded, and I had offered my cheek, but it was my lips he had touched with his, and his hand had snaked over my back, lingering longer than was necessary. I shudder.

Nina tells me how Ken has threatened to hurt not just her but Danielle, too, if she tells. Her voice cracks, and she starts shaking so much she can barely get the cigarette to her mouth. "I don't know what to do."

I lean over and put my arm across her back, I can feel the knobs of her spine. When she stops crying, she leans against me.

"Tell the police," I beg. "Are you sure he isn't just trying to frighten you?" But I'm aware I haven't fully taken in the enormity of what she's revealed.

"You don't know these people like I do. And anyway," she grinds the cigarette butt into the ground, "some of these people *are* policemen." She challenges me with a stare. "You have no idea what they're like. I'm not taking any chances."

I do not know what to say.

"Don't you believe me then?"

"Yes, yes of course I do."

She puts her head to one side and regards me frigidly, something hostile in her eyes, and then she crawls to the back of the bunker. "Turn away. Don't watch." And she levers out the brick from her hiding place in the wall.

When she comes back, her cheeks are red and there is a strange, heightened excitement in her eyes. Carefully, she fiddles in the bag and eventually pulls out a photograph. My heart begins to palpitate

"There."

I want to look, but my mind recoils, sensing I will see something that I don't want to. She presses it into my hand, and I turn it over. As soon as I glance at the image, I wish I hadn't. It will never leave me, not ever. It's a girl with blonde hair and sad eyes, her arms folded across her small frame, a group of men hovers. I place it face down. On the back, Nina has written a name — *Maria*. She is watching me, daring me not to look at it again, but it's too late, I don't need to see it again. I will remember it forever.

"You have to go to the police." My voice sounds insubstantial.

"That was my plan, but I told you, some of them *are* the police."

I can't argue, and, impatiently, she shoves the photograph back into the packet. Wrapping the bag around it. I wonder what else is there. I saw the envelope from which she took the image of Maria. There were more.

"Are there — are there ones of you like this?"

Her face says it all.

"But where did you get them?" I am aghast.

"From one of the places."

I don't want to think about these places, about this other life she has to endure. For me, home is dinner, arguments with Anna, television, getting nagged about homework, and bed. That is all. The worst things that trouble me are falling out with Nina or the bitchy comments that get passed around at school, and whether Scott will ever notice me. But what I have seen in the photograph seeps through me like a toxin.

"Who's Maria?" I try not to think about what I saw.

"One of the other girls."

I want to ask her if she has to do what the girl in the

picture is doing, but I don't want to know the answer. And part of me can't believe that this has happened at all.

"So you see. We have to run away, and we have to take Danielle."

My heart sinks. I will let her down. I don't want to run away and particularly not now that I've been told about Ken and his friends — I'm too afraid.

I gaze out bleakly at the woods. Over her shoulder, a magpie opens its wings and glides into the air. On the horizon, salmon-coloured clouds drift past the water tower, and I know that something is gone, gone forever. It will not matter now how brightly the sun shines or how beautiful the day is, some essential part of my childhood is over forever.

2016

DENISE

Denise parks at the back of the police station and then makes her way inside. DCI Mike Tennant's office is on the third floor and at the end of a long corridor. It has the advantage of two windows but the disadvantage of being situated above the canteen and, therefore, generally smells of whatever is being cooked for lunch. Because the canteen produces food that is largely unappetising, the room smells equally unappealing. The canteen is due to be dispensed with in favour of a self-service kitchen and facilities. A piece of news nobody mourns.

Mike is sitting with the Assistant Chief Constable, Barrett. They both look up with interest as Denise enters.

Today, the air clings to the odour of fatty meat and some vegetable that might once have been cabbage.

"I'd really like to give the case another look over. With Heidi's memory supporting the abduction theory, I could at least dismiss other lines of enquiry."

Barrett regards her doubtfully. "The abduction theory was covered pretty thoroughly last time, wasn't it? And how reliable a witness is Heidi?"

Denise sighs, "There were details in what she saw that support the truth of the memory — things she would have only known if she had been there."

Mike raises his brows dubiously. The hairs in them are sparse. Beneath his eyes there are fine wrinkles, but his square chin and steely gaze reflect a keenness of the mind. "Isn't there enough information on the internet for Heidi to have made such a statement without actually having a recollection of it? Is it possible she's producing this memory now to initiate another investigation?"

Denise pauses, the rehearsed speech dying before it can reach her lips. "Personally, I don't think so. Over the years, I've got to know her fairly well, and I have only ever found her honest. She's not suggested we re-investigate. She asked only for validation of what she recalled. Her memory is still very impaired, but she believes that things seem to be finally emerging, and I think there's every chance she'll recover more in due course."

Mike removes his glasses. "How long is it now?"

"Fifteen years."

Mike turns to his boss. "What do you think?"

Barrett sighs. "There's not nearly enough to reassign the case, Denise. Not yet."

"I understand that, but it's a perfect opportunity to check out the names that came up on the first enquiry," Denise says. "I did a lot of leg work on Heidi's case myself."

"It would be a waste of manpower. If it hadn't happened quite so long ago, or we had more forensics, you could argue its cause. We worked every angle at the time, and what you have here does not constitute sufficient grounds for another official investigation." Barrett gives her an apologetic look.

Denise thinks about Heidi. "I'm happy to work on it in my free time, such as that is. I see your point, but there's nothing to be lost by going over the old investigation and checking for any more recent convictions against the original names. And don't forget that Anna wasn't the only young girl who went missing around that time. There was another, too, and Heidi's memory means that we are now looking at two definite abductions. This changes everything, surely?"

"Holly Watts." Mike leans back in the chair and cups the back of his head with his hands.

Barrett shrugs. "I hope you have a lot of free time."

Denise feels a sudden flush of anger. "Look, these girls have never been found, and Nina's killer is still out there, as far as we know. Heidi has lost everyone she ever cared about and knowing what happened to Anna would be some kind of closure for her. Although she doesn't say it, every time she talks about what happened to Anna and Nina, all I hear is the guilt she feels."

Barrett nods. "Have a dig around, if you want," he stands, "and keep me updated on any developments if they come your way. It remains one of the force's greatest failures."

Mike and Denise get to their feet and watch his retreating back.

"I'll check the files out and take them home." Denise, too, feels the failure of the investigation. "I'll include the Holly Watts' files, as well. She was abducted first, and that's where I'll start. I'll want to re-interview anyone who was close to her."

Mike gives her a wry smile. "Good luck, Denise. You're going to need it."

2016

HEIDI

The taxi turns into Jason's tree-lined avenue. At the house, the gate has been left open and the cab drops me straight at the door. Before I can take money out of my purse, Jason is taking the steps, two at a time, and leaning into the driver's window with his wallet.

He gives me a smile that is both nervous and keen, then ushers me up the steps. Taking my coat and scarf, I follow him through the hall to the kitchen. Here, I study him curiously. He's tall and wiry with thick hair that's lighter than his sister's.

"Thanks for coming."

I feel small inside the open-plan room, the rear of which seems to be entirely composed of glass doors looking out to a landscaped garden. He indicates a stool, and I pull myself on to the seat and watch as he pours a glass of wine.

He takes a beer for himself and props himself opposite.

"I remember you." And in his dark eyes is the shadow of Nina's death. He may have wanted to see me, but he can't fully hide the anguish it brings, anguish and a nervous excitement. This means a lot to him. His complexion is fairer than Nina's, and his brows heavily defined. There is something of all his siblings in his face.

"I hope you're hungry." He slips off the seat and opens the oven.

"Can I help?"

He shakes his head. Now that I'm here, I feel a stirring of memory and that connection to Nina tugging at my insides and I wonder — if she had lived, would we still have been friends? Would I have met Danielle, Jason, and Scott at family get-togethers? I think of all the lost birthdays between then and now, birthdays marked by flowers on a grave. I suck in my breath and look away.

"Are you okay?" He is watching me carefully.

"I'm fine," I lie.

He pauses. I see he has so much he wants to voice. Instead, he says, "Would you like to see some photos of Nina?"

He brings out an album, pulls up the stool next to me and opens it, and I gaze down with fascination at a world I once knew, at faces I saw every day, faces that were almost as familiar to me as my own.

They're all here: Nina, their mother, Danielle, Scott, and Jason. Each image seems to knock at something deeper, particularly the ones of Nina. I try to imagine us at the park or in town or lying on our beds and discussing our hopes and dreams, the intricacies of school. And suddenly, I am hit by the profound weight of loss.

The photographs are random — a school shot followed by a blurred image of the two boys holding plastic swords outside a castle. There are only a few of the whole family together; the album contains no holiday snaps and leaves no sense of a family evolving as time passes. It's a sad testimony to their fractured lives, and I readjust my perspective. I pause at one of Jason as a boy, with hair long fringed over his pale skin. He glares into the lens with an expression that reminds me strongly of Nina. "What happened to your real dad?"

"I'm not absolutely sure who my real dad is." Something like a smile tugs at his mouth, but not quite. "Scott, Nina, and Danielle's lives in Manchester now, but there's no contact."

"And yours?"

He gives a grim laugh. "If he's the one Mum claims he is, he didn't hang around for long. And he's probably dead of an overdose by now."

I raise my brows in question.

"He was a druggie. Mum's had problems with stuff all her life. Now it's just the booze, I think."

I recall the aged skin, the red veins of her cheeks, and slurred speech. It's not hard to imagine.

"What about you?" he says.

Usually, I find ways of avoiding questions like this. I hate the pity I see in people's eyes when I tell them I have nobody.

Self-consciously, I explain my lack of family. I hear the slightly defiant note in my voice, but even so, a fleeting expression of empathy passes over his face.

"And will your mother get better?"

I shrug and realise that I have excised her so completely from my life that I no longer even consider an alternative. I visited once, but if she knew who I was, she didn't show it. Perhaps, one day, I will try again. Perhaps not.

"And you don't remember anything about the attack?" he asks.

I flush and, whether it's the wine or the need to share what I know, I find myself telling him of lying next to Nina and seeing Anna torn away in someone's arms.

His eyes open in surprise, and he leans towards me, his expression intense and focused. "So when did you remember this?"

"Recently," I admit.

"You didn't say anything when you visited my mum."

I flush. "It somehow didn't seem right, and it doesn't offer anything material."

"So, nothing else? No face? Could you tell anything about the man who had Anna?"

I shake my head and wonder whether or not I have done the right thing in bringing it up; in many ways, it offers no answers and raises only questions. The room is still. And his disappointment falls between us.

He turns the page, and I remember the sense of something passing between Carol and her children when I mentioned Ken.

"There are no photos of Ken here," I say, gesturing toward the album.

He gazes at me with a strange expression, gives a sharp laugh, and closes the album with a slap.

"Why do you ask about Ken?"

I don't answer.

"Come on, let's eat first."

From the oven, he removes a casserole covered in slices of crisped potato. He takes the food to the dining area of the kitchen, where we talk of other things.

"How did you learn to cook like this?" I say.

"I hadn't realised until I left home that proper food existed, if you know what I mean. I thought the best you could get came out of a paper bag with salt and vinegar. It's the way I relax now. On the rare occasions I give myself a holiday, I pick a location abroad and book myself on a cookery course."

As we eat, I try to explain my amnesia, but we don't talk of Nina or Anna. He fills my glass more than once, and, as the wine goes to my head, I find myself opening up. I tell him about my job, the books and films I like and, even though I

79

don't say it, I am aware that I'm revealing all the years of my loneliness. When the food is finished, I help him clear away, and he puts on the coffee maker.

As I take my first sip of the coffee, he places his hands on the table, and the skin around his eyes tightens. "You asked about Ken. Well," he pauses. I see him struggle with the words. "Nina came to me when she had nowhere else to go."

"How do you mean?" My heart gives an uneasy flutter.

"Stuff was going on for her. Bad stuff."

The anxiety comes from nowhere.

"Ken," I say.

His name drops between us like a stone. "He was abusing Nina."

Something in me shifts and a shower of images fill my head: her angry eyes; the thin arms as they cover her breasts; the way she smoked, fast and shallow, blowing the smoke out in a thin grey line as if emitting a stream of expletives. Ken, the pockmarked figure, now takes form, and I see him in Nina's back garden laying a path in the heat of the sun. He is bare to the waist, and his back, too, is pitted with acne scars. When he sees me, he gives me a slow wink. Nina and I walking back from the shops, Ken striding towards us, and Nina pulling at my arm and dragging me into an alleyway. As he passes, she ducks out and throws a pebble at his back that misses, hissing "fucking creep".

"Are you all right?" Jason is leaning forward; his hand is on my wrist.

I am shaken and sense that I had known already. The revelation sits inside me like poison. Did I know? Did she tell me, and if she did, what, if anything, did I do?

"Did she tell Carol?"

Jason gives a snort of derision. "I love my mother, but she isn't going to win any 'Mum of the Year' awards. I wanted to go to the police with Nina, but she persuaded me not to. She said Ken had connections with them, and it would make everything worse."

"The police?"

He gives me a curious look. "You think they couldn't be corrupt because they're the police?"

"No," I say, realising how naïve I sounded.

"Looking back, I didn't know what to do, but she was adamant. Ken scared her. She begged me not to take it further." There is self-recrimination in his tone.

The burden of Nina's abuse hangs in the silence.

"I can't forgive myself for not acting on it then, not doing anything ... and a month later, she was murdered."

I don't know what to say. Nina died forever trapped with her terrible secret, too afraid to get help.

"And I'm certain now that she was right, and that Ken did have associations within the force. He got away with it and was never arrested, not even for the abuse. Nina told me that someone would cover it up if she came forward and accused him." He looks at me meaningfully. "And I think she was right." He leans in. "I hired someone privately."

"You mean like a private investigator?"

"Seven years ago. He didn't get very far."

"No?"

"I've always believed Ken was responsible for her murder, too. Think about it: what if Nina told Ken that she had reached out to me, and then he was afraid that I would tell someone else or go to the police? After all, they can't all be bent. It would have caused problems for him. Maybe he tried to shut her up."

"But why try to kill me? And what about Anna?"

"Maybe you just weren't supposed to be there. Maybe Nina saw Ken coming and told you to hide and then you witnessed

Nina's murder? Afterwards, he saw or heard you — he would've had to silence you too. Maybe he couldn't bring himself to kill Anna ... I don't know."

Repugnance clutches at my insides, and I think about Ken, those reactions I first experienced when I saw the photo of him on the beach. I realise now that, among those emotions, there was also trepidation. Was he the one I saw in that returned memory, Anna in his arms? I can hardly bear to consider it.

"You think he killed Anna, too, don't you?"

Jason looks down. "I'm sorry."

"What did the investigator say about Ken?"

"Ken had an alibi. He was in Kintbury for a poker game. The people he gave as witnesses — the investigator looked into them."

"And?"

Jason shakes his head. "The guy was really enthusiastic at first, confident he'd be able to find some leads, but then he just dropped it."

"Why?"

"I think he was scared off."

"By who?"

Jason sighs. "I'm not sure. At the time I believed he must have come up against some pretty nasty people who probably threatened him. But later, I remembered a couple of times when he seemed to be alluding to a different sort of threat, and I remembered what Nina had said: there *was* police involvement."

"So, where's Ken now?"

"That's the million-dollar question."

"Nobody knows?"

"There are no work, DVLA, or address records for him.

Maybe he died. Maybe he moved abroad, changed his name, who knows?" Jason shifts in the chair. "He was always considered the main suspect. The police kept tabs on him for a long time. And then, with the alibi and nothing to prove he was there or to prove that he had even abused Nina, they had to move on. One of the main reasons I hired this man was to find Ken."

The idea that Ken is out there frightens me. If he tried to kill me once, he could do it again. "But he didn't find anything?"

"Nothing." His expression shifts, and the dark eyes are filled with something that I can't interpret. "And you, Heidi? You say you don't remember much, but did any of that about Nina ring a bell? You were her best friend, if she told *me* what was happening, isn't it likely that she also told you?"

Uneasy feelings move through me and I feel close, closer to some truth at the heart of my childhood. Then I recall Danielle's statement that both of us had changed. Was this the reason? That Nina told me? Suddenly, I am frightened, and my arm tingles with the memory of Nina's dead fingers.

"I don't remember," I say.

"You really don't know, do you?" I feel as if I have been on trial, that up until this moment, he has been hoping that I have been holding back. I almost want to laugh.

"I have lots of memories, but they're fractured. I lost more than I'll ever even realise. It's like..." I struggle to explain, "... it's like the numbness when you put a piece of ice on your skin... you still sort of feel it. I still have a sense of things. Sometimes emotions come back or a smell or sound, but when I try to go further, the memory stops."

"Will that ever change? Perhaps that flashback of the day is a sign that you're closer to remembering?"

I shrug. I don't want to tell him that I believe I'm finally thawing, that puddles of memory have been appearing out of nowhere.

"I don't know, not necessarily. Bits return from time to time, but it doesn't mean much."

And yet, even as I speak, new images of Nina's face flicker in my mind, along with the bunker, and the smell of the sweet shop we went to after school, and something else, something darker.

Jason gets up and switches on the lights, and I blink into a sense of unreality. Glancing at my watch, I realise how late it is. "I ought to get back."

When the taxi arrives, I put my boots and coat on. I feel that somehow, something has changed, and I don't want to meet Jason's eyes. "What's your next plan?" I ask, because I sense he has one.

He sighs, gazing into the distance. "I haven't made progress in years, but it's different now."

I look at him curiously. "How?"

"You know how, Heidi." His expression is masked in the hall light, and I shake my head. "Think about it, apart from the murderer, there were witnesses."

The chilled air brushes my cheeks.

"Anna and you. But Anna is gone." He leans towards me. "You're the only one left, and somewhere, inside your head, is the knowledge of who did it."

The taxi beeps, and he hurries me out into the dark and into the awaiting cab, pressing a five-pound note into my palm. Before I can thank him, he's turned and is making his way back into the empty house.

I can't stop dwelling on Nina and the photograph. During the days that follow, I realise the knowledge of what is happening to her has overlaid all reassuring sentiments I held about my life and our friendship. Every time I glimpse her dark head or catch her eyes, I am cramped with awkwardness and revulsion.

Our relationship has suddenly become complicated, and never far from my thoughts is the promise that I made to run away. At night, my dreams are interlaced with nightmares — monsters pursuing me through tangled woods, or in the corridors of vast houses. And beyond all this is my belief that Nina can be saved, that, if she told the right person, Ken would be arrested and taken away. I still don't fully believe that she can't tell the police — there must be plenty of policemen who are good.

Home is contaminated by the knowledge that Ken is just next door. He continues to wave and smile, have conversations with Mum. I avoid him at all times, and on the odd occasion when we cross paths, I have to hide my feelings. Should I tell Mum? But if I do, she will say something, and Nina will never speak to me again. And what if it's true that something will happen to Nina or Danielle if I told the truth? I could never live with myself.

Since her revelation, Nina has been more open, and it's clear it has been a huge relief. On occasions, when we are alone or about to part for different classes, she snatches my hand in her warm one and squeezes it gently. And she does not hide her grief or fear from me, I can see it in her eyes, as I can feel the renewed faith and trust in our bond. But her gain has been my loss, and it's as though the baton of horror has been passed to me, and my life is now tainted by the dark knowledge that has been shared.

"Are you okay, love?" Mum places a warm hand on my back.

"I'm fine," I lie, summoning as much of a smile as my face allows, but I see doubt in her expression.

"I'm going out tonight. Natasha is going to come over to babysit later." She can't hide her excitement.

"Who are you going with?" This is an unusual occurrence.

"A friend."

"Who?"

"You don't know her."

I don't believe her. "Where are you going?"

"Just a meal out, nothing special." But her eyes say something different.

"We don't need Natasha. I can babysit Anna."

"In a few years or so, not yet."

I storm out of the house. Ken's car is not outside, so I take courage and ring Nina's bell.

Scott opens the door and I flush. But I'm aware of him in a different way, too, and the thought of him kissing me is suddenly polluted by all that I know of Nina.

86

"Just go on up." He goes through to the sitting room, leaving me in the hall, and I wait until my heart stops pattering. How many months have I secretly hoped that he liked me? Moulding every tiny interaction into something I wanted to see. I lean against the wall and there is a lump in my throat. The thought of a boy wanting me scares me now, and I wish I could take away all those fantasies of my hand in his or that first time when he might have leaned in and touched his lips to mine.

Once I have mastered my feelings, I climb the stairs and find Nina in the room she shares with Danielle. In spite of the weather, she has raised the sash window and is blowing smoke from her cigarette into the back garden. She looks tired. I move some dolls and a bead set along Danielle's bed and sit down.

"Nina," I whisper. "I've been thinking..."

"Stop it! Not here." She scowls. "What you doing later?"

"Nothing. We could go to the bunker after lunch?"

"K." She leans out to stub the cigarette on the brickwork then throws it into the border.

Voices are raised downstairs. I hear Carol shouting and the sound of Jason and Scott.

"For fuck's sake, here we go again!" Nina scowls and lies back on her bed. "Mum's bloody well drunk again. No wonder we're all such screw-ups. Stupid bitch."

It's common knowledge that Carol drinks during the day — a constant embarrassment for Nina. I don't say anything.

The sun has come out and is warm on my cheeks as we climb to the bunker; but frost is still laced in the grassy hollows and along the twisted branches of trees.

"It's freezing," I say.

In the bunker, we light the candles, but the sense of excitement and secrecy I once enjoyed has been eclipsed by what I know. My eyes drift constantly to the bit of the wall where Nina has hidden the photos and money.

"Will they know you stole those pictures?" I ask. "What will they do if they find out?"

"Of course they don't know." She laughs dryly. "If they found out, shit. I daren't think of the consequences."

"So they... they would *really* hurt you?"

"You're so naive, Heidi. Think about it. Think about what they do. Do they give a shit about hurting me now? What sort of people do you think they are? They're hardly human." Her eyes are black. "And some of them, they don't have souls at all."

I am shocked by her vehemence. The stain inside me spreads. These men are so far outside my understanding of human nature, that I have never really considered them. I watch the news occasionally and see the newspaper headlines, but those cruelties that are sometimes inflicted on others seem too far removed to play a part in my life. And, up until now, they have never upset the balance of my belief that the world is generally a safe and loving place. I see how foolish I've been. I look at Nina and open my mouth to speak, but the chasm between us seems to grow in the chilled air, pushing us even further apart.

When we get back to our street, we part ways. Mum is in the kitchen preparing shepherd's pie, my favourite. Did she do this to make up for going out and not letting me babysit? Or because, as I suspect, she's not meeting a friend at all, at least not a female one. What happens if she falls in love and brings a man into our lives? He could be a man like Ken.

Suddenly, I find myself in her arms. She smells so warm, so nice, so mum-like, that I begin to cry.

"What is it? What's the matter? Heidi?"

The things I want to say are sticking to my insides — all corners and dangerous edges. I open my lips.

"Have you fallen out with Nina?" she asks. "You don't seem quite as close."

And whatever I might have said dies on my tongue.

Later, I cannot sleep. I am convinced now that she is with someone other than a friend. She wore too much lipstick and fussed over her hair for much longer than usual. I had followed her to the door hoping to see whoever she was meeting, but she said she was walking into town.

Natasha comes with chocolate and sprinkles and makes cakes with Anna. We eat them in front of a film. And when I go to bed, I feel alone and afraid — all the things Nina has said about the men tumble about in my head. When I hear an engine outside, I creep into mum's front bedroom to peer out of the window. The car is silver. It sits idle for a while before a man gets out of the driver's seat and comes round to open the passenger door. And there is mum — with flushed cheeks. She is smiling in a stupid way. *Liar, liar*, I think. *You bloody, fucking liar.*

I go back to my room, careful not to wake Anna, who lies on her side, facing me, her hair blown about her head like candyfloss. I watch her in the semi-darkness and listen to the sound of the key in the door and my mother's footsteps — the hum of her and Natasha's hushed voices. Then I pull my covers over my head and cry silently until I am empty.

2016

The more he observes Heidi, the more he recognises her determination. For the first time, he wonders if she has been underestimated. The past seems to have become a quest. He is learning about her through her habits and mannerisms: the way that she holds her body as she walks, the pace of her step, the small neat movements of her hands when she talks.

Sometimes, she and a few colleagues have lunch at a local café, and although he cannot hear what they say, he fills in the gaps himself — snatches of imagined dialogue and reflections, and later, at night, he tries to visualise the contours of her thoughts.

In her hesitant movements, he perceives femininity and weakness. Now, she is leaning back in her seat and adjusting her hair and taking a sip from the cup in front of her. The colleagues are laughing, but he can see that Heidi is just outside the circle of intimacy. Is this as a consequence of the attack? It's as though she is branded.

Heidi dresses more conservatively than her work mates; she does not advertise her body. He knows that she has no boyfriend, no lover, and no close friends. She seems to be entirely alone. He can relate to this. He, too, is alone, nearly — The Chief's strong face, the face he has loved for so long, comes to fill his mind and briefly reassure him.

Later, he follows her home. It is dark now, and he parks down the road at the rear of her property. Getting out of the car, he clings to the shadows and dark alleyways, feeling almost invisible. At the back of Heidi's house, the sprawled back gardens lead to fences and an allotment. He makes his way there now, brushing against the damp grasses and climbing over the rotting gate to crouch.

He zips his coat high and pulls gloves over his hands. From here, he can see straight into the window of Heidi's lounge and kitchen. Her figure moves across the room and into the kitchen area, where she is making a hot drink. The cat leaps on to the counter and arches its back. Heidi pauses, a hand on the cat's fur, but she is gazing off into space, somewhere else in her reflections. A small frown darkens on her brow. After a moment or two, steam pumps from the kettle spout. She pours water into a mug, but she is still distracted, putting things away and circling the kitchen, her manner hesitant.

The cat rubs itself back and forth along her midriff and, finally, putting the cup down, she lays her face against the cat's body and closes her eyes. Then collecting the cup, she switches off the light and moves out of his vision.

Behind the blinds, the bathroom is now illuminated, and he thinks about how she might brush her teeth, undress and put on pyjamas or a nightdress. Does she still bear the scars on her body? He wonders what they look like on her white skin.

Then he visualises her head on the pillow, her eyes closed, her hair spread against her face, the gentleness of her breath, the way the covers will rise and fall, her lips slack, and he wonders what she sees in her dreams. Is she forever running from a killer, running but never fast enough? Part of him wants her to know that she is watched, and more than once he has stepped away from the screen of darkness and into the light. This risk also gives him strange pleasure. One day, he won't have to hide, one day The Chief will give his instructions, and he will stand before her and her life will be changed forever.

2001

HEIDI

As I make my way through the woods, there are clumps of snowdrops in the hollows, and it's cool but not freezing. I pause to look around, see the shadows between trees and the stretching emptiness and imagine someone waiting and watching. The world no longer feels safe. I begin to run, my breath straining in my lungs, and hope that Nina will be at the bunker like she said.

At the top of the hill, I stop again and scan the wood. There is nobody here, no one behind me, although, more than once in the recent weeks, I have felt the uncomfortable sensation of being watched. I lean over and wait for my lungs to adjust and then make my way towards the bunker. As I near, I smell cigarette smoke and my heart lifts a little, and then voices drift in the air. Perhaps Danielle has come with her.

Nina has left the sheeting on the ground, and when I look in, I see Nina and another girl — a girl with dry blonde hair and small eyes. I realise with dismay that she's the girl in the photo, the one called Maria, and I am cramped by embarrassment. Why is she here? They stop talking immediately.

"This is Maria," Nina says pointedly, and I understand that I must keep quiet about what I have seen.

Maria gives me a tight and unfriendly smile. "Right, I better be off."

Nina follows her outside, waving a hand to indicate I should stay. Their hushed conversation reaches me but is too far away to interpret. I lean back against the wall and take a cigarette from the packet on the floor, lighting it with a candle. The smoke wafts like a dream.

"Thanks," Nina's eyes are bright and strained.

"Are you mates then? What's she like?"

But Nina's thoughts are far away. I reach forward to rub a patch of mud from the trainers I bought in town that morning. Usually, such things are enough to fill me with enthusiasm, not anymore.

She's watching me now.

"Why was she here?" I don't tell her I'm upset she's shared our secret place with someone else, another friend. Maybe Maria will replace me. They have more in common than we do.

"I asked her to come. She bought me some pills. You can have one if you like."

I shake my head.

She opens the bag and puts one on her tongue.

"So, she came to bring you pills? Be careful, Nina, you don't know what the effect might be."

She laughs. "Yeah, I need to be so careful with my amazing life. Jesus, if I can get off my head for a few hours it would be fucking brilliant."

My clumsiness makes me feel stupid.

"We talked about them." Her eyes stray to the woods outside.

"Did you show her the photos?"

94

"I couldn't." She pauses. "It would be horrible if she knew I'd seen them, and she would want to see the ones of me."

"Does she want to run away?"

She gives a dry laugh. "She thinks it's a stupid idea."

We smoke in the silence and after a while, she gets up and goes to stand outside. Her eyes have an unnatural shine. Whatever she has taken is beginning to work. "You should really take one of these. Everything looks amazing, seriously."

Slowly, she raises her arms and waves them in front of her face.

I reach across and move her cigarette packet and pick up the newspaper lying there. We buy magazines from time to time, but not newspapers. Maybe Maria brought it. I turn it over curiously, and it's as though an icy hand has reached deep into my chest and squeezed my heart.

It's her — the girl in the photo that fell from the envelope holding Ken's money. I read the headline. Her name is Holly Watts, and she has been missing from her home for two days.

2016

DENISE

From her study, Denise is aware of the whirring of the fridge and the occasional car engine. Her coffee has been left undrunk. She shuffles another file in front of her and reflects. Much of the information in Holly Watts' case she has forgotten, or had not worked on directly. The files are thinner than they should be, testimony of the failure to produce a perpetrator.

With a sigh, she returns herself to the photographs of the scene where Nina and Heidi were found and the timeline of events. It's hard to believe that somewhere, among all this evidence, a killer is not hiding just beyond sight — unnoticed in a passing comment or eluding consideration beneath the sheer weight of information. But if they are here, they were not discovered at the time, either escaping recognition or not deemed worth of full investigation.

The paedophile link between the cases has been explored extensively, with known offenders having been interviewed and asked to present alibis for the time of both incidents. Much energy had been invested in Ken being the perpetrator.

Denise remembers Ken with dislike. Before Nina's brother had come forward accusing him of abusing Nina, they had already discovered the accusation of abuse from the children of a previous domestic partner, but the CPS had dropped the case. It was more than likely that Nina had been abused, but how could it be proved? The medical examinations suggested abuse had taken place, but without Nina's own statement identifying the offender, a prosecution was likely to fail.

And then Holly Watts, seven years old, who disappeared in late January, six months before Anna. The rareness of such incidents, the geographical closeness, and the similarity of the victims made it likely that they were seeking one assailant. Denise, like everybody else, believed that they had a dangerous paedophile operating in the area, yet there had been no subsequent abductions, not within any compelling distance or time frame. And, in spite of the extensive work trying to find a connection between the two children, none was ever discovered.

If Denise could now uncover the piece of evidence that proved Holly knew or had met Ken, it would make all the difference. Ken's fingers are all over Nina's murder — the abuse, his history. It makes sense that he abducted both Anna and Holly. Maybe Nina had found something out. Something that incriminated him.

Denise empties her mug into the sink and puts the kettle back on to boil. The police station has changed a lot in fifteen years — much dead wood has been stripped away, and there was plenty of that, she recalls. As she continues to pore through Anna's files, she is less than happy with the quality of the police work in places. Things that should have been followed up are absent and, in her opinion, there does not seem to be enough work carried out exploring a possible link between Anna and Holly.

Feeling chilled, Denise puts on some thermal slippers and a large, woolly cardigan. On the way back to the kitchen she catches a glance of herself in the mirror, her hair askew, the vast jumper swaddling her like the pelt of a mammoth.

After making two rounds of bacon and egg sandwiches, she begins looking at the files on Holly Watts again. It makes tragic reading, and she switches to a glass of wine. Holly had been in the custody of social services for less than seven months following the death of her mother. Initially, she had been fostered by a couple in Oxford. There is no specific reason given for the termination of this arrangement, and Holly is then moved to Bayview Children's Home in Waterstone, 25 miles or so from Riverbridge. There are as many similarities as differences: both girls' abductions appear to have been unplanned and were probably opportunistic.

Holly disappeared sometime after school, when it was believed that she had followed some older children to a nearby park. There were no witnesses, although one person had thought they had seen her get into a dark green car. Ken's car had matched the description, but at some point between Holly's and Anna's disappearances, his car had been scrapped, and he had bought a new one. This meant it had not been possible to comb it for forensic evidence. This fact alone drew suspicion his way. But there are differences, too — Anna had been with Nina and Heidi. Had someone followed them to the bunker? It would be a huge risk to take Anna in front of two onlookers. And the murder and attempted murder of the two older girls points to a disorganised killer, one with an entirely different profile. Perhaps the killer had been there with the purpose of killing Nina. The way in which Nina's murder had been perpetrated suggested something more personal, rather than the chaotic manner of the attempt to kill Heidi. If Nina had been killed first, had Heidi and Anna been hidden then discovered and attacked in a panic?

She puts down her cup and stares into the night. Whatever the reason was for taking Anna from the scene, one thing is true: if Anna had been alive — and there was no evidence to suggest that she hadn't been — she would have been a witness. And if it was someone she knew, someone like Ken, it would make her survival an incredibly risky prospect.

Or were there, as was often mooted, two perpetrators? There are many unanswered questions. Witnesses stated that, on the day, Heidi left for the park, she left a good half an hour before Nina — they did not go together. This behaviour was a departure from their usual.

Denise chews on the end of her pen. Both Lynn and Carol had stated that, not long before the attack, there had been some friction between the girls, and, at one stage, a full-scale falling out. However, they had appeared to be friends again on the week of the attack. Had they fallen out again?

Did someone see Anna and think she was alone? Did he follow her as far as the bunker? What happened next? The girls' behaviour has always made Denise suspect that Nina and Heidi were already caught up in something — that perhaps they had fallen upon some piece of information that made them a threat. Could this have been Ken's abuse?

Would the abuse have justified the murder, attempted murder, and the abduction of Anna? This explanation does not sit well with Denise. Perhaps Nina and Heidi discovered something else, something far more dangerous. Lynn stated that, prior to the attack, Heidi had been withdrawn, moody, and more secretive, something Lynn attributed to her budding adolescence. But what if it was something else? And if it was — then Heidi is still in possession of it. A whisper of disquiet settles on her skin.

Yet again, as she begins to go through the files, there are areas of sloppiness and places where the records appear incomplete. The policeman who headed the murder investigation was Alf Claybourne. Denise had begun on the force after the Watts' investigation and not long before Anna was taken. She recalls Claybourne with distaste. There were many rumours of backhanders and intimidating police interviews. But what Denise remembers most is his arrogance and the covert racist and sexist remarks he made. Unfortunately, Claybourne is not someone they can question — he died of a heart attack several years ago.

Denise pauses, chin in hand. The trees begin to whisper in the rising wind, and rain spatters at the panes. She looks down at the photographs of the two girls she has propped on the desk. The silence of the room settles inside her, and, although it has been acknowledged many times already, she takes in their likeness to each other and experiences a prescience that there *is* a connection.

Finally, eyes dry, she takes off her glasses and sees that dawn is beginning to filter through the window, and the shape of the distant trees is now visible against the skyline. When she gets up from the chair, she is stiff. In the bedroom, too exhausted to undress, she pulls the covers over her and falls asleep instantly.

2016

HEIDI

I wake; the silence tells me it is very early, before dawn. There is coffee and alcohol on my tongue. Behind my eyes, a dull pain threatens to become a full-blown headache. Nina, I see Nina. She is holding a plastic bag and money is spilling to the floor, lots of money. The collar of her shirt is turned up on her slender neck.

The bunker; the smell of the woody earth, the sharp scent of animals that have taken shelter. Above, the discoloured bricks seem to press down. Suddenly, we are outside the bunker, where clouds have gathered on the edge of the woods and a breeze carries the sweetness of dried grass.

Nina's face, red with rage, her eyes black and uncomprehending. "*I hate you, you bitch,*" she screams. "*I hate you. You're supposed to be my friend.*" She's running down the hill away from me, light glancing off her hair. And I am standing outside the bunker as a sob starts in my throat then consumes me, and I lean into it. "*I'm sorry, I'm sorry,*" I am screaming, too, but she is too far away, and the cry of my voice is drowned by the hammering rain.

All morning, I wander dispiritedly about the house and the memory of Nina presses. Eventually, I can stand it no longer. I know I must return to the bunker. The bunker was where my old life ended and the new one began, the place where I lost two people that I loved. My skin pricks with dread but the compulsion is overwhelming. I change into warm clothes and stuff a torch and gloves in my pockets and leave the house.

The day is already on the turn, with clouds gathering. At the bus stop, I wait in the drizzle for the bus to come. The memories cling to me like a skin.

The bus driver gives me a smile, and my heels clunk on the metal as I ascend the spiral stairs to the top deck. Two teenagers slouch on the back seats, so I sit at the front, gazing out of the window distorted by raindrops.

The teenagers leave and a woman gets on, takes out a newspaper, and begins to read. We pass the street where Nina and I lived, and I look at the line of houses, seeming untouched by the trauma that was played out in them.

Eventually, I arrive and step out on to the chilly avenue, feeling a growing sense of anxiety. The scene is familiar, and I recall the park well and it's as if part of me slips out of my adult perception and becomes once again that of a child. I am visited by a faint sense of culpability that I do not fully understand.

Ahead, a little path winds up beyond a narrow gate, trees, clinging to the last of their leaves, tower on either side. The trunks stand close together casting a shadow over the lane. For a moment I falter, my feet cemented to the pavement. This is where we came so often, climbing over the gate rather than opening it, and I recall the mossy texture of its frame beneath the palms of my hand, cool and furry. At night, the green stains would still be caught in the ridges of my skin and beneath the nails.

Flicking the latch, I push it open and begin to ascend the path. Now that I'm here, I recall the geography of the woods clearly. Rain has softened the ground and there is the imprint of many feet.

A memory comes to me of sledging down this path, snow turning dirt brown as we furrowed the whiteness with our sleigh. Birds twitter in the branches, and I recollect how alive the park had been, how each clump of grass held a bee, a train of ants, or a bright butterfly.

I walk fast, feeling my heart pump and notice the sky is already streaked with red to the West and that the ground is suddenly darker. It's getting late. When I reach the top of the path, the area opens up. To the left is the wooded hill that leads to the bunker — a few resilient gold and red leaves cling to the trees.

Standing here, time falls away. Straight ahead, the sky stretches, and, in the distance, I see a crouch of houses, miniature streets. We would play football here on the open ground, hoping to attract attention of the boys who sometimes played on the weekends or after school.

It's then, at the corner of my awareness, I hear some movement, something out of place, and I freeze. Gazing out, my pupils take in every detail of the surroundings with perfect clarity: the trees, more defined, branches sculpted into the crimson sky.

Skin shrinking, I discern, halfway down the hill, the figure of a man. At first, my mind races to rationalise his presence, to make sense of his approaching bulk. Desperately, I search for the form of a dog, but he's not in the right place. He's not on the path, and I am consumed with some primal instinct that I am in danger.

His head is suddenly visible as he emerges from behind a tree, and my nightmare is confirmed — a balaclava covers his face. I can think of only one reason why this would be the case and terror bullets through me. He is still half hidden behind a shrub, but I can feel his gaze and the unwavering intent of his purpose. He is coming for me.

Wendy Martin, Holly Watts' aunt, lives in Milton Keynes — a good two hours' drive, but Denise considers it worth the effort. On the phone, Wendy had sounded anxious and a little shocked. Was there news of Holly? Had she been found? Denise had had to admit that they were no closer to discovering what had happened to her.

It's nearly 8 pm when she finally arrives on the quiet street. Denise takes the remaining half of the egg sandwich out of its plastic wrapper and eats it quickly, swigging it down with the dregs of lukewarm coffee she had bought at a garage. Grimacing into the mirror, she checks for stray cress between her teeth, then collects her coat and bag, and climbs out of the car.

Outside, the smell of woodsmoke wafts in the air. Wendy's house is a neat, square box with red tiles and a terracotta path leading to the front door.

The doorbell plays a tinny rendition of the opening bars to Beethoven's Fifth symphony, which is followed almost immediately by an insistent, high-pitched yapping. When Wendy

Martin opens the door, Denise sees an attractive, middle-aged woman. She offers Denise a chair in the sitting room, where the dog rolls immediately on to its back and offers itself for petting.

While Wendy makes tea, Denise takes a look round the room, pausing to study a row of photos above the fireplace. Her eyes fall first on a picture of Holly with her mother, Rachael. Behind them a Christmas tree is blurred with coloured lights. The image is a little faded, but Denise can trace their features. Holly is grinning, a tabby cat in her arms. Her hair is held back on one side by a rainbow patterned clip.

The other pictures largely depict what Denise assumes are Wendy's children. There are no images of a husband or partner. The children are grown-up, with offspring of their own. They all have Wendy's blonde hair and high brow.

Wendy returns with a mug of tea and a plate of biscuits.

Denise takes a sip from her cup. "Thank you for seeing me. I'm sorry I don't have new information about Holly."

Denise isn't sure whether it's relief or disappointment she reads on Wendy's face.

Wendy sighs. "Holly would be 22 now. All grown up. I have almost stopped expecting to know what happened her, but I'm no fool, I know she's probably dead." Her chin tilts a little defiantly, as if challenging Denise to contradict her. "So, if you're not here to tell me you have further information, why are you here?"

Denise puts down her mug. "I don't know if you're aware, but it was always believed that Holly's abduction may have been linked to another missing persons case that happened around the same time."

"Anna Bevan?" Denise nods, and Wendy sits forward. "You've found out what happened to Anna?"

"No, nothing like that, but a witness statement corroborates the fact that Anna appears to have been abducted, and I'm taking another look into the case."

"So you have a description of the person who did it?"

"I'm afraid the description is so vague as to be of no use. I'm here because I'm hoping you would talk me through all that you knew about Holly leading up to her abduction."

"I see." Wendy frowns. "That's a shame about the witness. It's a long time ago now, but I'll do my best."

The dog, sensing its owner's agitation, jumps up on the sofa beside her.

"I understand how painful this must be for you."

"Yes." Her gaze moves to the photograph of her sister and niece. "We had fallen out, you know, Rachael and I. I hated her new partner. And then she said some things to me that hurt — we both said too much. I didn't even know that she had died till the solicitor contacted me. She wrote to me once and tried to ring. This was only a few months before her death, but I ripped the letter up. And then, afterwards, Holly..." she tugs a hand through her hair, "Holly had to go into care. If only I'd known." Her face crumples. "I would have taken Holly, but it was too late by the time I found out. As soon as I knew, I was in conversation with Social Services and I had visits. They said I could almost certainly take her, but there was a lot of red tape. Holly was... she was a sweet little thing, you know. We would have welcomed her and loved her."

"So you knew very little of Holly and those in close contact with her before Rachael died?"

"That's correct."

"How long before she went missing did you last visit Holly?"

Wendy shrugs. "Not long, about a week or so. It was a Saturday. They let me take her for a burger in town." The memory makes her bite down on her lips. "She had extra chips."

"How did she seem?"

"Well — as you'd expect, I suppose. She'd lost her mother and her home, but she seemed excited about coming to live with us."

"And prior to that?"

"I visited Holly in Bayview about four times in all. Social Services said to take it slowly. I'm ashamed to say, Rachael and I had not been in touch for nearly five years by then, and so Holly couldn't remember us at all."

"What happened wasn't your fault."

"I know that now, but I wish with all my heart it had been different." She sucks in her breath. "I pray now that we'll find out what happened to Holly, whether she's alive or dead. The not knowing is worse. I'm glad Rachael never lived to see it — though it probably would never have happened if she hadn't died."

"So, over the four times you saw her, did she change at all? Apart from the distress over her mother's death and having to go into care, did you sense that anything else may have been troubling her?"

Wendy runs a hand absently over the dog. "I don't know how much attention I paid, if I'm honest. I was devastated over Rachael's death and wracked with guilt. I hadn't long found out that Liam, my ex, was having an affair, and I was trying to juggle my kids, work, and a divorce. It was a tough time."

"Did you have any ideas or thoughts about what happened to Holly?"

"No, none at all."

"You say you fell out over Rachael's ex?"

She nods her head. "She deserved better, or I thought so.

He was flirting with me the first time we met. I didn't trust him. Rachael was a couple of years older than me, and I looked up to her. When we were younger, there was a lot of jealousy — just the usual, but I think we both bore grudges. Anyway, we said things we could never take back."

"Were they together when she died?"

Wendy gives a bitter laugh. "No, he'd left her a few years before that. I learned this later, of course. I didn't like him, but he had no interest in Holly. And I'm assuming he was thoroughly checked out at the time."

Denise consults her notes. "Yes. We have no reason to believe he was involved in any way. What about Holly's biological father? It says here he had moved abroad and had never been a part of Holly's life."

"That's true," Wendy acknowledges. "Poor Holly."

Denise drains her tea and brushes the biscuit crumbs into her palm, which she puts on the empty plate. "I'm sorry to have raked up such difficult feelings for you."

"I have grandchildren now." She waves a hand at the pictures on the fireplace. "I consider myself fortunate."

There is a quiet wisdom to Wendy Martin that impresses Denise. "I really appreciate your frankness."

"I wish I had something to offer that could help you."

"It's never easy," Denise asserts. "I think one of the hardest things that families discover is that, as much as they want to, they often cannot help." Denise adjusts her position in the chair. "I must ask you not to discuss what you learned today concerning Anna."

"Of course. I understand. But you said that you're looking into it again?"

"I'm just making some preliminary enquiries at the moment and seeing if anything comes up."

"Which doesn't sound like a great deal."

Denise feels her sadness. "I'm not calling a halt to it yet. There are avenues I still intend to follow up. If the status of the investigation changes or we learn anything, I promise I will let you know right away. Did you inherit Rachael's effects?"

"Yes, such as they were."

"Did you get papers, diaries, things like that? Anything that throws light on her day-to-day life?"

"There were a couple of boxes."

"I didn't find anything at the station. Did the police look at them last time?"

Wendy frowns. "No, now you mention it, I don't think that the police ever asked."

Denise swallows a huff of frustration. "Do you still have them?"

"I couldn't bear to throw them away or to look at them."

"Are they here?"

"In the garage. You can take them." Wendy leaves Denise with the bruised silence of the room, returning a little later with two cardboard boxes.

There is nothing more left to say, so Denise stands and hands Wendy her card. "If you think of anything, anything at all, please let me know."

The dog follows them to the door, and Denise is relieved to be stepping out into the night air. A breeze whips around her ankles, and she clips hurriedly to the car where she places the boxes on the back seat. It's a two-hour drive home, and Denise switches on the radio. A debate on hunting is followed by a discussion on books, but she is unable to follow the conversations — her mind remains on Holly and the tragic final months of her young life.

VERONICA SLATE

2016

HEIDI

Although it's too distant for our eyes to connect, there is a cord strung between us as fine as the thread of a spider's web, and, as if sensing my decision for flight, he starts to run. Adrenalin empties my brain of all superfluous thought, and I know only the keen awareness of what I must do. It's unlikely that he knows these woods as I do. So I veer off fast to the left. Here, the park dips to an open space of wild grass. Beyond that, and leading to where the railway lies, is an area of dense oak and shrubs.

I head for the copse, my breath banging into my lungs. Glancing behind me, I see that he has not peaked the hill — yet. *Hurry, hurry.* The thud of my feet is muffled on the ground. My breath flashes hot on to my cheeks. My teeth chatter. The copse is close, I see it ahead, a darkening thatch of trees that spreads out like a black stain on the horizon.

I risk another glance back and see, to my horror, that his figure has emerged on to the hill. Seeing the direction I have taken, he's clearly altered his course so that he is now much closer to me than I had anticipated. *Stupid, stupid.* Faster, I push myself until I nearly fall, tripping over my feet, my body propelled beyond their stride. With effort, I manage to correct myself but hit the first tree with a bang.

With too much force, I put out my hand to soften the impact, and I wince as my wrist flares into pain. Now I have to change my pace. I turn and see that he is gaining on me. Oh my God. Oh my God. Crouching as low as I can, I jump and twist through the shrubbery.

As I enter the copse, the sky shrinks, and I realise that it's nearly dark. Finding an area of thicket, I begin to crawl. Pausing, I listen. It is still. Looking back, the distant hill is now a dark smudge. I realise that I have come a good way into the woods. Desperately, I scan for his form and then I see him — he is close. He, too, has stopped, and I watch as he turns his head from left to right, its angle cocked; he is listening. I hold my breath until it nearly bursts from me. He pauses and his eyes find the covert where I'm huddled. *He sees me, he sees me.* I muffle the impulse to scream as he starts to run in my direction. With all my strength, I push myself further backwards into a dark maze of bramble, thorns tearing at my face and wrenching at my hair. A trickle of blood tickles my cheek. I hear the ripping of my coat, but I push in further, barely aware of the pain, and squeeze into the smallest form I can make.

Now, when I gaze out, little is visible — only the last band of red in a black sky. I can't see him. I breathe into my coat, and some childish impulse makes me want to shut my eyes — if I cannot see him, he cannot see me.

Suddenly, from nearby, there is a footfall, the crunch of twigs. He's close. He's above me. Another step, and the huff of his breath falls on the silence. Tighter, I press into my coat, then, like the sound of a bullet, a noise resounds followed by a crunch. I have a sick instinct for what he is doing. I shrivel inside my nest and feel the stick he has fashioned from a branch reverberate as he jabs and hammers into the brambles.

From time to time he stops, and I feel him listening. These times are the worst, as I can't guess his exact location, or perhaps he's seen me, sensed me, and is standing just above the spot where I'm hidden, and I panic that my body will betray me. When he pauses, I hear the noises of the night — low scratchings from the undergrowth, the hoot of an owl, or the distant rumble of a train. He's been quiet for so long now that I almost dare to move, to ease the pains shooting through my compressed legs.

Just as I decide to alter my position, his footfall comes again, somewhere close, and I give a jolt of dismay. I wonder if I've made enough noise to attract his attention, but the whoosh of his stick rushes through the air as he attacks a different area of scrub, and I lean forward, gratefully giving my legs room to stretch. Pain goes through me as blood once again begins to circulate.

It is pitch black now, and I wonder how he can see in the darkness. Please go, please go, I beg. In all this time, he has not spoken. The only sound has been his heavy breathing and his footfalls. Is this Ken? The man who killed Nina, who took Anna?

Some instinct draws him back again and again to the thicket in which I'm huddled. I begin to shiver uncontrollably. From the way he tramples heavily on the undergrowth, I know that he's impatient now. My readjusted position has given me a tiny view through a gap in the brambles, and I see a dusting of moonlight has settled on the trees.

Suddenly, there is a change in the noises he makes, a new sound, and I hold my breath. Gradually, I understand what has happened. He is on all fours, at my level. Straining my eyes, I see him, his body facing my way, the terrifying black mask, as he pushes scrub aside in his effort to seek me out. And then a click, and light is thrown to where I am, and I press my head to the ground hoping my hood will hide the redness of my hair. My mouth is dry, the earth damp on my lips and tongue, and I catch a brief and horrifying scent of his warm breath. My heart beats so loudly that I'm sure he must hear it. Then the light is extinguished. He pauses, listening. He rises to his feet, and I see his legs — dark and long like saplings. Time passes as he stands motionless and poised in the moonlight.

Finally, he begins to walk away, back towards the hill where the heavy moon throws a pool of silver on to the grass. As his footsteps retreat, I shiver more violently but am still too afraid to move — it could be a trick. It's deathly silent now, and I push forward, pain numbed by the underlying shock and try to find him in my field of vision.

Most of the wood is in darkness but I scan the patch of hill with longing, hoping to see him at the top and prove that he is gone. It feels as if I wait a long time, but then he is there. He stops, turns, and gazes back towards me. The mask still shields his face. For a long while, he stares into the trees before turning and moving off.

With a sob of relief, I try to pull myself into a position that's more comfortable. My hand finds my pocket, and I try to get to my phone and gloves. The noise of the zip rips through the stillness, and I stop, terrified that he'll make his way back. The phone has no signal. With despair, I realise that, even though he appears to have gone, I don't have the courage to leave my hiding place. As much as I long for the safety of home, the idea of trying to find my way through the woods with this man possibly in wait is too much.

Having made the decision not to move, endurance is easier. Gloves help a little with the temperature, and the adrenalin is numbing. At times, I almost fall asleep, my head resting on my arms.

Eventually, a pale light filters through the trees, and I shift my stiff body. I am so deeply embedded in the thicket that it's impossible to see my surroundings. Straining my ears, I listen and hear only the early morning noises of the wood. I begin to squeeze my way out to the damp morning air.

Overnight, it's as if the entry I forged through the brambles has conspired against me, and the exit is almost as difficult. Thorns rip at my skin and coat and catch in my hair. Twigs and branches block my way. Every minute or so I stop, listening hard, trying to gauge if he has returned.

It is nearly light when I eventually emerge. For a while, I crouch, taking in the full panorama. There is no sign of the man. I stand, painful spasms shuddering through my legs. I don't return by way of the bunker but instead head further down, deeper into the woods. If I continue this way, I'll come to the railway line, and from there I can cut out to another exit. With the frosty dawn numbing my lips and mist still clinging to the hollows, I make my way through the silent woods, feeling the presence of invisible eyes at my back.

It is barely 7 am when, finally, I arrive home hobbling and with pain flaring in all my joints. I pause at the door and take another look around for sight of a figure. The street is quiet but for early workers and dog walkers.

Inside, I lock the door and lean against it for a moment and wait for the fluttering of my pulse to still. Then I call Denise.

2016

DENISE

It's drizzling when Denise pulls up and turns into the sweep of grey tarmac. A chrome climbing frame, its bars bubbled with rain drops, and a sandpit lying half filled with water stand outside. Denise rings the doorbell, hearing it echo in the hall beyond. The door is opened by a girl of about nine in a pair of blue glasses that sit at a slight angle to her face. She's covered in spots and smears of calamine lotion.

Behind her, a woman emerges in an overall that is covered with garish pansies. She looks to be in her mid-fifties with wiry grey hair and an unhealthy complexion.

"Detective Inspector Gilzeen?"

Denise steps into the hall. "Yes, and you must be Heather Lockburn?"

The woman glances down at the girl. "Thanks Tania, now haven't you somewhere to be? If you feel better, you could have a look at some homework."

Denise follows behind the bulky, flowered figure to a small office at the back of the house, which the woman opens with a set of keys. The room is shabby with plastic chairs stacked against one wall and a row of dusty filing cabinets. By the window is a desk on which sit a box of papers, a newish looking computer, and a pot of pens.

Heather shivers and takes one of the chairs for Denise before seating herself behind the desk. Through the window, a doll entangled in a football net resembles the victim of some bizarre ritualistic bondage. Heather does not smile. Noises from the rest of the house filter through, voices, a vacuum, the distant bass of music.

"I'm not sure we can help you much. I've only been here six years."

"But you keep a record of staff?"

"Of course."

"Did you find a list of staff leading up to the time of Holly's disappearance?"

The woman nods. "You're lucky. To be honest, after so long, I would've expected these records to have been archived. I can't let you take them, but you can make photocopies."

"Thanks. What about workman, people like that that may have had access to the home?"

"I'm not sure. Your best bet is to ring the Local Authority. They may keep stuff like that."

From upstairs, there is the sound of running feet and laughter, a shout.

"Does anyone still work here from before?"

Heather pauses. In the fading light, the pansies on her overalls look nearly black. "I think Wilf was probably here. He's the gardener. I know he's been around a while."

By the time Denise has finished photocopying, it is gone 2 o'clock, and her hands are stiff with cold. The smell of lunch, which has come and gone, hangs in the air, and the house

117

seems quieter. Not long until the children return from school. She collects the photocopies she has made and finds Heather in the kitchen. "Thanks, I've got everything I need now. I left the original file on the desk." She turns to go.

"Wilf turned up a while ago. I mentioned that you might want a chat."

Putting the papers down, she follows Heather into the garden where, in the distance, a hunched figure is spreading organic material over a border of turned soil. At her approach, he straightens slowly, easing out his muscles with gnarled fingers. His pink cheeks and clear eyes bely the age he must surely be. Thick white hair grows about his face and over his domed scalp, and, in spite of a curved spine, Denise gets the impression of vigour. He leads her to a squat gardening shed where there are two chairs and an electric kettle and makes Denise a hot and very welcome cup of instant coffee.

"You wanted to ask about Holly?"

Denise nods. "Do you remember her?"

"It was a long time ago now, but yes, I do remember her."

"There must be so many children that pass through. What was it made her stick in your memory?"

Wilf considers. "Apart from the fact she went missing, you mean? Each child is given a plot of garden if they want. Most aren't interested. They've better things to do, 'specially the older ones." He raises his eyebrows. "Of course, if they could grow cannabis, I'd never keep them away." He chuckles.

The shed is damp, and Denise warms her fingers on the mug.

"But Holly was excited about her bit of earth. I think wherever she'd been before she hadn't had a garden. She wanted to grow sunflowers." He pauses and gazes out of the grubby window. "She was a nice girl. A bit shy, but friendly enough."

"Did she talk about how she was getting on here?"

118

"Not much. We talked about the garden mainly, and she liked the birds. I showed her an old blackbird's nest I found in one of the apple trees."

"What impressions did you get from her?"

"I always had the feeling she was sad, but, then again, wouldn't you be to be in a place like this? And she hadn't long lost her mum."

"Was there anything that seemed out of the ordinary before she disappeared?"

He shakes his head. "We only chatted a few times."

"And what about staff, people coming into the home? Did you notice anyone taking a particular interest, anyone she spent a lot of time with?"

Wilf drains his mug and takes a pipe from his overalls, which he stuffs with tobacco. The smoke is sweet and pleasant.

"I can't say I noticed anything like that." But his eyes shift uncomfortably.

"Does the name Kenneth Finch mean anything to you?"

He shakes his head.

"What about friends? Did she make any here?"

"She seemed like a bit of a loner. I felt sorry for her."

"What about staff? Anything unusual happen leading up to Holly's absence?"

He is silent for a while. "One thing. The staff here tend to be pretty regular, but a while before Holly went missing someone was sacked — a new worker. There was a lot of fuss about it, and I heard things."

"Heard things?"

"Nothing specific, but there were raised voices, and, I don't know, I just got the impression that it was a big deal."

"Can you remember the name?"

He nods. "His name was Mark. Mark Lyell."

Denise waits to see if he will say more. She senses that he's holding back, but there's something resolute about his expression, and she doesn't believe she'll get more out of him. Her eyes drift to a pot of dried sunflowers, their crêpey petals as thin as skin.

"Thanks for your time and the coffee. Did Holly ever get to grow her sunflowers?"

"She was gone by then. You're wondering about those?"

Denise nods.

Something crosses his face. "As I say, she was a sweet girl, and, after she disappeared, I grew one for her, you know, just in case... but she never did come back. It's a sort of habit now. Call me sentimental, if you like, but each year I plant a sunflower for Holly."

"There's that policeman that helped us when the shopping bag broke." Anna pauses and puts her hand on my arm. "You know the one who took Scott to the police station when he was naughty. He's called Charlie."

"Shh, he can hear you," I hiss.

"He went to your school to talk about drugs."

"Be quiet."

Ahead, he reaches the end of the path and shuts the gate. The spring sunshine is hot on my neck. Although I look away, embarrassed, he sees us and pauses. He's not in uniform today, he has a sports bag swung over one shoulder with the head of a racquet emerging from a corner.

"Is that your house?" Anna says.

"It is indeed," he laughs. "How are my budding gangsters today?" He looks down and winks at us.

"Is that a tennis bat?" Anna asks.

"It's a badminton racquet."

"They're never called bats," I add.

"So where are you lovely girls going? Off to rob a bank?" He is looking not at us but at Mum.

Mum laughs. "We were thinking of the one on Friar Street. What do you think?"

"We're going to rob a bank?" Anna's eyes are round with awe.

"No, stupid," I say. "It's a joke."

Anna tugs at her socks, which are constantly falling to her ankles. "We went to see Cinderella at the cinema, and then we got me new shoes."

"Ah."

"They're red," she adds, holding up the bag. "Has Scott been in the police station again for being bad?"

"It's called 'arrested'." I shove Anna.

"Anna, you can't ask the policeman that." Mum gives her a look.

"Has he though?" And, in spite of Anna's glee, I watch his face carefully, eager for gossip.

"Scott's a good lad really."

"Can you come to our school about drugs?" Anna asks. "Me and Danielle would clap."

"When you get to big school I will."

I recall the pride I felt when I was able to point out that I knew the policeman who was giving the talk. He's not young, but he's definitely handsome. I had whispered my knowledge to several school friends. Not in front of Nina though — because it was coming out of her house that we first met. He had brought Scott back from the police station. We had been returning from the supermarket and Mum had dropped a shopping bag — he had helped collect runaway apples from the gutter.

I study him now and cannot imagine that he is one of the men involved with Ken. There is a reassuring intelligence to his face, and I remember what Carol had said about him. If it weren't for Charlie, Scott would have been charged.

I look at mum slyly. I can see she likes him. Perhaps they will go out for a meal together. I like the idea of that, better than the other man.

His glance turns to me. "You okay?" he asks, and there is something steady and kind in his eyes. My anxiety for Nina rises up and presses against my ribcage, and I have the urge to blurt it out. I imagine being taken to the station and a flurry of officers listening to my story. Ken would be arrested and taken away. Surely, Nina is mistaken about the police and, after all, they can't all be bad.

"Is this your house?" Anna asks.

"Anna stop being so nosy," Mum says.

But Charlie laughs. "Yes, it's where I keep all the dead bodies."

Anna squeals with delight. "I want to see a dead body."

"Perhaps I'll invite you in for a cup of tea sometime," he's looking at Mum again, "and I'll show you the dead bodies after your custard creams."

"Can we come now?" Anna begs.

But he pulls up his sleeve, revealing the golden hairs of his forearm and checks his watch.

"Can we come in now, please?" Anna says again.

He gives me a wink. "Not today. I'm meeting a mate at the sports centre. Another time, though?" For the slightest moment his gaze rests on me, something like a question in his eyes. "In the meantime, if you need a copper — you always know where I am."

2016

HEIDI

I'm sitting in Jason's car and can't quite believe how I came to be here. His call had come just as I was getting ready to go out.

"I've found out where Ken's mother is," Jason had said.

"Where is she? Is Ken there?"

"The private investigator doesn't think so."

"You hired one again?"

"I thought it was worth another try. Don't you?"

"But didn't you visit her last time you tried to find Ken? She must be a sort of step-grandmother to you."

He had laughed. "It didn't occur to me before, and I don't believe any of us ever met her. If Ken had a relationship with her, it was kept away from us."

When he rang, I hadn't been sure I wanted to meet Ken's mother, and I couldn't think of a good reason why she might be prepared to agree. At the back of my mind was Anna — and the thought of her had given me purpose.

I turn to him now. "Are you sure she will even see us?"

He doesn't answer me.

Joan Finch lives in Herefordshire in a small village called Ruardean.

At lunchtime we stop at a roadside café, and Jason buys us lunch. He seems distant and preoccupied. He eats quickly and without interest, leaving most of his food at the side of the plate. Instead, he drinks three cups of black coffee. His dark hair is longer than when we first met, and a lick falls across his forehead. Stubble darkens his jawline, and he seems suddenly older. We talk in hushed voices, discussing the strategy he wants to adopt with Ken's mother.

"What if she knows where Ken is and tells him about me? As you pointed out last time, I'm probably the only remaining witness."

He frowns, his expression intense. "Heidi, why don't you come and live with me for a while? I'm concerned about you. Have the police found the man who chased you?"

I shake my head.

"You'd be safe with me." And I read in his eyes the single-minded determination to find Ken regardless of the consequences.

"We should have left this to the police." I'm suddenly angry.

"The police can visit Joan Finch any time they like."

And I have to acknowledge the truth of this.

He gets up from the table abruptly and puts on his jacket. I stand and wrap my scarf around my neck, watching as he pays at the counter, and follow him back to the car. He puts on the radio and music fills the air, consuming the spaces for conversation.

It's 4 o'clock when we finally arrive in Ruardean. Houses have been replaced by fields and woods. At one point we have to stop as a herd of short-haired cattle stutter across the road from one field to another. The ghost of a moon appears behind a stunted hedge, and my trepidation increases. Jason turns off the radio and turns on the Sat Nav, where the address has already been added. He mutes the volume, and the silence is louder than the music was. His tension hums. He lights a cigarette, pumping fumes into the car.

The house is set at the end of a narrow lane bordered with bushes and trees.

"Is this it?" I ask.

He exhales breathily. "I guess so."

The property is quiet. No sound of traffic, just the rustling of wind in the leaves. Where the tarmac ends, the lane becomes a muddy path bordered by a privet hedge.

As we approach the house, we come to a squat 1970's bungalow. Once white, it's now streaked with stains, and paint on the front door is peeling. Anxiety skitters up my spine. Jason rings the bell and then knocks hard. The sound is like a gunshot in the silence. After a few minutes, a light appears in the frosted glass, and I hear the lock being turned.

A woman of about 75 opens the door. She is tiny, her skin a mass of creases that reminds me of elephant hide. Behind the creases, a pair of watery, blue eyes gaze up at us.

"Hello."

"Mrs Finch?" Jason holds out his hand.

"Who are you?" she asks. Her words are slow and drawn out with a strong West Country accent tinged with Welsh.

"My name is Jason Carpenter. Could we talk to you, please?"

Her face furrows with agitation, and she shakes her head, trying to push the door closed.

Jason holds it open. "Mrs Finch, you know why I'm here. You may know nothing, and I will respect that, but I have come a long way to see you."

"I know who you are, and you're right, I don't know anything." Her eyes are wary.

"Please."

She coughs wetly into her hand, fiddles with the button at the neck of her blouse, looks at me. "And who's that?"

"She's a friend. She was a friend of Nina's, too. Please, I know this must be difficult for you. I don't hold you responsible for Ken's actions, but he was my mother's partner for many years. I would really appreciate it if you would talk to me." Jason's voice is authoritative, but I can hear, interwoven with it, the thread of desperation.

"I know nothing of Kenneth," she says with grim finality.

"My sister was murdered. There will never be peace for my family."

Something in what he says, or the quiet way in which he says it, causes her to hesitate. "Come in then, but I don't know what you expect from me." There is a well-used defensive tone to her voice.

The hall smells of mildew, barely masked with the odours of furniture polish and air freshener. We are led to a small sitting room stuffed with cheap furniture and ornaments. A fire blazes in an open grate and chintz chairs vie with paisley curtains and a patterned carpet. A television is propped on a table in one corner and on the other side a caged budgie. As we enter, it trills, and its beak ticks on the metal frame, filling the room with a tinny tattoo.

"You may as well sit down."

Jason takes one of the sofas, and I place myself beside him.

She nods, sinks her body into the chair with a small sigh and wheezes. The short walk to the door and back has made her breathless.

"Do you still see Kenneth?"

"I told you — not for a long time."

"When did you lose contact?"

"More years than I care to remember. I'm sorry about your sister. I can't imagine what that's like, but Ken didn't kill no one." She falls into a spasm of coughs.

"If he didn't, there's a good chance he knows who did."

She's quiet, turning her head to gaze into the fire. "God knows he's done bad things, but he's no child murderer."

How do you know? I want to ask. *How can you know what depravity he's capable of?* But I keep the words locked in my throat. She shakes her head, waves a thin, mottled hand. The veins are dark and lumpy, and I am reminded of a blue-veined cheese.

"Before Nina was killed, he abused her."

She doesn't look up. "I know what he was accused of, but there was never no proof of it." Her indignation isn't convincing.

"I was Nina's friend," I say. "She told me about Ken's abuse."

She pouts, pushing her lips out then sucking them back in. The only sound in the room is the spitting of the fire. Eventually, she gives a defeated sigh. "I suppose it's too late to go protecting him now. What's done is done. The truth is, he liked them, you know, girls, not women." Her voice cracks with shame. "There was a girl round here when he was younger. You do your best, and they come out like that." A blob of spittle shines at the corner of her mouth.

"Another?" Jason asks.

"She were about 11. The daughter of a friend. Kenneth were only 16 at the time. I thought it were a mistake or a phase..."

"There were more?"

She doesn't reply, but her face says it all.

"Don't go thinking I approved. Of course I didn't. I tried

everything I could, but it didn't matter what I said. It's the way he was. It's why we didn't talk much. It was hard for me," her voice falters, "and he isn't all bad, whatever you think. He was kind, too. He rings me every birthday and Christmas."

I feel Jason stiffen beside me. "So he still contacts you. Where is he?"

"I don't know. He won't tell me, and he isn't welcome in these parts anyway. People have long memories." She leans forward and stirs the fire with a poker. Slivers of ash and wood spit on to the tiles.

Jason takes something from the inside pocket of his jacket, a photograph of Nina. It's not one that was in the album I saw, and I look at it curiously. In it, Nina is standing in a garden. Her smile is so broad that it bisects her face, and sun dances in her eyes and glitters on the sheen of her black hair. Her arms are long and slim. One of her hands is pressed into the whorled bark of a tree — the other hangs idly, a small posy in her fingers. My eyes take in what she's wearing, and for a moment my heart stops. I remember the dress, remember each stitch, each detail. The dress belonged to me. It had been bought for one of my mother's friends' wedding. I remember not just the dress but lending it to Nina for some occasion she was to go to. He gets up and passes it to Joan Finch.

Joan frowns down at the picture. "Pretty girl. I don't suppose it matters now, what I say." She's quiet, staring into the flames, reflectively. "After Ken's father, I was married to another man. Neither of them were much good." She looks at me pointedly. "Choose wisely. You have no idea how hard it is to escape once you let them put a ring on your finger. I was barely 18 when I met Kenneth's dad, and he was no older. Too young we were to have a baby. Not that we intended, you know…" She looks at me. "We was only together for five years, and then I met John. He was older, more sophisticated. I fell for him hard."

She pauses and is once again assailed with a fit of coughing. She leans into her hand then gets up from the chair.

"Can I help?" I ask.

She waves me away and shuffles to the kitchen. Jason stands impatiently and paces the room, pausing to examine a small pile of cards and presents.

Mrs Finch returns with a glass of water. "John had a son to another women — Chuck he was called." She spits the name out. "Never liked that boy. John had him at weekends. He was older than my Kenneth by a few years." She looks at Jason, raises a frail hand, and picks at the antimacassar on the arm of the chair. "If anyone was the ruin of my Kenneth, it was that boy." Her eyes fill suddenly with tears which slide over her skin — water over a dried riverbed.

"Kenneth was a nice boy. A good boy. I told John not to bring that Chuck here, but he did."

The heat of the room and the smell of air freshener are making me light-headed.

"I didn't mind much when it finally ended between me and John; he was sleeping with half the women round here by that time. Apart from that, he was a good man, really. Even after it was over, he took Kenneth to football at the weekend and often trained with him at night. He was a better father to Kenneth than his own. My boy was very fond of him. What I didn't find out till much later was that, when he took Kenneth out, he had Chuck, too. He pushed those boys together. They became best friends, or, so he said. The age difference never rang true, and I didn't like the way Chuck was with him. It always felt wrong." She frowns, and I see regret etched into her skin. "It was Chuck that ruined my boy. Kenneth was too weak." She leans forward. "I'm sorry if he hurt your sister. He wasn't brought up like that."

"Where is Chuck now? Do you know?"

"I don't know where he is, and I don't care to know. He left these parts a long time ago. Fancied himself, he did. I heard once that he'd done well." She gives a disbelieving shake of her head. She launches into another coughing fit. "Bloody cigarettes. They come back and get you in the end."

"What was it about Chuck that you didn't like?" I ask.

Something between a groan and a growl escapes her throat. "It was more than a sense. Clever boy, he was, but I never trusted him. Would smile and look you in the eyes as soon as stab you. They caught a hedgehog once, in the back garden. Kenneth were only eight or nine. Chuck didn't think I could, but I saw what he did to it," she shudders. "Told me later it had been dead already. I would have believed him, except that I'd seen it for myself." She shakes her head. "He had a bad reputation round here. One summer, he lost the tip of his little finger. The story they told was that he had caught it in some farming equipment. The rumours were different, though. I had it on good authority that he had been badly bitten. A cat this time." Her mouth sours with distaste.

Jason goes over, takes back the photograph and edges it carefully back into his wallet. "Did Ken tell you about Nina or about the girl who went missing?"

I hold my breath. Mrs Finch is still; the air pregnant with things unsaid. She looks up and fixes his gaze. "I think he knew something, but he didn't do it."

"What do you mean? He saw Nina killed?"

"He came to me," her voice crackles. "The police were after him for it. He broke down here. Afterwards, he told me that he'd got involved in something horrible and didn't know how to get out. He said there were a lot of nasty people, and it got your sister killed. He didn't see your sister murdered, and he didn't take the little girl. That's what he said."

"And you believed him?"

"I love my boy. I love him like you love your sister." Her voice is quiet now and tears run unchecked over her cheeks and on to the collar of her blouse. "I think it changed him, what happened. I hope it did."

"Does he use a different name now?" Jason asks.

She shrugs. "I don't know. I hope he's living a decent life. If he is, and if you find him, tell him he can come and see me and tell him not to drag his feet while he's at it."

The bulk seems to have been sucked out of her, and I see now how loosely her clothes hang on her body and feel a tug of pity.

"The girl," I can hear the tremor in my voice, "Anna, the one who went missing. Did he say anything about what happened to her?"

She looks at me steadily, searching my face. "No, he didn't tell me what happened to her."

"But he knew?" My heart is beating fast.

She can't look me in the eye, and I feel my body trembling.

"Did he say if she was alive?"

"He didn't say anything, and I didn't ask." She frowns. "Perhaps I should have been braver, but I weren't. Truth is — I didn't want to know."

Jason writes his number on a piece of paper and hands it to her, and, as we leave, I study her face a final time. What little colour there may have been once is drained from her skin, and her cloudy eyes seem focused elsewhere. As I look, I see confirmed my impression that she is not just old, but ill. Briefly, she touches my hand and seems about to utter some last word, but instead pulls the door shut. We are barely out of the porch before I hear the clanking of the security chain.

I find I'm trembling. Above us, the moon has risen and is the colour of skin, pale and freckled in the dark. Stars shine, white pinholes in the sky. When Jason looks at me, we do not need to use words. I can see what is in his eyes, and he will see the same in mine. Not just triumph, but agony, too.

2016

DENISE

The phone rings just as Denise has tucked her chair into the desk and decided to grab coffee and something to eat. In the background is the hum of phones and clicking of keyboards. It had been a late night working another case for all of them, and they are all suffering. She is thinking about chocolate, something sweet — the sweeter the better. When Denise takes the call, she has to track back before she remembers what it is all about. It had slipped her mind, and part of her had not expected the information to be still available.

The man on the other end of the line seems to express the same sentiment, and there is a tone of bewildered triumph in his tone. "I found the invoices with the name of the company on it. The work at Bayview was carried out in the time frame you mentioned. I can't tell you more than that."

Denise writes the name on a piece of paper — *Ward Builders.* Grabbing a telephone directory, she flicks to the business section and finds the name there. They're still a registered company. It is a long shot, but, at this stage, she's determined not to leave any avenue unexplored.

She scurries for her coat and heads for the car. It's colder now, and the sky has darkened. Puddles of greying slush are showing a dangerous glint of ice. As the town gives way to the suburbs, she enters a whiter world, where little hillocks of snow garland the walls and fences.

Graham Ward lives in a detached house in a tree-lined street. When she first sees him, she decides he must be somewhere in his mid-sixties with a pink, cleanly shaven face. He shows her through the hall and into a large sitting room where a gas fire pumps out a wonderful wall of heat.

She accepts the offer of tea and gazes round at the family photographs that line the shelves — children, grandchildren, rows of smiling faces. Above the fire, a picture of shire horses grazing by a stream and hay bales catching the sun in the fields behind.

He returns, with a slightly bow-legged gait, bearing a tray with a pot, a jug of milk, and a plate of biscuits. She allows herself to sink into the chair and enjoy the tea. She decides that she likes Graham Ward and not only because the biscuits are mainly covered in chocolate. He has an honest, open face; heavily lined, but the lines are kind ones, ones made if you laugh and smile a lot.

"Do you remember much about the job that you did at Bayview Children's Home, in Waterstone?"

He looks away, rubbing his thick fingers over his jaw line. "We did a few care homes."

"It's the one Holly Watts went missing from."

"Ah. That's why you're here." He nods sadly. "I won't forget it now. We built an extension and installed a new kitchen. Quite a big job in the end. Yeah, I remember it well. I worked on that one myself."

"How many of you would have been involved in the job?"

"That's easy." Graham gets up, takes her cup, and refills it.

"Both children worked with me then — my son Billy and daughter Rosy, that is. I can't remember if Eddy was still around. He was with me from the beginning, but he must have retired at about that time." He shakes his head. "I could find out if you wanted."

"Just his name will do for now. What about other people? Were there others who came and worked for you?"

"No, I kept it fairly small. I had a few come and go before the children joined me, but after that, not really. We wouldn't have done the plumbing or electrics then, mind. Rosy trained as a plumber, so we do that ourselves now, but she wouldn't have been qualified then." He places his cup on the saucer with almost dainty precision.

"I don't suppose you remember who was contracted to that, do you?"

"I seem to think he was a chap called Colin Ford, something like that. He was a one-man band. Did a few jobs with us. There would have been an electrician, too, but I can't remember who."

"And did anything strike you as odd or off at the home? Anything that didn't feel right?"

He gazes off into space and shrugs. "I'm sorry. Nothing."

Outside, through the patio doors, snow begins to fall again.

"Do you still keep records of the jobs? Who the subcontractors are?"

"I keep everything," he says, "but I store it at an office we have in Bundlebury. Shall I look it up for you?"

"That would be fantastic. Thank you." She gets up, reluctant to leave, but there is little else to say. She gives the fire one final, longing look.

"It's been nice meeting you, and thanks for the tea." Denise gets into her coat.

"Let me know if I can help any further. I have grandchildren myself now. I hope you get whoever took her."

Denise takes the path carefully across the new snow.

"I often think of her and wonder what happened." His eyes are troubled. "I don't suppose you'll find her alive."

"Probably not," Denise concedes.

He seems to consider this. "I watch enough police programmes to know that. They say they are usually dead within the first few hours."

"Unfortunately, yes."

He pauses for a moment. "I always hoped some absent father or relative had snatched her."

"We may never know." There is snow on her lips.

"Off you go," he says. "Look, here I am keeping you out in this temperature while you have more important things to do. Don't mind me."

Just as she reaches the end and unfastens the latch of the gate, Graham Ward calls out from the front door.

"I just remembered. We didn't do the roof either. It was an awkward sod of a job, but the care authorities organised it. They'd used him before. He was good at his work, too. Professional. I asked him if he'd consider contracting with us on occasion. I remember the name — Ken. Kenneth Finch. Nice chap." He gives her a happy grin, looks up at the sky and rubs his hands together. "It's going to be a chilly one."

2001

HEIDI

I am a coward, and I lie in bed, my head pressed into the pillow and facing the wall. Eyes open, I stare, unseeing, at the chipped paintwork stained with Blu Tack and Sellotape. Holly. She has been missing for over a month now. I should tell someone. Girls are taken and they never come back. I had told myself that this would not be the case with Holly, but even the newspapers have stopped featuring her on the front or second pages. She will never return, and I imagine her dead — her white hair drifting like weed in a stream, or perhaps she is deep in the earth, at a grave site that will soon be overgrown with spring flowers. What do I do?

Everything I know tells me Ken is connected to the men who took Holly, or, worse, he did it himself. Ken and the man with the posh house — Brandon. And Nina knows, too.

At the bunker, I had read the newspaper article and then put it face down where I found it. When Nina and I had returned home, making our way down the hill with the smell of wet leaves, she was still high, and conversation would have been pointless. The further I get from that moment, the harder it is to broach, and I know now that I don't want to hear what she has to say about it. I will never ask her.

In the past weeks, I have become more aware of our vulnerability — me, Mum, and Anna. I think of Anna and her gappy smile, and Mum with her small hands and hopeful eyes. There is nobody to protect us. Nobody.

Perhaps I could let someone know what happens to Nina without drawing attention back to me — an anonymous letter. But would they believe it? And who would I send it to? Who can I trust?

I hear the door and the sound of Mum and Anna.

"Heidi," Mum calls, and Anna's feet thump up the stairs. The door is pushed open.

"Dinner time," she gushes.

"I'm not hungry."

"She's not hungry," Anna shouts.

Slower steps and then Mum sits on the end of the bed. "Come on. You must want to eat something. I've made your favourite."

My thoughts grate against the inside of my skull. I can't imagine feeling happy or safe ever again. She puts out her hand and strokes my back in a way that reminds me of when I was very young. "Are you poorly, love?"

"A headache," I lie.

Her cool fingers touch my forehead, and her skin smells of baking and soap. I close my eyes. "Well you haven't a temperature. Did something happen at school today?"

"It's just a headache for God's sake," I snap.

"I'll bring up a squash and some painkillers, and I'll leave dinner to warm. We'll eat in about half an hour? Okay with that?"

I don't know what to say, so I pull the covers over my head and keep my eyes shut.

She closes the door on her way out, and I hear her on the stairs and then the sound of Anna and Mum — they are laughing, and I feel as if I'm on the outside looking in.

2016

HEIDI

It's late when the doorbell rings. Danielle is standing outside, drops of rain freckled on her hair and red circles on her cheeks. A bitter wind rushes into the hall.

"Hi Heidi…" She looks flushed and uncomfortable.

"Come in." As she steps over the threshold, I experience a shiver of anxiety.

I look at her curiously while I take her coat and put the kettle on. She paces the sitting room nervously.

"Is everything okay? Where's Robby?" I ask.

"Mum has him."

"It's nice to see you again." And I realise, despite my trepidation, it is. I put tea bags into two mugs. "I'm guessing Jason told you about our trip to Ken's mother."

"Heidi."

I turn and her face brings my heart to a stop. "What is it?"

"I lied," her breath comes out in a rush. Tears begin to roll down her cheeks, and she buries her head in her hands.

"What do you mean? Who did you lie to Danielle?"

"It's all my fault."

"What's your fault? What are you talking about?" I put a tentative arm along her shoulders, and she looks up. "I lied about that day."

My heart begins to thump. "I don't understand."

"I lied to the police." She takes a deep breath. "It was true — I was poorly that day, and Anna had come over and given me the ball-bearing maze. But I told you that was the last time I saw her."

I clench my fingers into my palms.

"Anna came back. After lunch a few hours later, I think."

"You saw her again?"

"She always came through the kitchen at the back. She said she would bring me some biscuits, and I was hungry. Mum said I shouldn't eat because I'd been sick. I felt better by then, and I was really bored. She said she was going to play spies on you and Nina."

"The police are already sure that Anna was at the bunker. It doesn't really matter that you saw her later, but why did you lie about it?"

She sits completely still. "Ken came back to the house later, too." Her eyes hold mine. "When he said he wasn't there."

I recall the uneasy memories his face elicited. "You mean his alibi? What time was this?"

"I'm not sure, but after 4. I knew that because I switched on the television in Scott and Jason's room and watched cartoons. He was in the bathroom. I heard him being sick, so I went in. I thought he had caught the bug I had."

My anxiety grows.

"He was … there was something wrong. I know I wasn't very old at the time, but I could see how agitated he was. Not just agitated, shaking. He was scary. When he saw me, he got so angry. Really angry." Her skin pales. "He told me that I mustn't tell anyone that I'd seen him. That if I did, he would come back and kill me. He told me to say that Anna hadn't been in the house at all, but she had already been and left me the maze. So I had to."

"Didn't your mum or brothers see him?"

She shakes her head. "Everyone else was out." She sees the look on my face. "Mum didn't think leaving me alone, even at that age, was a big deal."

"You didn't say anything later?"

There is a tense silence. "You have no idea what he was like." She turns her head, and I see the curve of her chin. She is quiet for a while, and I wait, sensing that she's finding the courage to say more. There is so much pain in her face. "It wasn't just Nina he was abusing."

"Oh God," I take her hand and squeeze it hard.

"I never told."

"Nobody?"

She shakes her head. "You are the first person. The police did wonder and took me to a special room and asked lots of questions, but I lied." Her eyes are full of anguish. "It had just started... and I didn't want to be in more trouble with him... for him to think I'd told."

"I'm so sorry, Danielle."

"It's in the past. What haunts me is knowing my lies kept him from being prosecuted. He did it, Heidi."

My heart bangs.

"In the bathroom, there was blood on his shirt and in his nails. He knows I saw it. He tried to cover his shirt, but it was too late. He killed Nina. He took Anna."

Anger and bewilderment leave me speechless. I recall his thin face with hatred. Did he kill Anna, too?

I get up, my hands shaking. Recalling Joan Finch leaves me furious. Did she know more about her son than she was letting on?

"Why didn't you say something later?"

But her eyes are full of guilt.

"You could have told Jason?"

She shakes her head. "He was almost the one person I couldn't. He was so angry over Nina, and the longer I kept quiet, the worse it seemed. I feel I let him down more than anyone."

I put my arm around her and pull her into me while she weeps. Her soft hair against my neck could be Nina's.

"You shouldn't blame yourself, Danielle. Ken was a monster. He did monstrous things. Of course you did what he told you." I feel no anger for her, just an immense pity.

"I know that, but it doesn't stop me thinking that if I had said something earlier, he might have been caught and punished. I let them all down. They always believed it was Ken."

"We have to tell the police now. You know that, don't you?"

"I need to tell Jason and Scott first. Then I'll go to the police."

Later, sleep is difficult, and I toss and turn, waking in the hot imprint of my sweat. Ken's face looms in my dreams, and the rage I feel shakes me into wakefulness. I try to build the man who held Anna from the small glimpse that I recalled, but it refuses to grow.

And then I am blinded by a memory, and I am there again with the damp brick swallowed in darkness. I am watching Nina with a knife, its plastic handle worn to smooth edges.

She is crouched in concentration, using it to extract a brick from the wall of the bunker. She doesn't know that I'm watching. My heart begins to thud heavily, as though struck. Like a gong, it resounds and clamours — awaking a seam of vivid memory.

Everything has changed. Now, when I glance at Nina's dark head or catch her eye, I experience a thread of resentment. The relationship has become complicated, and never far from my thoughts is the promise I made to run away. At night, when I close my eyes, I feel as if I'm falling. There is no landing place. I worry about Mum and Anna. Nina will never speak out. If something is to change, it's me that will have to do it. I imagine Ken being taken away, and, for a brief moment, the relief is dizzying.

After school, Nina is meeting her brothers at a coffee shop, and I decide to go to the bunker — the secret hiding place and what it contains has generated an overwhelming compulsion in me. I must satisfy a grim curiosity and see what else she has secreted there.

As I begin the ascent to the bunker, there are tremors in my belly, both for what I may find and also for this act of betrayal. In my school bag, I've hidden a knife, and I intend to lever out the brick just as I saw Nina do.

The afternoon is not as it was on the Saturday that Nina

made her revelation. The sky is blue and birds trill in the branches above. The trees are in leaf, and soon Nina will want us to run away. I pass a group of children — the boys kicking a football and a huddle of girls on a bench watching and giggling. Long after I've left them, their laughter drifts in the air.

As soon as I reach the bunker, I realise that it no longer holds the spell it had woven when we first discovered it. It is spoiled, polluted by my knowledge. I sit at the entrance for a minute, feeling my fingers tremble at the prospect of what I have planned. From our box, I find a cigarette and matches. With a strike that fills my mouth with a sulphurous aftertaste, I light a cigarette, and by the time I blow out the last smudge of grey smoke, I am sure of what I am about to do.

First, I crawl to the end of the bunker and, with the torch, study the bricks. I know the approximate location from seeing Nina. The torch throws light on to the wall, illuminating each lump and grain of ageing mortar. It doesn't take me long to find the loose one, and, with the knife, I push at the little space underneath and edge it towards me.

I'm now able to remove it and place it on the ground. The space looks very small, and I wonder if my arm is too thick to go through the opening. Closing my eyes tightly and gritting my teeth against the fear of spiders, I reach into the cavity until my fingers find the thin crackle of the bag. My heart is thumping so hard. I can hear it resound in my chest. I crawl to the front of the bunker and lay my find down.

The parcel comprises several carriers, and I unwrap them nervously, not allowing my thoughts to dwell on how wrong this feels. There is the money, bundled up in a rubber band, and also the packet of photographs. The wallet is blue and carries no markings. She has put it inside a waterproof envelope. My fingers are clumsy as I open it and take out the pictures. The first is of Nina, and I gasp. My anger for Ken is so fierce that I bite down on my lip drawing blood. I go through each vile image knowing that what I see can never be erased or deleted. These pictures will remain in my mind forever and will poison every other experience or memory that comes into contact with them.

When I have finished, the nervous anxiety has been replaced with a strong feeling of repugnance and shock.

Outside, bees hum among the clover, and I wish that I were at home. I can't bear the weight of Nina's secrets, and an idea begins to insinuate itself into my thoughts more insistently. Charlie. I remember his open face and sympathetic eyes. I even know where he lives.

I can't understand why I haven't thought of it before. With one photograph, I could effectively demonstrate what these men are doing and remain anonymous. I don't even have to use one of Nina. There had been one with Maria where Ken is visible in the background. My heart beats faster. And Nina need never know.

Carefully, I open the packet again and flick through until I find the picture of Maria. I take it out, slip it into my pocket and then wrap the bags up as I had found them and place them back inside the wall. Afterwards, I feel jubilant. I will post this through the policeman's door when he is at work, and nobody will ever know it was me.

2016

HEIDI

The early dawn does not seem to touch me, and I remain sitting in bed watching the images flicker and play though my mind. I am leached of emotion, as though my body has been robbed of all other sensitivity in order to accommodate this sudden wealth of memory. Nina is no longer just a photograph, a snatched scene in the back of my mind. She is real. I see her in full colour: the pitch of her voice, the way that her hair smelt, and the exact shade of her eyes. In my head, the bunker is as it was when I was 13, and I finally remember her hiding place. She has told me about Ken. I remember her pain, but I feel no triumph at her confidence. I feel nothing, only a consuming numbness. Nina seems more real to me than I do to myself. What Danielle told me last night barely registers. I have to go back to the bunker — see if the photographs are still there. I feel no fear that I will be followed. It is as if that day belongs to another time. There is no emotion, just the pressing urge to find her hiding place. This time I pack a thin-bladed knife.

I walk to the bus stop with no sense of dread or threat. I

149

am aware of how I put one foot in front of the other, and how my hand reaches for my purse when the bus rumbles towards the stop, but I could be elsewhere, looking down, rather than the person who hands the coins to the driver. The journey passes in a blur until, once again, I am back at the moss-covered gate and the lane shadowed by trees.

The park is damp and mulchy underfoot, but at least it has stopped raining hard. As I ascend through the woods, a film of moisture attaches to my face and hair. Not once do I turn to see if I have been followed.

At the top of the hill, the weak drizzle becomes a full downpour again, and the wetness leaks inside my coat and through the seams of my shoes.

Finally, I reach the bunker. Crouching down, I push away some brush and gaze into the darkened opening. It is like a gaping mouth, and I draw back. The bricks are stained with ash and a faded ribbon, all that remains of some funereal bouquet, is caught in thorns of a briar. The air is earthy and dank. A small creature darts out from the shadows, across my feet, and into the wet bramble.

Inside, I pull down the hood of my jacket and unstrap my rucksack. I take out the torch and knife. My breath is a fog before my face, and rain drops fall from my sodden fringe to drip into my eyes. The torch throws a beam into the blackness, and I crawl across the floor, unfeeling of the sharp points of stones against my knees.

Crouching in the place that I remember seeing Nina, I play the light along the brick. The soot is thicker here and it takes me a while, exploring with the knife, to find the loose one. When I do, it comes away easily. Removing coat, jumper, and shirt, I reach my naked arm into the icy cavity. Brick scrapes my skin, but I don't feel pain.

Eventually, my hand alights upon a decomposing bag —

the plastic is stiff and almost completely degenerated. I go in more than once until I am sure I have recovered everything.

Now, I look at what I have. The money is damp and water stained, but I find the photo wallet and a notebook. Inside the wallet, the envelope shows only a trace of its original blue. The notebook is dulled with moisture and age.

I open the envelope. The pictures inside are faded to white in parts but still intact. I gaze at the first image, shudder and pack them into my rucksack.

It's barely midday when I reach home. Discarding my coat and shoes, I slump on the sofa. I know I should ring Denise, but, first, I retrieve the envelope of photographs and the notebook.

There is something deeply disturbing about the notebook's cover, scattered with ladybirds and their curling antennae. My mother had bought two, one for me and one to give to Nina as a gift. Mine had been full of my childish activities, accounts of what I had done with Nina and at school. And all the while, Nina was filling hers with the dark, terrifying truth about her life. It is cool in my hands. I switch on a lamp and am aware that my fingers are sitting in the imprint of hers.

I open the cover and inside, beneath the words *This Book Belongs To*, she has written her name in biro — *Nina Carpenter*. The N and the C have been double drawn and beneath that a flower, long stemmed and leafed. The ink is faded and patchy. Trying to prise apart the following pages is not possible, and I lay it down with a sigh.

Cleo whines round me, and it is only with great effort that I get up and feed her. Afterwards, sensing my alien mood, she runs through the cat flap and into the rain.

My phone is full of messages from Danielle, Jason, and Denise, but I ignore them all. I am remembering again the day

Nina told me that she was abused by Ken. I recall her pain and the burden of trust she gave to me. And, as though I am a vinyl record, stuck forever on a scratched groove, the image of her as she passed me the picture of Maria replays over and over in my brain. It's not my responses I remember, but the dual emotions that flickered in her black eyes, the thin triumph of proof weighted against despair. Not even the memory of telling her that I would run away with her softens my heartache. I recall how soft her cheek was against mine and the smell of cigarettes on her breath and in her hair.

I must ring Denise and Jason, and I try to imagine Jason's reaction. He will want to see the photos, the proof of the men who abused her. But what would those images do to him?

I glance down at the packet of photos still exuding the smell of damp. I unwrap them, my mind resisting looking again, but I must do it. Hidden amongst those figures might be the one who took Anna, who killed Nina. I shiver as I open them, half afraid of the memories that might be spilt from me. It isn't easy; I have to hold back my reactions to what is there. As I scan the faces of the men, apart from Ken, none elicits a memory; but there, on the back, Nina has labelled them — *Ken, Ray, Brandon* — the list goes on. Halfway through, I have to place them down and swallow the rush of horror.

At the back, there are a dozen or so of Maria and then a group of photos featuring boys. I don't know why I should be surprised, but, somehow, I had not imagined that. When I have finished, I am trembling.

Snatching up my phone, I begin to type out Denise's number, then pause. I consider Jason again and his hunger to find Nina's murderer — he, unlike me, may recognise someone here, but I cannot let him witness the atrocities. A plan forms in my mind. I will have to find an excuse to explain the delay to Denise. Before I can analyse too closely, I wrap the photographs into several paper bags and stuff them to the bottom of my bag.

In the bathroom, I shower quickly. I dress for work and leave the house again.

During lunch, I wait for everyone to go then make my way to the copier. The room is dry with a lingering scent of ink. Locking the door, I photocopy each frame and, afterwards, I fold the copies into an envelope with the originals and tuck them back into my bag.

When I return home, I take the photocopies and cut Nina and the other victims out of the pictures leaving only the faces of the men.

The house is chilled, and I am aware of a profound silence. Grief presses up against my chest. I want to cry, but not now, later — now I must call Denise. These images will change everything.

Cleo returns and stretches beside me. I feel her thin skin and beating heart, conscious of the fragility of our bodies, and I have a flashback of Nina, her mouth hugging a cigarette, and how the light caught her hair. It had a blue sheen like the feathers of a magpie's wing.

My heart is sore and it remembers. It remembers how it once felt to have a best friend.

DENISE

Denise is sitting with Mike in his cluttered office.

"This is much, much bigger than we ever imagined."

Denise tugs a hand through her hair. "However many men are in Nina's photos, you can guarantee this will only be the tip of the iceberg. This changes everything."

"Barrett's on his way."

They wait for the Assistant Chief, and Mike flicks through the images with distaste. "Do you recognise any of these men?"

"Apart from Ken, no. But, hopefully, when we compare what we have with records of registered offenders. We may be able to identify some of them."

Barrett doesn't knock and waves a hand when Denise and Mike push back their chairs to stand. Denise hands him a pair of gloves, and he studies each photo with silent concentration. When he has finished, he removes the gloves and places them on the desk. Denise senses his anger.

"This is quite a catch."

"Heidi can take the credit."

"What does she remember?"

Denise updates Barrett on the latest, while Mike bags and labels the items.

"You mentioned a notebook. Where is that?"

"We weren't able to read it. We bagged it up and sent it off to forensics earlier. Hopefully they'll be able to recover some of what was written inside. We have a team at the bunker." Denise pauses. "Although I don't suppose there'll be much left to find."

"What does this say about the abductions of Anna and Holly?" Barrett adjusts his cuffs.

"Ken Finch is squarely back in the frame for Nina's murder now. Nina's sister came in a few days ago and kicked his alibi out of the window. She also stated that his shirt was bloody, and he was agitated. We can also put Finch at Bayview during the time Holly was there."

"Finch was always our first suspect," Barrett says.

"But these photos have to change our perspective — we now know that we're dealing with a group, and this must give a much wider net to the abductions. Even if Ken was responsible for Nina's murder, it doesn't necessarily follow that he abducted Anna or Holly himself — perhaps Anna and Holly were trafficked, or someone else within this group took and killed them. God knows how many children passed through their hands."

"Christ," Barrett shakes his head. "Any news of Heidi's masked pursuer?"

"Nothing," Denise admits.

"Do we think it's related to the case?"

"We can't say for sure. There was an incident in Theale a month or so back that bears similarities."

"I am astounded that she considered returning at all."

Denise nods, but inside, she realises that somehow, she is not surprised.

"If you believe now that Nina confided a lot in Heidi, and we don't fully know what was happening in Heidi's life before the attack, make sure you have a watch on her."

Denise is grateful for Barrett's concern.

"What's most important now is finding Finch," Denise says. "The very fact that he appears to have dropped so thoroughly out of sight is incriminating in itself."

Mike's face is grave. "I think we can all agree that this new evidence is more than enough to justify reassigning manpower to the investigation."

"Agreed," Barrett nods. "Come and see me later, and we'll sort out a team." He rises to leave, meeting Denise's eyes. "Keep me updated. I worked this case from beginning to end, too. It means a lot to me."

When he has gone, Denise leans back in the chair. "I hope you'll let me head the new investigation?" She feels a strange thrill.

"You've earned that."

"Good, because I already have a few things that need to be followed up. I spoke to someone at Bayview where Holly went missing, and apparently a worker there was sacked just prior to Holly's abduction. We've managed to track this individual down, but he's on holiday at the moment. We'll interview him when he gets back." She pauses. "I visited Holly Watts' aunt. Holly's mother's effects were left to her. I'm not sure that the police looked through what was there last time. They may not contain anything that links to Holly's abduction, but everything needs to be analysed. There's something else, too."

Mike watches her closely.

"This was an organisation, and there is always someone at the top. I don't think Finch would have been clever or powerful enough. Whoever headed it managed to hide a large paedophilia organisation, avoiding police notice and keeping the victims quiet. I think there are people in this with a lot of power and leverage. Even now, fifteen years later, nobody has come forward and hinted at what was happening. The original police investigation was inadequate, possibly deliberately so, and I think we're dealing with someone with far-reaching influence. Far enough to reach into our pockets."

Mike leans forward on the desk and absorbs what she says. "Claybourne?"

"I don't know, maybe. Claybourne was a poor policeman and a pretty sorry excuse for a man. He wasn't the smartest, either. My money would be that if he was influenced, it was from someone else."

Mike links his hands behind his head and sighs. "I truly hope not, Denise. The last thing we need now is to find one of our own wrapped up in this. I'll talk again to Barrett. See what he thinks, but he won't like it." Through the dusty window, it begins to rain.

The grey night passes by through the bus window, streetlamps furred in the rain. Part of me still remains at the bunker. So much of my life now involves living in the past, falling over sudden recollections or trying to prise them from the locked places in my head. The photographs have leaked a Pandora's box of ugliness into my thoughts and, behind that, a growing sense that I am somehow responsible. Denise has spoken about survivor's guilt over the years, but this feels different. I remember what Danielle had said to me in the coffee shop — that something had been troubling me before Nina's death. Was it Nina's abuse? Or something that I'd done?

Disquiet scratches at me, too, over not telling Jason about the photos. The photocopies remain hidden. I haven't had the courage to show him yet.

My face in the glass is a white smudge with hollows beneath the eyes. I get off the bus at the high street where there is a small supermarket, and, pulling off the hood of my coat, I push open the door.

Tinny music drifts in the aisles along with the smell of

meat and floor cleaner. From the rack, I pick up a basket and put in eggs, cheese, and bread, along with a microwave meal. Above, the lights are harsh and yellow, emphasising flaws in the lino and the discoloured plastic of the fridge units. I have to stop as a boy blocks the aisle with a trolley of lemonade. He begins to manoeuvre it to the back of the shop with painful slowness.

There is one assistant at the tills who stares off into space. Her blue-checked overall is loose on her thin frame. She yawns, turns and looks at me, and I get a strange sense — as if she has been conscious of my presence all along. Immediately, she averts her eyes, and I glimpse her gaunt face in the reflection of the window. I often shop here and have seen her on more occasions than I can remember, but this time my breath catches in my throat. I know who she is.

She's watching me now, I feel it. Her gaze falters, but it's too late — she knows that I recognise her. With a stiff jerk, she gets up from the swivel stool and walks briskly away, through a door at the back of the shop.

I can't move. The boy starts to unload his trolley on to the shelves. Two people stand at the empty till looking at the ceiling and muttering angrily under their breath. The door at the back of the shop opens, and an older woman with a huge chest inches sideways into the seat with a smiled apology and begins to check the shoppers through.

I gaze at the door at the back of the shop willing her to return, but it remains firmly closed. A flurry of new customers enters from the rain, a baby begins to cry, and I move like a robot to the checkout.

As I arrive at the front of the queue, the shop assistant gives me a tired hello and begins putting through my items. Beside her, there's the bottle of water the first attendant left. It has a white label on it, and I don't need to read the name to confirm what I know. I read it anyway, over and over again, and, as I do, I see not this girl's handwriting, but Nina's slanting letters — *Maria*, she had written on the back of the photograph, *Maria*.

It's drizzling outside the shop, but there is an alley to the side, offering shelter, and I prepare myself for a wait. Rain taps thinly on to the hood of my coat. Occasionally, a bus or car passes and light flashes across the crumpled crisp bags and cigarette butts on the road; water drips from a leaky gutter and pools at my feet.

People walk by on the street, and, as it gets later, the bell that pings every time the supermarket door opens becomes less frequent. At ten o'clock, I hear the clanking of metal shutters as someone begins the process of locking up for the night. I move deeper into the shadows and watch the entrance. The older woman comes out first, fastening a plastic hood over her grey curls and zipping a mac over her bulk.

I wait, and the boy who had been stacking shelves slopes out and begins to walk up the street, hands sunk deep into the pockets of his jacket. Then the door beeps once more, and it's Maria wearing a short red coat with a fur collar and trainers. The coat looks thin and inadequate for the weather. She fishes in her pocket and lights a cigarette, blowing a bubble of smoke into the air. A car passes and the headlights glance across her face, defining the sharpness of her cheekbones and the paleness of her skin. Adjusting a satchel on one shoulder and picking up a bag of shopping, she takes a quick look round and begins to walk away from me.

My heart is beating hard now, but I slip out of the alley and follow at a distance. At the end of the road, she presses the button at a crossing and puts the shopping on the ground. Her posture is hunched. I move behind the pillar of a doorway and watch as she passes to the opposite pavement. Here, she turns right and quickens her pace. I wait until she's further down the path and then cross over and walk behind.

After a while, the shops peter out, and we pass a garage. Ahead, the concrete columns of the housing estate begin to emerge. Her red coat is easy to keep in sight. Light shows behind curtained windows and in others, where curtains are not drawn, I see the flicker of television screens, somebody washing up, children in a row on a sofa.

The traffic noises recede. In the daytime, the estate is busy. When I pass by, I usually see teenagers on bikes with alarming haircuts, cigarettes between index finger and thumb, and black track suits. Rain is all it takes to drive them inside. I try to follow her, but, from time to time, she turns and scans the landscape, as though sensing she is followed.

The main path now converges to a series of link ways, and I wait so long, keeping out of sight, that I lose her. My back aches, and my feet and fingers are numb. Then, through the lit interior of a hallway, I see her red coat ascend a spiralled stairway. On the third level, she puts down her bag, opens her purse and fishes for a key. Once she's inside, I follow.

The entranceway smells of frying oil. Right-wing graffiti is sprayed on the walls, and a heavy-bass drumbeat resounds from behind one of the flats. My footsteps echo back to me as I climb the steps. At the third level, I pause for breath and feel the racing of my pulse. Maria's door is grey, no letter box, just the number 12 and a spy hole. I press the bell. The sound of a television or radio floats from somewhere inside.

There are quiet footsteps that stop just on the other side. Silence. She's waiting, and through the barrier I sense her uncertainty, her hostility. I remember the way her eyes darted away from me in the shop, and I know. I know that she knows it's me. For a moment, I hold my breath, and then there is the sound of a chain and the door opens.

"You better come in."

The flat smells of smoke. The television is playing some soap opera, which she pauses. "I knew you'd come, right?" In the overhead light, I see the brittleness of her dyed hair and the tiny lines around her thin mouth. She leads me to a kitchen, where she drains her glass and pours another. "You want one?"

Why not? I think. "Thanks." She pours me a vodka and Coke.

"You've been going in that shop as long as I've worked there. I thought you'd never remember me now. Today though..." Her eyes narrow slightly.

I take a sip.

"Want a cigarette?" She pulls one out then stuffs the packet in her jeans, and I follow her to the living room. "So, we may as well get this over with. What do you want to say? I didn't know Nina very well, and I haven't got a clue who killed her or who did that to you." She blows the smoke out of the corner of her mouth and takes a long swig from the glass. There is no expression on her face.

"I guess you know that I lost my memory."

"Yeah, I heard."

I look around at the patterned wallpaper and stained white rug. The furniture is cheap. There are no pictures or ornaments along the shelves. Fake flowers sit in a blue vase on a cabinet, and a door stands open at the end, through which I can see a bed, a duvet spilling to the floor.

"Nina was being abused," I say.

Maria plays with her cigarette and raises an eyebrow. "It's all history now, isn't it?"

"Is it?" I say. "Not for me. My sister's still missing."

There is a sullen set to her mouth, but something moves across her eyes. Sympathy?

"Anna," I say. "Maria, I know you were one of those girls, like Nina. I know you were being abused, too."

For the briefest instant, the mask slips, and I see the fragility beneath. Her eyes grow hard.

"Says who?"

"I know."

"Did Nina tell you?"

"Yes, she did."

"Fucking bitch."

"I'm sorry."

"Well it isn't any of your, or her, bloody business. All that was a long time ago, and I don't need it dragging up now." She lights another cigarette, refusing to meet my gaze.

"It is my business — I lost my best friend *and* a sister."

She gets up, coming back with the vodka, which she slops liberally into her glass. "What do you want me to say? I don't know who did that to her or who took your sister."

"But you must remember who they were. You must remember Ken. You're a witness. God, do you know how hard I've tried to recall that day? Ken almost certainly killed Nina, but Anna may have been taken somewhere else." The thought makes my insides shrink.

She looks startled.

"Danielle, Nina's sister said he was at the house later. His alibi doesn't hold. He was agitated. There was blood on his shirt."

She looks away and shrugs, but I feel her shock. "If you know all this, why are you here?"

"Anna is still missing. Ken wasn't alone in abusing Nina. Do *you* think he killed her?" My voice cuts the air.

She watches me for a moment. "Honest? Ken was a cunt, but I don't see him as a killer."

"What if Nina threatened to tell?"

She shakes her head. "Ken wasn't like that. Some of them," she lowers her eyes, "some were brutal. They liked to hurt. It's what they got off on. Ken wasn't one of those. That probably sounds mad to you."

"A bit."

"Well it's not easy to talk about, or think about, all that stuff. In some ways, the older you get, the worse it is. I went to a counsellor once, but I couldn't hack it." She gives a shudder. "I saw one of *them* quite recently, you know."

"One of the men?" I lean forward. "Who?"

"God knows what his name was. He came into the shop. He bought a bottle of our expensive wine and some fucking posh cheese." She pauses, as if trying to digest the memory. "He recognised me, gave me a smile, and I couldn't say or do anything. I just put it all through the till and gave him the receipt." Her face tightens with anger. "Then he winked."

She gets up and paces to the window, where the thread of Thames glitters in the distance. Her shoulders are hunched. "So you remember meeting me, do you?"

For a moment, something dark touches me. I have a vague recollection of her at the bunker.

"I was at that den you and Nina had. You turned up," she says.

I don't say anything.

"So, what do you want?"

"Please go to the police, and tell them what you know. You must remember some of their names at least."

She is still. Her reflection is unforgiving in the glass.

"You need to know something, anyway — the police have re-opened the investigation into Anna and Nina."

She turns, and I see now what she has been trying so hard to hide — fear. "Why?"

I don't want to tell her about the photos. "I'm beginning to remember stuff."

"You remembered Nina and I were being abused, and you told the police? Is that what you did?"

"It doesn't matter why. The police already knew about Nina. What happens next is what's important."

"The fucking police!" Her words are beginning to slur. "Well *that's* going to make all the difference."

"What do you mean?"

She comes over and sits on the edge of the sofa. Her eyes are heavily kohled, but behind that they are a startling and beautiful blue. "How do you think they all got away with it for so long?"

"Are you saying the police were involved?" I think of what Jason said.

"Involved and paid off. Yeah, that's exactly what I mean."

"This was fifteen years ago."

"You think they change? These disgusting bastards never change. All that changes is the kids. One lot gets too old, so they find another lot. That fat cunt with the wine and the cheese, you think he's a nice, old respectable man now?" Her anger grinds into the air. "So, how come the police are 'looking into it' again? Are you telling me that you remembering her abuse is what did it?" Her tone is mocking.

"I remembered some photos."

She is momentarily stunned. "What photos?"

"Nina stole them — they were pictures of the abuse. I found them again."

Maria seems to shrink. "When?"

"She took them years ago. Maybe she planned to take them to prove what was happening. I don't know. She hid them at the bunker. I remembered. They were still there."

"Jesus." Maria leans back on the sofa, a frown between her

pencilled brows. "Nina was always full of surprises. She kicked one of those wankers once, where it hurt. She had some real guts." She looks at me now with something like sympathy. "She was... she was all right, Nina, you know. Clever and funny. I liked her." She looks away and takes a deep breath. "So, you took these pictures to the police?"

I nod.

"Fuck. I get it now." Her skin pales. "I was in them, right? Not Nina. It was me. That's how you recognised me." Her features crumble — her pain hits me like a rock.

"Nina was in them, too. I'm sorry," I say.

"That's that then." She fills and drains her glass. "You're going to tell them where I am, as well."

"I want to. If you can identify these men, maybe they can find out what happened to Anna."

"Fucking hell." Her voice is squeezed from her throat. "You have no idea what you're asking."

"You said it: they're probably still doing it. Someone else is suffering as you had to, as Nina had to."

Her fingers tremble as she lights another cigarette.

I stay until late. I get drunk, and Maria gets drunker. At 2 in the morning, I guide her to the small bedroom and help her into the bed. Her eyes see past me now, past everything. I pull the covers over her. In the darkened room, with her face slack, she looks younger, and pity for her swells inside me. I check that no cigarettes are left burning and tidy up the glasses. In the kitchen, I find a pad and pen and leave my number and a note. Then I call a taxi. And when it's time to leave, I descend the empty stairwell and walk into the night.

2016

He sees her. She waits in the alleyway, as wind blows rubbish along the pavement, and tugs at her hood. There is something tense and watchful in her posture. Leaning low into the seat of the car, he is confident that he cannot be seen. He tries to work out how he feels about her now. There she is, still standing as the storm blows around her, and it will worsen. Who knows who will be recognised in the photographs and where it will lead?

And then a woman in a red coat comes out of the supermarket, and Heidi reacts immediately. He sits up, turns on the engine and turns the car round. Heidi steps out of the shadows and begins to follow the woman. He waits, keeping his eyes on their progress until they reach the estate. Driving forward, he parks, pulls up his hood, wraps a scarf across the lower part of his face, and follows, taking cover in the shadowed doorways. But he needn't have worried — they do not see him. The woman in the red coat enters one of the blocks of flats and climbs the stairs slowly, the weight of her shopping pulling at her shoulder, her body angled to balance the weight.

Wind whistles through gutters and down the concrete passageways. Once the woman is inside the flat, he sees Heidi, white faced, taking the steps at a quicker pace. At the top, she pauses. Her hand reaches out and then falls to her side. He watches as she gathers her courage. There is a pause, he can almost feel the tension, and then the door opens. There is a movement of lips, an adjustment of her body, and she steps inside.

Back in the car, he closes his eyes and sees the image of the red coat against the stark lights of the hallway. He sees the blonde hair and used face. And something comes back to him, a flash of memory, the slightest thread of surprise. He recognises her. She was one of their girls. For the tiniest moment, this recall pulls at deeper memories, plunges a hand into the places he keeps tightly locked away, and threatens to lift the lid — just for an instant. He wrestles with the thoughts and pushes them firmly back.

He sits forward and examines his face in the mirror, his eyes; *his* eyes — at times they do not seem to belong to anyone he knows. Maria is the name of the girl. She was a friend of Nina's. And suddenly, when he thinks of Heidi, he experiences a shudder of blind anger.

2016

DENISE

It's dark as Denise begins her journey to Mark Lyell. Loose flakes of snow hit the windscreen before dissolving against the wipers; around her, and on the road ahead, there is the pale brush of whiteness where it has begun to settle. Denise drives slowly through the villages to Allingham. The afternoon has turned colder, and she turns up the heat in the car and tries to listen to the radio through the rush of hot air.

Mark Lyell's home is an end of terrace on a picturesque street. The door is opened by a young woman in her late twenties or early thirties. The woman is effortlessly beautiful with dark, shoulder-length hair and generous lips. She gives Denise a tight smile and calls for her husband.

In the sitting room, Denise has to negotiate an assault course of children's toys before coming to stand by the open fireplace. Mark comes in, nearly scraping his head on the top of the frame. In his arms, he holds a chubby baby with green stuff all over its face.

Denise watches him carefully, trying to gauge his reaction to her. "I hope you had a good holiday, and thanks for seeing me. I'd like to talk to you about your time at Bayview Children's Home."

He holds the baby closer, bouncing it protectively against his chest. There is anger in his face.

"What do you want to know?" Hostility hovers in his eyes.

"Is there somewhere we could talk?"

"Are you really investigating Holly Watts? Look, I don't even want to talk about it here. Can we drive somewhere?" He hands the baby over and grabs a coat from the banister and puts on a pair of heavy boots, then, reaching out, gives his wife's arm a brief touch. "I won't be long."

Snow has settled on the railings of the fence, and Denise feels it on her cheeks. They climb into the car, which retains a little warmth, though the footwell is chill against her legs. "Where do you want to go?"

"Anywhere, just drive for a bit."

"I was hoping to take notes, if that's okay with you."

"Am I under investigation?"

"No, this is just informal."

They drive for about half a mile, then Denise pulls into a parking space beneath the glow of a streetlamp. She takes the notebook and a pen from the glovebox. "Thanks again for talking to me. Can you tell me about Bayview and about how you came to leave?"

Mark leans back in the seat. He smells of onions and baby powder. He is silent for a while, and Denise waits. "I'll tell you what happened. I always wondered if this would come back to haunt me one day. In a way, I'm glad it has." He glances at Denise. "I was sacked after being accused of a theft. It was a false charge. I've never stolen anything in my life."

"What happened?"

"What, indeed. I borrowed a camera from one of Ray Watson's mates. Watson was Bayview's manager, and this man was often there, and he offered to lend it. I had been asked to take pictures for a friend's twenty-first. Next thing I know, the police accuse me of stealing it."

"Why do you think they did that?"

Mark looks down, fiddles with his watch strap. The street-lamp glances on his features and engraves lines of anger on his brow. "I caught the owner of the camera with a girl at the care home. A young girl."

"Tell me." Something icy grapples with Denise's insides.

"I lived in a bedsit about a mile away, but it was part of my duty rota to cover about three night shifts a week at Bayview." His face works with emotion. "One night, I wasn't actually supposed to be there, but I'd left my rucksack and came back to get it. It was late. Bayview was quiet, but I went upstairs out of habit, just to check everything was okay. I found him, the man who lent me the camera, coming out of one of the bedrooms. He was astonished to see me there. Made a ridiculous excuse and left. I went into the room, and the girl was crying." He grimaces, and Denise can see he's holding back his feelings. "She was only six or so. She told me what he'd done." He gazes angrily out of the window into the blackness. "The next day, the police came to my bedsit, found the camera in there, and that was that. He must have decided to invent the theft when he realised I knew what he was up to."

"Did you report the incident with the girl?"

"I didn't have time that night. It was late. I had somewhere else to be, but the next day, the police were at my door before 8 am accusing me of theft. They took me to the station and took a statement about the theft, wrote down everything I said. I tried to tell them about what happened to the girl. The officers seemed hostile, and I could tell they weren't inter-ested. Every time I tried to make a report about what I'd witnessed, they shut it down. I was sacked straight away, and later that night two policemen came back to the bedsit." He pales under the streetlamp. "Basically, they said if I 'forgot' what I'd seen, then all charges would be retracted. But if I ever tried to report it again or tell anyone, then they would make sure I regretted it. I believed them."

In the stillness of the car, Denise feels the weight of what she might be up against.

"Do you remember the name of the policemen at the station?"

His lips tighten. "Claybourne."

Her instincts about Claybourne were right, and she wonders how involved he was — and was he involved because he shared their appetites? Or perhaps, like so many weak men, because he was just greedy and got paid for his part.

"The whole thing was a cover up, you know. That place — Bayview. In retrospect, much more was going on than I realised even then. I just didn't want to believe it at the time, or now."

"Go on."

"Once, in the beginning, I was covering a night duty, and two of the older girls arrived back late. One of them was in a right state — very drunk and crying hysterically. I couldn't calm her down. The other girl was also drunk but kept telling her to shut up. She was distressed, too. I was trying to get them to tell me what had happened when Ray — Ray Watson, he was the care home manager — came in and got rid of me. He said he was used to dealing with stuff like that. It happened a lot."

"What? Girls coming in late, upset?"

"The kids going AWOL. Often for a complete night — girls, boys, whoever — and Ray always insisted on dealing with it. I don't know if you know, but there are procedures in place that are supposed to be followed in those events. If kids don't come back at night, it's supposed to be reported to the police and go in the incident book, but he always persuaded me not to. He didn't want to make trouble for them, he said. But after a time, I saw patterns. Certain nights, like Thursdays, one or another would go missing. And there were the absences from school." He swallows and draws his hand across his chin. "And then, around town, I saw Ray with them more than once. You know, when he shouldn't be — in a car, when they should have been at school, or late at night. He always had an excuse — the police had found them somewhere or something — but he never wrote them up. And the kids..." Denise witnesses a tremor. "I don't know, but I began to suspect abuse. The way they were around him, cautious and edgy. And looking back, he tried to find out where my preferences lay, you know — whether I liked underage kids." His eyes darken. "There were odd comments about a particular girl or boy, inappropriate comments. And once there was a magazine in the office that he showed me. It was a pornographic one, young women dressed up to look like very young schoolgirls, that sort of thing. He said he'd found it under one of the kid's beds. Asked me if I'd like to keep it for my own pleasure." He swallows in disgust. "In retrospect, he was just fishing, wasn't he?"

Denise stares out of the window where snow spins in the streetlamp's penumbra.

"And then there were the visitors. Different people — men."

"Do you remember the name of the man who you saw coming out of the room, whose camera you borrowed?"

"Sorry, no. I'd chat to him now and then, but he was one of Ray's friends. He was always there. I hated the way he was round the kids, particularly the little ones. Always sucking up to them, bringing them sweets, little gifts."

"Why was he visiting the home?"

"He was really into his photography. He came to encourage an interest in the children. He had a club." Mark gives her a hollow look.

Denise pulls her coat closer. Snow falls steadily now, and the flakes settle, leaving a mantle of white where they fall. She shivers, even through the hot blast of air.

"And what about the other policemen who came to your house later? The ones who threatened you — did they give a name?"

He shakes his head.

"Can you describe them?"

"I couldn't say if they were policemen or not; I always assumed so. One was tall, heavy set, but not fat, with blonde hair, and he was handsome. The other one..." He shrugs. "He was average, nothing notable."

"At a later date, would you be prepared to make an official statement about all this? Look at some photographs of serving officers or suspects?"

"Okay."

"And the children — this girl who was abused that night? The other kids? Do you remember their names?"

He sighs. "I've tried to put it behind me. Forgetting is simpler than remembering."

"Does a Ken Finch, Kenneth Finch, mean anything to you?"

He shakes his head.

"There was building work going on when you were there. There must have been a fair few workmen. Did anything strike you as off with any of them?"

He purses his lips in reflection. "The work was nearly finished when I started. I don't remember anything striking me."

"And Holly Watts. You said you remember her?"

"Holly." Another flurry of snow whirls against the car. "I remember her. I don't want to imagine what happened to her," Mark captures her in his hunted gaze, "but I do know one thing — she was a sitting duck for one those monsters."

"Is there anything else you remember that might be significant?"

"Not really. No."

Denise closes the notebook and is about to return it to her bag when Mark leans forward. "Wait — there is one thing. At the time I was there, there was this social worker that used to visit. Once, when Ray wasn't around, she took me to one side and started asking me questions."

"Questions?"

"Yeah, leading questions. It was before I began to notice stuff, so it didn't really register, but later, after I was sacked, I remembered her and what she was getting at. You know?"

"So you think she knew?

"I think she had an idea, yes. Yes, definitely she knew. And I got the feeling she was frightened. She hinted that powerful people were involved. Dangerous ones. She was scared." He bites down hard on his lips. "At the time, I thought she was being overly dramatic. Now, I'm not so sure. If anything happens to me..."

"This was a long time ago."

"But someone in the police made sure I kept quiet the first time." He fixes her with accusing eyes. "I have my own kids now."

"Do you remember the social worker's name?"

"No, I'm sorry. All the kids had social workers but not necessarily the same ones. I can't even remember whose social worker she was."

2001

HEIDI

I have the photograph of Maria folded inside an envelope and hidden behind the loose front panel of the piano. Mum doesn't know about this place, because it was me that knocked it loose. The knowledge of the photo's presence makes me afraid. What would happen if Mum or Anna found it? How could I explain it? I don't trust myself to keep Nina's terrible secrets.

"Are you okay, love?" Mum strokes my cheek, pulling me into a hug. "You look tired. Is there something worrying you?"

"I'm fine," I lie. The skin of our walls and the narrow space between our and Nina's house is not thick enough to protect me from the knowledge that Ken lives next door.

One morning, I see Ken getting into his car, dressed in work overalls and carrying a lunch box. He grins and waves. My heart judders, and I'm rooted to the pavement, my school bag heavy in my hand. I feel naked in the thinness of my blouse and am conscious of the shortness of my skirt. For a moment, I feel as Nina must feel when he looks at her.

Glancing up at the windows of their house, I imagine Nina

and Danielle in their room just down the hall from him, passing him daily. I have seen him playing with Danielle and Anna, lifting them high in his arms and giving them piggy backs.

And behind all this, the shadow of Holly's disappearance. I still haven't questioned Nina, and I know now that I won't. I don't want to know.

Each day, Ken's presence burrows itself more deeply beneath my skin and into my fears, and, with it, the reality of the other men in the pictures and men who may be like them. In every male I see, I now imagine a monster such as those Nina encounters. They're everywhere — sitting in parked cars, strolling towards me on the street, drinking coffee at the bakery where Mum works.

Often, I find myself trailing after her or sitting close to her when Anna is in bed and feeling the words in my mouth, my despair choking the back of my throat. The effort of holding it all inside strains at my lungs. Once, she found me crying under my covers after school. Her warm hand on my back, her gentle words, her concern, could not pull the truth from me, and I made up a story of some fall-out in the lunch break. The relief in her tone made me sob harder, carrying me further away from being able to tell her the real reason for my agony. And all the time, the photos, Nina's horrible ordeals, and my promise to run away, bleeds into my world.

Finally, I know that there is no other way, and when nobody is around, I take the envelope from the piano and worry it into a little gap in the lining of my school bag where no one will find it. All day, I can't look at Nina, who seems to cling to me even more than usual. After school, we pick up Danielle and Anna, but at home, we part ways.

"Mum asked me to pop to the bakery. She's working there late tonight."

Hand in hand, Anna and I walk to the bakery. The weight of what I am to do hangs heavy in my limbs. I drop her off, telling Mum that I promised I would go to a friend's house and lend her a book.

The house of the nice policeman, Charlie, is a mere five-minute walk from the bakery. As I near, trepidation flutters in my belly. What if Nina is right? What if this will find its way back to Ken or to one of the others? But if I don't do something, this will go on and on. For a moment, I worry in case Charlie sees me. What will I do if he's there? I push the doubts aside and imagine him again in my mind's eye — his light hair, his strong features. I trust him. I grab tightly on to this hope and hold it close.

At the house, I hang about on the opposite side of the road by the bus stop. The house tells me nothing, whether he is there or not, and all the time, my mind slips from one conviction to another. Should I, or shouldn't I? I remember the invitation he extended to me. *"If you need a copper..."* And the jokey manner he has. The exchange outside his house comes back to me.

"What happened to your finger?" Anna had asked, and my embarrassed gaze had been drawn to the missing tip of the little finger. "Oh, that's criminals for you. Lots of sharp teeth." And he had smiled at me, as if to say, "don't be embarrassed".

The photograph of Maria gets heavier and heavier on my conscience. Time passes, two buses arrive, pick up passengers and disgorge them, and I watch the dark windows trying to see beyond the blackness for signs of life. There is no car outside and no light behind the glass, and, as time elapses, I convince myself that he can't be there.

Suddenly, the skies open and rain falls fatly on to the concrete. The smell of earth and drains drifts up. Passers-by begin to run for shelter, the slap of their feet mingling with the downpour, and I know that this is the moment — if I don't do it now, I never will, and Ken will be there forever, just a finger's touch from me and Anna.

Rain hammers on to my hair, cleaving it to my scalp, and runs warm into my mouth. Before I can let my doubts catch up with me, I pull the envelope from its hiding place, cross the road at a run, race up the narrow path and to the letterbox where I push the envelope through. Then I turn, fleeing from the house as fast as I can.

I reach the bakery, my uniform dripping and limbs shivering from doubt or cold. My heart bangs furiously in my chest, and as I pause for breath, I look up and see that a rainbow, impossibly vibrant, arcs across the blue heavens. Fear and triumph battle for precedence, but suddenly, I am cowed by a shrinking terror that I may forever regret what I have done.

2016

HEIDI

I have stopped using the supermarket where Maria works, and I have not told Denise that I recognise her. So many secrets sit inside me now, secrets from Denise and from Jason and Danielle. They do not know that I have the pictures. And all the time, my past seems to be leaking back into my life like a stain. At times, I wonder if it's been worth it. Beyond all that, I am haunted by a sense that what happened is somehow my fault: it eats at me, causing me to wake early in the pre-dawn with images of Nina and Anna stamped in my head. Sometimes, I hear Anna's voice, from some moment in the past, asking for a glass of squash or telling Mum she's too full to eat her broccoli. Sometimes, I hear the sound of Nina's laugh. It's unbearable, and I bury my head into the pillow and wait for the pain to ease.

On the bus, I pass the shop again, as I have every night, and I peer through the glass. Yet again, Maria is not there, and I feel anxious. Is she on holiday, or off sick, or stacking shelves somewhere at the back?

Impulse finds me jamming on the Stop button and exiting

the bus just along the road. Inside the shop, I hear the hum of the freezers and the same meaty smell hangs in the air. I walk around aisles, pick up a box of tea bags and stand at the till.

The big woman is there.

"Is Maria around?" I ask.

She looks up at me.

"She's not been in all week."

"Is she on holiday?"

But the queue is building up behind me, and the woman gives me only a brief nod of affirmation.

Outside, the pavements are slippery with ice. Instead of catching the next bus, I walk back and find Maria's flat. The stairwell is silent now, no bass thumping through the air.

I put my ear to her door, but there is no sound. Shit. Unease begins to prickle through me. I ring the bell, waiting in the stark hallway for an answer, but none comes.

Taking out my phone, I scroll through the numbers to Denise. My fingers hover over her name. What if Maria has done something stupid? Did the threat of me going to the police destabilise her? I had promised that I would give her time before I told the police that I had recognised her. But now, I find myself sending Denise a text. I look at it for a few seconds, and then I press send.

As I enter my flat, I'm aware of the chill, and when I look around, I see that the sash window has been pushed up. Immediately, I back out of the front door, my pulse skittering wildly. Outside, I lean against the wall and attempt to steady my breathing. Gazing up, I try to see if my neighbours in the flat above are in, but the windows are black. I send out a call to Denise, who is engaged, and then I text her again. Then, I remember Cleo, and I'm crippled with panic.

The hall bulb leaves a puddle of light on the mat, and I gaze through into the darkened sitting room to the open window. A breeze tugs at the curtains, and the fabric swishes as it passes across the sill. The air seems chillier inside than out. Without fully entering the room, I let my eyes travel the walls and floor, but there is no sign of disturbance, and no sign of Cleo. Still, I dare not call out. Nervously, I walk in, my ears attuned to the noises beyond, but the house is utterly silent, and I sense that I'm alone. An icy tongue of air touches my cheek, and I slam the sash window shut. "Cleo," I call, but she does not come. Heart beating, I check the bedroom and bathroom, but there is nowhere for someone to hide. Whoever has been here has gone.

I take my time looking for signs of interference. The first place I check is the hall cupboard, but the intruder has missed the photographs. In the bedroom, I open the bedside cabinet. Nothing has been disturbed, and I think of the day I was chased and shudder. As well as dismay, I experience a bullet of rage at the violation of my home. There is no sign of Cleo, and I hope that she is outside chasing through the undergrowth in search of mice.

I race to the back door, calling her and scanning the garden and eventually I see her, prowling through one of the allotments, caught in the light from a window.

Denise rings back, telling me they are on their way and not to touch anything. I pace the house, trying to contain the tumult of emotion. Finally, I sit on the bed and put my head in my hands. There is an unfamiliar crackle beneath me. Folding back the duvet, I see an envelope. For a moment I am filled with a profound sense of menace. I imagine someone here — in my space, in my house, and in my bed — and I know I should wait for Denise, but I slide my finger across the top anyway and pull the flap open.

Inside, a black-and-white photograph that is stippled with flaws does not give up its image easily. But as my eyes begin to make sense of the scene, revulsion clogs my throat. What appeared at first to be a slab of pale stone is now identifiable as the back of a woman's body. The links of her spine ladder along her skin. The torso is swollen and discoloured with bruising, and mud clings to the dip of her waist.

Around her flesh, twine is tightly bound, cutting deeply into the tissue. Her misshapen neck is fringed and loose where the head must once have been. I sit down heavily but can't draw my eyes away. What is left of her lies on a bank dotted with curling leaves, her legs disappearing into the black river.

In my imagination, I can smell the dankness of the water as it turns the mud, and the chill of the scene is sucked into my bones. Some of the binding from her body is caught in the knotted roots of a tree. My brain refuses to explore beyond the immediate horror of her remains to the living person that she once was. I only feel the threat that is so clearly articulated. Turning it over, someone has written a message: *Memories are not for the living*.

I look out of the window where the night sky reaches up to a crescent moon. The darkness stares back at me, and I feel naked beneath the ceiling light. Out there, in the tangle of winter gardens and alleyways, he may be waiting, and I recall Ken's thin and sallow face. Whoever has been here can easily see me through the uncurtained glass. Perhaps he's watching me now, gauging my reaction, enjoying the emotions he has elicited. But I can't move, cannot prise my legs from the duvet or stand. So I gaze into the blackness, lips open in shock, and with dread weighting me to the bed as my world disintegrates further.

And then something else begins to filter into my consciousness — a smell, earthy, raw, and foul — and my gorge rises. A sense of something terrible loosens the muscles of my belly. I look down and see that my hand is stained; a patch of colour seeps from underneath the duvet, and new terror shakes me further. I don't want to look. I know it will be something worse, much worse, than any image captured on a piece of paper. I rip the cover back.

When I finally translate the mess of blood and fur, I see that it is a rabbit, or what remains of it — its belly ripped open and the contents spilt across the sheets — dark-rimmed eyes that once scanned the wooded horizons now cloudy with death.

2016

He makes the call from his car in a nearby village. It is early evening, too early for the pub to begin filling up. Most people are at home eating their evening meals. He sees lights in windows, the flicker of televisions, a child at a table — head bent over a phone.

If he takes his attention further inside, he imagines the smell of food, the chatter, the demand to complete homework, to wash hands before dinner, the volley of mundane exchanges. Envisaging other lives, he conceives something other than his — somewhere where the rooms are always warm, where a mother and father exchange amicable conversation, and dinner arrives at approximately the same time. His life has never been like this.

The past is like a faulty video, damaged, edited and re-edited. But there are times when everything threatens to spool out of its box like a trail of bloodied intestines. His childhood feels more distant than the actual passage of years justifies. He wonders what life would be like without *him* to frame it. And now, as he gazes at the little patches of light behind the curtained glass, the stories he weaves are somehow comforting. And for a moment, his world is less full of edges and pitfalls, is less empty.

The phone is answered swiftly.

He turns from his thoughts to listen to the voice on the other end. The measured and familiar tones. He imagines the calm gaze of the eyes and the reassuring jaw.

"They suspect what was going on at Bayview." The Chief does not sound overly concerned.

He has only a vague recollection of these people, and Bayview was not somewhere he knew.

"More worrying is that there was a social worker back then who had suspicions, and she has the sort of information that could potentially be difficult to manage. We shut her up the first time, but they'll put all their efforts into tracing her again."

"What do you want me to do?"

A car passes, and its wheels hiss on the wet road.

"Ray Watson will never cough, but I want you to sort the social worker out — shut her up again. It'll take a while for the police to find her, and you have a head start. Any more on our little amnesiac?"

He tells him about Maria.

"Who the hell is Maria?"

"She was one of the girls."

There is a long silence, "Heidi's quite something, isn't she?" The Chief's tone is brittle with controlled fury.

He stares out to the street and wonders why The Chief has risked keeping Heidi alive. She has already caused so much damage.

"Are you there?" The Chief asks.

"Yes, I'm listening."

"Anything else I should know?"

"Nothing." He visualises Heidi and the fear that she is constantly trying to master. "I think the photo and rabbit worked though. She's running scared."

A laugh of satisfaction. "Well, that's something." And the call is ended.

2001

HEIDI

I don't see him until I hear the slam of the car door, and Ken's skinny frame blocks my path. He is wearing a jacket and drainpipe jeans.

"Heidi."

My heart lurches.

"Nina's waiting for you at the shops. I said I'd drop you off."

I can't look at him, and my face flames with embarrassment and fright.

"What's up?" He gives me an easy smile, leans against the door of the Renault. "Come on, you haven't been in this new car yet." Over the years I've taken many lifts. We all have. It's different now, though, now that I know.

He reaches out and pats my cheek. "What's the matter, Carrots? Anyone would think that I'd done something wrong."

And he's so natural, so easy, that to not get in the car would give me away. The hairs on my scalp prickle. He doesn't know. How could he? Soon, Charlie and the police will come and take him away, and it will be fine again.

The car smells of petrol and cigarette smoke. There's a newspaper on the polished dashboard with a picture of the Queen on it. I rest against the seat and try to stay calm. The ugliness and brutality of what he's done creeps through my skin and into my mouth. But it won't be long before I'm away from him. The shops are only round the corner, maybe three minutes, and then I'll be with Nina.

The car starts with a cough. I think of the photograph, and of what I've done, and shrink against the seat. Because I don't want to look at him, I turn and gaze out of the window at the passing street — two girls with a puppy, an old man cutting a hedge with a pair of shears, a boy balancing on a skateboard, houses, pavements, lamp posts. Scenes of everyday. Nothing is wrong. Nothing is wrong. Ken whistles through his teeth and time stretches. The sweet smell of his hair cream mingles with my distress.

"Beautiful day, love, isn't it?"

I make the mistake of turning to answer. He is no longer smiling. His eyes are angry in his cratered face, and, just as we should be turning into the car park, he revs the engine, and we shoot past.

"No," I try to say, but no sound leaves my mouth. His thin smile knifes through me, and I fumble with the door handle, but the car's going too fast.

"Stop. I want to get out." My heart thunders in my ears.

"Don't try anything silly. You're in a lot of trouble."

It was a trick. I am brutally aware of my vulnerability, the prison of the car about me, his hands as they curve across the wheels, the terrible things he does to Nina. I want to be sick. He will do them to me. I start to cry. He knows about the photograph. He knows because Charlie must have given it to the wrong person. Nina was right — it was never safe to tell.

I am stupid. A child in my belief. The sense of my understanding of how things are tips again, and I am pitched into a grown-up world where people get torn apart and the things that happen to Nina happen to others, too. Everything that seemed ordinary and safe has been flipped over to reveal a dark and terrifying underbelly.

"I'm not going to hurt you."

I want to believe him, but I feel as if I have no skin to protect me as we hurtle down the road ever further away from home and towards the countryside.

I consider winding down the window and screaming, but we are out of Riverbridge already and racing along the wooded lanes, past the crossroads at Hexley and the church at Littlestone. With every minute, I am conscious of how far away we are from safety.

Finally, he pulls into a rough track that cuts through a bank of trees, and, ahead, I see what looks like a farm building with yellowing walls and a flat roof. Still, he doesn't stop until we reach the heavy doors.

Terror sings through my body. Tears dry in my throat, and I wrap my arms about myself. Without the engine, it is silent, and I'm aware of him in a way that I have never been before — of his skin, his smell, the flesh and blood realness of him — his man-ness. He grins at me, and I know how terrible my error has been in getting into the car.

Lighting a cigarette, he turns on the seat to face me. "When did Nina give you the photograph?"

My mouth is dry, but I shake my head vehemently. "No, she didn't," I try to say, but the words are thick and unwieldy, vowel-less. I look at the fields around me. I could get out and run. If I hear a car, I will leap out and run back to the road.

"We know where the photos came from, and we know Nina must have stolen them."

"She didn't give it to me. I took it."

"But she showed you?"

I nod.

"Where?" His eyes are sly. I don't want to look at him. There are no cars coming, only silence.

I've betrayed Nina again. I start to cry.

"For fuck's sake, shut up." He sounds impatient. "Stop snivelling. I just need to know how you got the photo, okay?"

I look up into his eyes. "I took it from the bunker."

He leans closer to me, and I back away until I feel the door handle digging into my back. "And who else did you show?"

I understand now what this is about. This is about keeping the secret. It is what Nina had said. There is nowhere to run, no one to tell. Again, I experience that terrible shift between the world as I knew it and how it actually is. Why hadn't I trusted her?

"Nobody. I didn't show anybody."

"Your mum?"

"No!"

And I sense that he believes me.

He throws the cigarette stub out of the window. Then he lunges at me, his fingers digging into my thigh. I try to scream, try to push him off, but he is too strong, and I am helpless in his grip. I think the worst is going to happen, but he pulls away, leaving his hand still burning into the skin of my leg. I am shaking and crying again.

"If you ever, ever tell anyone about Nina or the photographs or this — you know what will happen, don't you? Think of your mum and Anna, how easy it would be to drive a car on to the pavement when they're walking back from the bakery. Or the doors to your home with their flimsy locks. Think about that tonight, when everyone else is asleep, and you are lying awake and going over what's happened today."

"No!" It does not come out as the scream that's building inside me. It comes out as a whisper.

He opens the door then goes round to my side and drags me out. My limbs are boneless. From his pocket, he takes a set of keys and unlocks the door.

"What are you going to do? I'm sorry. I won't tell, I promise." But even to me my words sound meaningless.

He pulls me into a large room with a high ceiling and lots of wires and frames clamped to the walls. The space is partitioned into different areas. He stops and watches my face.

"See here."

I nod.

"If you did tell, and I get taken away, this is what will happen. I'll get one of those men you saw in the pictures to come and get you." His face is terrifyingly near to mine, and again I bite down on my lips. "And there's Anna, too." He crouches to meet my height.

His eyes are the most terrifying thing that I have ever seen. "If you tell, I'll find out one way or another." He puts out his hand and strokes my cheek. "How do you think I know about the photograph? Do you understand?"

I'm unable to move. His fingers are unbearably intimate on my skin. His eyes bore past mine and drill into my soul and I know that I will never tell. Never. Ever. Ever.

2016

DENISE

It's late when DC Marion Brown is putting on her coat to leave. She has changed into a pair of jeans and a scooped top. Her hair, out of its customary ponytail, curls above her ears. Denise wonders if she knows how pretty she is.

"Have a nice weekend. Good work this week," Denise says.

She gives her a white-toothed grin. "How's Heidi? I hear they managed to identify the photo."

"It was a police photo from back in the 1970s. A domestic, apparently. We don't think it can have had anything to do with this case."

"A threat then." She cocks her head. "Quite a nasty one. Shouldn't we have her in a safe house?"

Denise sighs. "I think the consensus is that if they wanted to kill her, it would have been done already, and all the local safe houses are full. She's staying with Jason Carpenter, who seems more than capable of looking after her, and the house is pretty high-tech with alarms. We have someone passing by on a regular basis, too. Any luck tracing Maria?"

"No, she seems to have booked a holiday rather suddenly, but she should be back next week."

Denise makes a note.

"Denise?"

She looks up. "What is it?"

"This police photo. Do you think there's someone on the inside involved in all of this?"

"If there is, it's our job to bring it to light. I'm not one of these coppers who think it's okay to protect the guilty or break the law just because they might be a colleague." Denise realises she sounds fiercer than she needs to.

Marion frowns. "From everything I'm learning about this case, I'm not sure we did justice to it the first time around."

"I have to agree with you."

She puts on her scarf and begins to button her coat. "I meant to say, the stuff they picked up from the bunker is on one of the tables in Room 25. We had a good look this afternoon, but it's pretty much as you'd expect."

After Marion has gone, the flowery scent she wears lingers in the air. It makes Denise feel unutterably old. The doughnut she's been saving is slightly stale, and she dunks it in the coffee listlessly.

The corridors where the administrative staff work are virtually empty now, and she's aware of the strange quality of silence that remains after a usually busy building is left unoccupied. In the stairwell, with the raw overhead lights, she is even more conscious of being alone.

Room 25 is not locked, and Denise walks to the table where the bagged and tagged items recovered from the bunker make several sad piles. The main body of the girls' den elicited only a few items: a cigarette packet, empty wrappers — nothing, she suspects, that is of any use. It had been thoroughly combed the first time.

Nina's hiding place appears to be equally disappointing: a pile of damp notes, a pen, a lighter, and a dirty hair clip. Denise picks up the bag with the clip and examines it, turning it under the light, and, as the beam catches it, she sees the coloured enamel and her heart thumps. It's common enough, but she's seen this design only days before. She's sure of it. Christ. Taking out her phone, she calls Wendy Martin, and then she sits in the quietness of the room waiting for the reply.

It takes less than a minute for Wendy to send Denise the image. Using her thumbs, Denise enlarges the photo of Holly's face, watching as her freckles become more pronounced over the up-turned nose. But Denise pays scant attention to that. She hovers over the clip to the side of the blonde hair. And to the way the light plays across the rainbow enamel.

After a restless night, Denise makes her way into the station. Its familiar noises and faces are a home away from home, but today, the weather has put undue stress on the inadequate heating system, and none of the radiators are working. The small electric heater in Mike Tennant's tiny office is woefully deficient, and when Denise enters — clad in coat, and thick boots — she can detect the dry aroma of his overheated trousers and whatever the sauce was that covered the canteen's pasta bake.

Denise gets straight down to business. "We've arrested one of the men from Nina's photos. They matched someone already on our files as a known offender, but he's saying he wasn't part of the group. He'd shared pictures with someone he used to drink with in a pub and had been invited to one or two of their parties. He couldn't, or wouldn't, identify the others. Hopefully, his computer and a house search will turn up more."

Mike raises his eyebrows.

"He's frightened. He said it was a very tight organisation run by someone with a lot of clout. He wouldn't give us a name, just said they called him 'Chief' or some such."

"Great. Nothing more than that?"

"He said some of the others referred to him as Blondie."

Mike gives an uncharacteristic laugh. "Well, that narrows the field. Was Claybourne blonde?"

Denise shakes her head. "He was bald when I knew him. And Finch certainly isn't. What does Barrett say about Claybourne?"

"He agreed with you. He says the police investigation was shoddy, and he suspects Claybourne deliberately stopped or redirected avenues of investigation. What do you make of the hair clip we found at the bunker?"

"It's a tough one," Denise says. "There was nothing to definitively prove it was Holly's, but there is a partial on it that matches Nina. I think Nina took it. I think she knew that Ken had abducted Holly and wanted to prove it. This puts Ken even more in the frame for Anna." So far, it's the only explanation that Denise can come up with.

"And what about Holly and Anna's abductions? Has anyone given information?"

"Still nothing. If they know something, they're keeping it under wraps. And there's been no evidence that they were even abused by the group beforehand. In Anna's case, almost certainly not." She pauses, taps her pencil on the table. "I think something else happened to them. Abduction is dangerous behaviour and, even in a group like this, I wonder if they would have risked a step this far."

"It happens, though. Do you think it was someone else?" Mike's eyes are steely.

"Not really. The links to the group are too strong, and

Finch is clearly connected. No, I think it must have been someone within their circle, but out of character."

"And no other abductions since. So what happened to the abductor? Behaviour like this is compulsive."

"I'm hoping one of the names will match prison records and point to the offender having been locked up for the last 15 years, or perhaps it's Finch, and we'll find Finch is dead." Denise pauses. "But I'm concerned with the police association, Mike. I think it's very likely that there was either direct police involvement with this group of individuals, or the police were coerced. Mark Lyell's statement certainly backs this up. Watson, Bayview's manager, is in custody, but he's not going to crack. We've charged him. Some of the photographs are indisputably him. There is one thing I got from Lyell that we're following up — apparently a social worker at the time expressed concerns about abuse within the home. With a clear timeframe, it should be easy enough to find out which social workers had dealings with Bayview then."

"Great work. But no luck finding Kenneth Finch?"

"Nothing." Denise experiences a bite of frustration. "Did I tell you that we know who one of the other girls in the photo is? Heidi recognised her."

Mike looks startled.

"Her name is Maria Reilly. She's 27 and was a friend of Nina's. She's on holiday." Denise sighs.

The phone trills, and Mike picks it up impatiently. Usually calm, she watches his expression change, and when he finally looks at her, she can see the heightened anticipation in his eyes. "Forensics got access to Nina's diary."

As they drive through the frost-filled morning towards Forensic Services, the brick facades and office blocks give way to countryside, where the wet verges are strewn with leaves. Denise's stomach thrums with expectation. She wonders what's in Nina's diary. Does it identify more clearly the men who abused her? Or worse?

She studies Mike's profile surreptitiously, seeing his strong jaw and feeling his tension simmer in the car beside her. She thinks about what Danielle had said regarding Ken's blood-stained appearance on that afternoon. Will something be revealed that could lead them to understand what happened? Ken was dangerous even before Nina was murdered. And Anna, did he take her for himself? Or traffic her elsewhere? If she had been killed at the scene, he would surely have left her body there, unless he was trying to hide evidence. The thought sickens her. Her suspicions are strongly in favour of Ken being the person who took Anna and Holly and then passed them on. But to whom?

After negotiating their way through security, they are escorted to Forensic Services, located in one of the buildings on site. Here, in one of the square white rooms, they are shown the separated pages laid out behind glass.

"We've not managed to get a lot. Unfortunately, too much of what was there has been destroyed. Everything's been processed forensically, though there is nothing much that you wouldn't expect." As she listens to the discussion, Denise's eyes are drawn to the sheet of paper where Nina's childish writing is magnified. The horrors she lists make Denise swallow a lump in her throat. The lab technician hands them two folders.

"It might be easier to read from these." She leads Denise and Mike to an adjoining room with twin desks.

Denise puts the folder in front of her and, with trepidation, begins to read what Nina had written. Occasionally, they glance at each other. Mike's expression is tense.

Someone plants a cup of coffee at her elbow, but it remains untouched.

There isn't much to read through. She and Mike finish at approximately the same time and exchange looks.

"Let's get straight back."

They shake hands with the lab staff before leaving. "Great work, thank you." He gives a rare smile that reminds Denise that, beyond his police work, he is a family man. A man who laughs, who has another life.

The car is chilled.

"We need to find out who the hell 'The Chief' is," Mike says.

Denise cannot shake her anger "It's no help anyway without a name. It's a damned shame so much of what she wrote has deteriorated beyond restoration."

"She keeps mentioning 'Brandon' in connection to Holly. It looks possible that Nina knew who killed Holly? Wasn't there a Brandon written on the back of one of the photographs? Read it to me again."

She opens the folder and skips through until she finds the entry. She reads aloud, *"Brandon has chosen another girl. Her name is Holly Watts and now she's missing."*

"Holly is *another* girl? There were more who were abducted prior to Holly... unless he chose Anna first, but didn't get an opportunity to take her... but this doesn't make sense with the crime scene and Nina's murder."

"It's January. Too early to be Anna," Denise concedes. "So who went before Holly?"

Denise closes the folder with nervous fingers. "There's a Brandon whose name came up in the original enquiry — a Brandon Velker. He was one of Ken's alibis. My money's on it being him. If what Nina says here is true, then that's good news. We have a name."

He turns. "And the bad?"

"The bad news is that a 'missing persons' was filed on him straight after Anna's abduction, and he's still not surfaced."

"Jesus. That also explains the lack of a further abduction. Has he family?"

"No family."

"Odd," he frowns.

"Either way, he's a dead end at the moment. There's nothing on file except for the fact that he alibied Kenneth Finch."

Mike clutches the wheel. "Kenneth Finch again. All roads seem to lead back to him."

"We really need Finch. But Nina suggests Velker is the one who took Holly. Maybe Ken gave Holly to Velker."

"What else do we know about Velker?"

"He's very, very wealthy. The sort of man who could pull strings." She turns to meet his eyes. "He's the sort of man who could buy anything he wanted. If his tastes ran to young girls... Nina's diary suggests she was selected." Denise shivers.

"Did he have blonde hair?"

"I'll find out."

"Could he have absconded with Anna and Holly?"

Denise folds her hands. "Anything's possible. Of course, what Nina says is all hearsay — we don't know how she got her information. It's hard to believe she was told, but she may have overheard or guessed. These children would have been coerced and threatened. Brandon's name being cited as an abductor may have been used to frighten her off."

"And yet, we do have missing girls, don't we?"

"Nina's description of the locations she was taken to is interesting, though. It sounds like at times she was taken to a proper studio."

Mike's brow deepens in distaste. "I don't suppose either

girl is still alive now. Where did this Velker live? Is the house still in his name?"

"There's a property in Kintbury. No utilities on it, so I assume it's unoccupied. I contacted the associate who reported Velker missing originally. He thinks it's possible Velker could be abroad. He has properties all over the world."

"Broaden the search to other countries. Contact Interpol. Perhaps he did escape with Anna. And get a warrant for the property, ASAP."

Denise gazes out of the car window to the wintry world where the trees shiver with light on the hillside, and she feels a boundless sadness.

"Nina dated everything in her diary," Mike gives a deep sigh. "She was a clever girl."

"And a brave one. A brave, brave girl." Denise pulls her arms around her body but is unable to quell the heartbreak Nina's short, sad life has called forth.

I wake from troubled dreams to the unfamiliar room with its unfamiliar smells and remember the rabbit. The world descends heavily. Something uncomfortable sits in the pit of my stomach, a sense of blame and despair, and I lean over, feeling faintly sick. From the kitchen, the aroma of coffee filters into the air, and I get up slowly, my head thumping and mouth dry. In the en suite, I have a quick shower and dress for work.

Denise had arrived promptly, followed shortly by Jason. An hour later, I had left Denise and two other policemen at my house checking for fingerprints. Denise had said that they would arrange for the locks to the windows and doors to be changed and for the mess in the bedroom to be cleaned away. When nobody was looking, I had collected the envelope of photocopied photographs and slid them into my suitcase. Denise had arranged for the neighbours to have Cleo, and I had wanted to cry as I ran my hand along her fur in a brief farewell.

Now I emerge into Jason's kitchen.

"I'll give you a lift in, if you like." Jason hands me a mug of tea and pops a piece of bread in the toaster.

I swallow a lump in my throat. His kindness is disarming. "Thanks, but walking would clear my head."

"Are you sure? I'd feel better if you let me take you." Jason observes me carefully. Last night Scott, Jason, Danielle, and I had picked through what we knew, but I felt apart — apart and too close. The fear is getting to me. I try to think back to the past, but it seems so far away. Did I ever feel safe? I think of my mother in Fair Mile and wish that she were well.

At the back of my mind is Ken, always Ken, whose sallow face and watchful eyes fill my nightmares. And there is something else. It kept me awake half the night. Something is coming loose at the back of my mind — another memory. As I had sat in Jason's car, gazing out as the world flashed past, a scene with Nina began to play out in my mind. I don't want it, but there it is anyway, as if it were yesterday — I am standing on the doorstep with Nina in front of me. She is squinting slightly against the brightness. Behind her, the sun blasts on the metal of car roofs, and a cat jumps down from a wall opposite and stretches. It's morning, and the heat already pumps up from the concrete. Suddenly, the shrill tone of a house alarm clamours in the air, and I look up. Two boys with a football saunter down the pavement, eating from a bag of sweets. Nina leans forward, so close that her breath brushes my cheek. Her eyes meet mine, and the urgency of what she is trying to communicate is like a Taser to my heart.

But the memory stops there. Buried, somewhere, is the sense that this is important. But I don't like the way it makes me feel, do not like the wave of guilt that shadows it. And my memories so far have bought only misery, and so, this time, I do not scratch at it or reflect on it, instead I push it firmly away and out of sight.

Nina can barely look at me. Her body is taut with suppressed rage. I know that she knows. What do I say? I am already crying. Nina is walking faster than me towards the park, and I have to run to keep up.

"I'm so sorry, Nina. I'm so sorry."

She says nothing, and I stumble after her slim figure as she jumps over knotted roots and clumps of fern. The sun has baked the earth hard. I am panting when we reach the bunker. She sits down inside the entrance and glares at me from between her lashes.

"You took a photograph."

"I know. I just thought..."

"Do you know what you've done?"

I nod. My legs tremble, and I sit down. "Ken took me." And I begin to cry again. I want to tell her about what he did, how he tricked me into the car, how he touched me, threatened me, the dreadfulness of him.

But she isn't listening. "You stupid fucking cow." She gives a barking laugh, leans towards me, the sun reflected in her black pupils. "I told you. And now they'll kill me if I don't give them back. They will probably kill me anyway! And what are *you* crying for?"

"I'm sorry. I'm sorry. I didn't know."

"I told you what they were like. I trusted you." She is shouting now, her cheeks red with fury.

"Can you just give them back?"

A strange expression passes her face and she gets up, finds a packet of cigarettes from the box and lights one.

"They won't kill you, really? Not really?" I say, but I know that they could. I've already seen what Ken can do.

She draws deeply on the cigarette and blows the smoke out fiercely between her clenched teeth.

I sit, wiping tears from my cheeks and sniffing. Suddenly her eyes find mine, a knowingness in them. "So Ken got you, did he? Did he hurt you?"

"No." But tears drip down my face, my nose runs.

She sighs heavily, throws the butt into the grass in a violent gesture. "Are you okay?" Her voice is softer now.

I shake my head.

"You were an idiot. He recognised you. Please don't tell me you actually gave him it."

"No, I wasn't that stupid." But I know that I have been, and as I explain how I delivered the photo, my naivety cringes inside me. I remember the empty windows and my belief that nobody was home, rain hammering on to the pavement.

"Is he one of them?" I ask, recalling his kind smile and reassuring strength.

"One of them?" She leans in close, so I can feel her breath on my cheek. "You have no idea, Heidi."

She says it in a whisper, but I can see something in her eyes that makes me recoil.

"Ken won't really kill you though? Or me? I mean, I was only trying to help..."

"Ken said that you may have told other people about it, like your mum."

"But I haven't. I didn't. I promise you. I just thought..."

"And you are supposed to be my friend. I thought I could trust you." Her voice rises.

"We can run away. Let's just do it," I beg.

"Run away? Yeah, right. Like that was ever really going to happen."

Clouds gather overhead and it feels suddenly chilled. Swallowing, I say, "But all that money and stuff. We could go to London."

"We would have the whole country looking for us! Two 13-year-old girls and Danielle. Get real."

"But what can we do?"

"What can *I* do you mean?" And she stabs at her chest. "I was in enough shit before you put your bloody oar in."

"Will they hurt me?"

"I don't know," she yells.

"If you give them back, they'll leave us alone, right? Nina — just give them back."

"You think they'll leave *us* alone. Have you forgotten what this is about? They will *never* leave *me* alone."

And I am shamed. In all this, I have forgotten what her life is made up of.

"I hate this place."

"Riverbridge?" I say.

"This bunker, this stupid fucking kid's den. And I should hate you, too."

My heart is breaking. I can feel its mass pressing against my chest, a tearing anguish and emptiness in my gut.

"Our bunker?"

"Yeah, I bloody hate it. She grabs the picture of the cat and hurls it into the depths, grabbing everything she can, smashing and kicking.

It begins to rain.

Nina is crying now. "How could you?" Fury burns in her eyes. "I hate you, you bitch. I hate you. You're supposed to be my friend." And then she stands and goes outside, flying down the hill, leaving me standing at the top and watching her retreating back.

The sob starts deep in my belly, and I lean over trying to hold it in, but it escapes anyway. I howl with grief as the rain soaks my hair and falls coldly on my cheeks, blind to everything but my misery.

2016

DENISE

It's late when she and Mike return from Forensic Services, but the station is still bright with electric light. Although Christmas is some weeks away, someone has brought in a tree and decorated it with shiny baubles — instead of a star, a police helmet adorns the top.

Getting a warrant for Velker's property is now urgent, but, first, she pulls up Velker's driving licence details. His hair is fair, but is it blonde? If the colour had been more definitely blonde, the possibility of him being "The Chief" would be more likely. They all want this, because, if Velker's not "The Chief", there remains a possibility it's one of their own.

But now something is niggling, and she flicks though her notes and tries to identify what it is that bothers her. The box of papers she took from Wendy Martin has been painstakingly documented. Was it something there?

She finds the box again and heaves it into the office. It is with Rachael's invoices for work that she thinks she recalls it. Her fingers tingle, and she wants to be right so much that her head buzzes.

There, at the bottom, she finds it — a receipt from Sunningdale motors — a straightforward payment for 15 hours bookkeeping. But underneath the garage's name is another — Castle Enterprises — and her heart begins to hammer. She does not believe in coincidence. Castle is the house name of Velker's property in Kintbury. A name that is unusual. She remembers Holly's face and shivers.

Through the window, clouds skim the winter sky, and the ghost of a moon appears high above the frosted rooftops. From the drawer, she takes a packet of chocolate biscuits. The smell of sweetness drifts up, but the scent snags in her throat, and she puts them down, placing her palms upon the table where the surface is cool against her skin. She thinks of Holly and Anna and feels the working of emotion. Another time, she tells herself, she can give her sadness room, when they know everything — when it's over.

2016

The afternoon sun leaves pale shadows beneath the trees as he walks slowly up the path and to the house. Light catches the glass of the bay windows. Margery Fordham answers the door, and he enters the narrow hall. A terrier with fierce eyebrows jumps up at his trousers to be petted.

"Finn! Get down," she grimaces apologetically.

The house smells of stale cigarette smoke and curry. Although she has made efforts to tidy up, the sitting room is a mess — newspapers, books, stacks of mail, and magazines cover the surfaces.

"You said on the phone that you wanted to talk about Bayview?" Her eyes are wary.

"Yes, I must thank you for seeing me. I understand you worked there?"

"Sit down." She points to a space on the sofa. "What's all this about?"

"We're making enquiries into possible abuse that took place during the time you were a social worker."

Sitting opposite, she watches him closely, reading his face.

"I didn't have much to do with Bayview. You're speaking to the wrong person."

He tilts his head to one side. "We have a witness who says differently."

She shifts her weight uncomfortably on the chair and shrugs her shoulders. "What did they say?"

"They say that you asked questions, leading questions, about the children there and about Ray Watson who ran it."

"So why is it being looked into all of a sudden?"

"In the course of investigating another case, we came across the accusations concerning Bayview."

She gets up and paces to the window.

"Mrs Fordham, it seems to me that there has been a great injustice somewhere. Don't you owe it to the children, whose welfare was your concern, to tell us what happened?"

"The police were not so..." she turns, "...keen to address the injustice last time."

"How do you mean?"

"I mean that the police did not want an enquiry in to what may have been happening at Bayview."

The room is silent, just the whisper of wind at the eves. "Can you tell me what happened? Are you saying you reported it?"

"Yes." She talks so quietly, he can barely hear her. "One of the girls on my case list made a very serious allegation. Coincidentally, I also had dealings with another child who had spent time there. I asked him. Told him what had been suggested. He confirmed the abuse there." Her face is grave.

"So what did you do?"

She gives a humourless laugh. "You think I didn't do anything?" She is angry. "I spoke to my supervisor and then the police. You lot."

"What happened?"

Pulling her arms around herself she begins pacing again. Finally she stops. "I was threatened."

"Threatened? By who?"

"Some police officer. He came to the house. He had pictures. Pictures of *my* children — leaving school, in the playground, with me and my husband at the park. He made it very clear what would happen if I pursued the allegation."

"So you dropped it?"

"I asked to be moved within social services. I didn't want any more dealings with children, if I could help it."

"And your supervisor?"

"We never discussed it again. She probably got scared off, too."

He runs a palm along his chin and frowns. "Do you remember the name of the policeman?"

Her mouth clenches, and he sees how much she had been frightened. "He was very intimidating. He may not even have been a policeman — I never heard from the station again."

"Do you remember the allegations the girl made?"

"Yes, I remember some of those. There was more than one abuser involved. It was an organised body that assaulted the children there. Ray Watson, Bayview's manager, facilitated it."

"And did she name the abusers?"

"She did. She was very detailed. It was probably the most appalling thing I have ever heard." She turns. Her eyes glitter. "Then and since."

"She didn't go directly to the police?"

"She was terrified. The threats. If I was scared off, can you imagine how much more frightening it must have been for a young girl? I think the only reason she finally told someone was that she had given up hope." Margery crosses the room to a crammed shelf where framed photos fight for space amongst the clutter. For a moment, she gazes at the pictures. "My daughter lives abroad with my grandchildren now. I was always afraid for them."

"I understand that, Mrs Fordham. I understand how hard this must have been for you."

She takes another deep breath, runs her hand over Finn's rough back.

He wonders how much of the anger she expresses is for herself for having given in to the threats, or for the men who abused the children.

"Do you remember the names of the men she cited?"

Her eyes shift uneasily, and then she seems to make a decision. Leaving the room, she returns a minute later with an envelope. "I couldn't risk my family, but I wrote down what she said. It's here."

He takes the envelope carefully in his fingers. "Is there anything else? Any more notes or records of what was said?"

She shakes her head.

"Would you be prepared to make a statement?"

She frowns.

"Those days are long past. It's very different now. We have other witnesses, too, so you're not alone with these accusations, but we need all the help we can get to trace the children who made the allegations and also the perpetrators involved."

"Okay. I will." Her face is pale but resolved.

"Thank you. If you have time, I'd like to get your statement now. It won't take more than an hour, but we need to do this at the station. I'm sure you understand."

He waits while she goes upstairs to change, giving his eyes more leisure to roam. He can hear the bang of a door and her steps on the floor above. When she returns, she is dressed in a smart skirt and jacket. Armour against her feelings.

She follows him to the car, and he watches her through the

mirror, her head turned to gaze out of the window. In the sunlight, she looks strained and nervous.

As the car picks up speed, the trees and verges pass in a blur. The car is warm, the vibrations of the engine subtle. Her eyes are glazed, absorbed in her thoughts, but eventually she takes in her surroundings.

"Which station are we going to?"

"We're going to Abingdon."

"Why? I assumed you were from Riverbridge. Does Abingdon even have a station?"

"Oh, yes," he says.

She is alert now, tense, and he is acutely aware of her altered mood.

He turns off the dual carriageway on to a smaller road, grooved with dips that have collected puddles. The wheels gather momentum, and there is a hiss as they pass over the ruts and spray hits the windscreen.

"Where are we now?"

"This is the quickest way."

The landscape becomes more wooded, and the road darkens where branches knot together overhead. On either side, the damp hollows cling to wet grass and fallen leaves. Her fists are clenched. She meets his eyes properly in the mirror, and he sees the flicker of doubt and trepidation.

He is nearly there, and, when he sees the track, he takes a sharp left, but not before he clicks the door locks into place.

It is clear she does not want to admit to herself that she has misjudged the situation, but her expression is strangely calm. Even her fingers are controlled as they pluck uselessly at the door. "What do you want?"

He likes her face, the tired blue eyes, the strength and frailty of her mouth, the fact that she is prepared to come forward now, so many years later. But he has to make her change her mind.

"What did you say your name was?"

"I didn't."

"Are you a policeman?"

He doesn't reply.

"What are you going to do?"

He does not want to answer this question. He does not want to accept, even to himself, how easy this has become, or that there is a part of him that will enjoy causing her pain. He wonders if she will fight. He does not think it will take much to win her silence.

"Why?" Her voice breaks a little, crumbles at the edges. "Are you going to threaten me or kill me? I was silent once. You think I can't be again? You don't have to do this."

He does not want her to cry.

"You're too young to have been one of those monsters. You really don't have to do this."

Perhaps she thinks if she keeps talking something will intervene, some random event that will change the course of the immediate future.

"Who's making you do this? You can let me go. I won't speak."

In the distance, two bay horses tug at the patchy grass, their eyes shadowed.

He turns and meets her gaze. There is enough fear there already. A punch here or there, and he can make it fill her life again.

Still, she does not panic, but there is a subtle alteration in her expression as she studies him, and then something is born in her eyes. "You were a victim, too, weren't you? They did it to you, didn't they?" A fleeting look of pity.

For a moment, he is disarmed. Of all the things she could have done or said, even pulling out a gun, nothing could have had such impact. But it is an unforgivable insight that she has fallen upon. Unforgivable — he was never one of "them", one of those throwaway skins. No, he was more than that. He was special. A memory slides behind his eyes, pulls at something messy there. He closes it quickly, but when he looks at her again, he feels an uncontainable loathing and rage that changes everything.

He hauls her from the car. Now, her flesh is cool beneath his skin, and, as he squeezes and pushes, he can feel her blood and the pulse of her heart at his fingertips. Her desperate noises are muffled by the rain as it begins to fall, touching the back of his head and slipping on to the skin of his back. She is strong and twists her body like a landed fish, but he pins her with his knees. Anger ferments along his veins and into his palms that shake as he pounds again and again against her with a fury that seems to come from someone else altogether.

2016

HEIDI

It is Saturday morning, and I lie in bed, suspended between dreams and wakefulness. The house is wonderfully warm, and I close my eyes and turn over. Recent events spin in my head. I want to forget and go back to sleep rather than remember, but light filters through the curtains, stealing my drowsiness, so I sit up with a yawn.

The bathroom mirror is a reminder of the past — the uneven skin tone stretches down the left side of my torso. It is such a familiar sight that I barely notice it now.

In the kitchen, Jason is pacing, his shoulders square with tension. He turns when he sees me, and his eyes bristle. "It's Ken, Heidi. I've found him!" He sounds breathless.

"Ken?" My heart lurches. Through the window, the garden is swimming in mist, and the trees are as pale and blurred as ghosts.

"Are you going to tell the police?" I ask, though I know the answer.

"The police had their time with him. It's mine now. "Do you want to come?"

"How did you find him?"

He cannot hide the bubble of triumph. "Joan Finch. There was a card from him on that pile in her sitting room, and a pot of organic honey with an Oxfordshire farm label. It made me wonder, so I got back in touch with that investigator. He checked out the address and confirmed Ken lives there, off the radar. She knew where he was all along."

I feel alarm, but also a hunger to search the face of the man who destroyed our lives. Perhaps, in the depths of his eyes, I will be able to find some answer to Anna's fate and judge whether he lies or whether he tells the truth.

Within minutes, I am sitting beside Jason in his car, my coat on the seat behind me. I am grateful it has happened so quickly, and that I have not had time to mull over what this meeting means. I feel safe with Jason.

"How has he been able to keep so hidden? Denise said that he's top priority, but they haven't managed to trace him."

"If he doesn't use a bank account or own a house or car in his name, I suppose it's easy enough. Seems he's some sort of handyman. If it's a cash arrangement, then there's no money trail." His fingers are tight on the wheel. "He keeps himself to himself, works on the farm, buys booze at the local off-licence, and doesn't appear to have many social contacts. At least, that's what the investigator gleaned."

Too soon, we have left the comforting houses and shops behind us and are deep in rural Oxfordshire. Frost is pale on the fields and fence posts, and, even with the heater on, the cold that lies outside filters up through the floor of the car.

We reach the rough track to the farm, and my belly fizzes with anxiety. Looking at Jason beside me, I see the tightening of his jaw. He stops the car at a gate and turns off the engine.

It is utterly silent. Ahead, the shape of a run-down barn bulks in the mist.

"We walk from here," he says.

I rest back on the seat. "Let's wait a bit, see if we can see anything."

Jason gives a snort and opens the door. An icy wind whips into the interior, so I reach behind me for my coat and button it up with shaky fingers.

Jason holds the gate open, stamping from one foot to the other with impatience. I follow him, trying not to slip on the hard, furrowed surface. Chickens squawk from a nearby shed and a rooster pecks in the dirt, its crown swaying from side to side as it regards us with a red-rimmed eye. My breath is white on the air.

"His caravan is on one of the fields at the back," he whispers.

Light glints in the farmhouse windows, but I see no movement. Ahead, an ancient building and tractor stand in the mud, and beyond that the fields are shrouded in mist.

"Jason." My teeth are chattering. He glances at me. I am going to tell him that we should turn back, leave this for the police, but his granite face tells me that is not going to happen. So I shiver and follow in his wake, nearly running to keep up with his long strides.

The caravan comes into view — a greying rectangle of metal on a rusted frame. A trickle of steam rises from the top, and the windows are opaque with condensation. A gravel path leads to the door, where Jason reaches forward and slams hard with his fist. From inside, the sound of a television trickles out. My heart hammers in my chest.

Ken opens the door, a cigarette dangling from his thin mouth, and I recognise him instantly: the pock-marked skin, the dyed-black hair, combed back, but now sparse enough for his sallow scalp to show through. He looks from me to Jason, recognition springing to his face. Surprise is smothered quickly with hostility, but before he can slam the door, Jason pushes him backwards against the wall. Ken scrambles to regain balance and launches out with his fist, but Jason catches it and throws a punch at Ken's jaw that sends him flying across the caravan.

"Stop!" I cry.

Ken is getting up, both hands in a gesture of submission.

"Okay." He backs away to sit on the pull-out couch, rubbing his face. "All grown up then?" His voice is smoke roughened.

I feel the violence of Jason's rage, and I put a hand on his arm, stilling him.

Ken's gaze moves between us. "Sit down." He takes a packet of tobacco from his pocket and rolls a cigarette between his stained fingers.

Jason remains standing. "You fucking bastard."

I swallow, trying to read Ken's reactions. Something like fear flits in his eyes, but his expression is slippery.

"You know why I'm here," Jason says, his rage simmering.

"Yeah, I reckon I do." Ken's voice, like his mother's, has something of the West Country in it.

"You bastard. You ruined her. You killed her." Menace radiates from him like a furnace.

Ken shifts. "I didn't kill her."

"You fucked with her. And Danielle."

Ken pales a little.

"She told us how you came back that day and there was blood on your shirt. You threatened her. You filthy shit."

"It doesn't matter what I say. You wouldn't believe me. Just do what you came to do."

"I should kill you."

"Jason, please," I say.

"You have five minutes to tell me the truth."

Ken's hands tremble. "Everything you say is true about Nina and Danielle. But when I went to the bunker, Nina was already dead."

"You expect me to believe that?"

"Probably not," he concedes.

"And the blood. If you didn't kill her, why were you covered in blood?"

"There was blood everywhere. I had to check. I thought maybe she was alive."

"Who did then?"

Ken takes a tug on the cigarette. "I don't know."

"Of course you bloody know."

"No, I don't." He looks up, meeting Jason's eyes steadily.

"You fucking liar. You destroyed her life, and then you killed her." Jason launches forward, pushing hard against him, and Ken is flung back on the seat, banging his head on the metal wall.

"Jason!" I yell, tugging at his jacket. I keep hold of his arm.

"You deserve to die!" He screams, shaking Ken and slamming him over and over against the seat.

"I didn't kill her. I swear." There is real concern in Ken's face now. "Lay off. Look — she was dead already, okay? I promise."

Jason pulls back. He is panting. Water drips on to the caravan roof with a hollow rap.

Ken puts his hands to his temple, where blood trickles from a thin wound. "I went to find her. She was there, just outside. You both were." He looks to me.

"If you didn't kill her, why were you there?"

"You want to know why I was there? Didn't *she* tell you?" His gaze shifts to me, and Jason turns, frowning.

I glance between them in confusion.

"What do you mean?" I ask.

"Don't you remember?" Ken says.

I shake my head, but something ominous clamps itself to my chest and time seems to stop.

"Nina stole some photographs. You took one, though, didn't you? You posted it through someone's door. Someone you shouldn't have."

Time distorts, and I feel dizzy. "No," I mouth, but already I can see myself crouched in the bunker, levering out a brick, and a house with black windows. Rain. Rain thundering down on to the pavement and bouncing upwards to soak my legs, and I am running through the droplets, hair moulded to my scalp, shirt clinging to me, and posting an envelope through the dark mouth of a letter box.

"No," I whisper. But I hear Nina's voice as if it were in the room with me — *"I hate you, you bitch! I hate you. You're supposed to be my friend."* A groan is wrenched from my throat.

It was me. I got her killed.

Jason's eyes are wide with questions.

"It was my fault." The truth tears me open.

"Heidi? What did you do?"

"I never meant to hurt her." My voice sounds distant. "I posted a photo through the door of someone I knew was a policeman. I thought he would save her."

"What are you talking about?"

"Those photographs — the ones Nina stole to prove what was happening to her — she wouldn't use them, because she said they would get her killed. I didn't believe her, so I took one." I pause and think. "I thought it would stop it. I thought they would take *you* away." Fury at Ken swims dizzyingly in my head, making me feel faint. "Do you know how you made her feel? What you did to her? You're an animal." My voice becomes a scream. Somewhere, a dog barks.

Ken wipes his cheek where he is bleeding heavily. "I went

to the bunker to get the photos back, but she was already dead."

"So who did it?"

"I don't know, and that's the truth."

"You're lying." Jason breathes, kicking the table and sending it to the ground. A half-empty mug of coffee crashes to the lino, followed by an ashtray. Glass fragments rattle across the floor.

"*She* knows it wasn't me. Don't you?" He points to me. "You tell him."

But I shake my head. "I don't remember that day. I don't remember what happened ..."

Ken stands, regards Jason with a panicked expression, looking ready to run. "I promise you. I don't know." He plays with the ring on his left hand, twisting it nervously.

"You lied to the police about being there. Why?" Jason says.

"Isn't it obvious? They would have got us for it, even if we weren't guilty."

"Us?" Jason moves even closer to him.

Ken's face blanches at the slip.

"Us?" Jason says again. "You owe me, Finch."

"Okay, okay." There is something resigned about his expression. "Someone else was there."

"Who? Who was there?"

"His name was Brandon. Brandon Velker."

"Why was he there?" Jason says.

"To make sure we got the photos back. He was good at that sort of thing. If he hadn't been with me already, I would have guessed it was him who killed her." He glances at me, "We thought you were dead, too, I promise. It was your blood on my shirt." When he gets out his tobacco pouch, his hands are shaking violently.

"Was Brandon one of you?" I ask.

Something that is almost pity inhabits his eyes, and the answer is there. "Anna?" I gasp. "Anna wasn't dead, was she? She was there. You must've seen her." My heart is pumping too fast.

He can't meet my eyes. His thin face sags, each crease deepening in his rough skin.

"Where is she?" I whisper. It can't get worse.

"He took her."

"Who? Who took her?"

"Velker took her, okay?"

He got her. I cannot bear it. My heart spasms. She was taken. And it was my fault. The guilt that has been just beneath my skin for weeks devours me. I was the one who put Nina in danger, put Anna in danger. For the first time, I wish with all my soul that I had died, too.

"Jesus Christ," I say, my voice strangled in my throat.

Jason is staring at Ken's bloodied face, clenching his hands. "Go and call your friend, Heidi, before I kill him."

I rise, trembling to my feet, and call 999. In a trance, I relay a garbled message and then pass the phone to Jason who gives our location. From beneath his seat, Ken grabs a bottle of whisky and swigs it neat from the neck. His head hangs limply. The skin of his cheek is shiny and swollen, and one eye is half closed. Blood drips on to the floor from his split lips.

"Are you the one who chased me? Who left me the picture? Left that thing in the bed?" I ask, almost beyond caring.

There is genuine confusion in Ken's expression. "I don't know what you're talking about."

"You piece of shit," Jason says.

Ken takes another slug from the bottle, but Jason springs forward and slaps it from his hands, sending it smashing to the floor. Alcohol fumes fill the room.

"You deserve to die for what you did." Jason's voice is tight.

Ken opens then closes his mouth. His face slackens, where age and life have carved deep fissures, and, in the distance, the silence is split with the wail of sirens.

I stand shakily, longing to feel fresh air, to clear some space in my head. Jason opens the door and steps into the field, letting in a gust of unforgiving wind. The sirens draw nearer, and I can see the flashing of blue lights in the window. It's with a start I realise Ken is beside me.

I gasp, reeling backwards, but he clutches my hand and pulls me towards him.

His eyes are bloodshot, but he leans in close. "I'm sorry about your sister." His breath is stale, and I flinch. "I tried to stop him. I really did."

The sound of running feet approaches, and suddenly the courtyard is populated with uniforms. Five cars, lights rotating, a sea of dark, uniformed bodies.

Not seeing Denise, I call her. "Brandon," I splutter. "Someone called Brandon took Anna."

Denise's voice is calm. "It's okay, Heidi, I promise. We're already on to it."

Someone puts an arm on my shoulder, and I crumple. "It's my fault," I whimper, and I throw my grief into the officer's chest, feeling the fabric of her coat against my cheek. I feel her strong arms around me pulling me closer, pillowing my cries.

2001

HEIDI

The air is hot already, and Mum has taken Anna and I to the bakery, where Anna chooses a doughnut and then lays out her colouring book. Her felt-tips have been lined up neatly, leaving little space on the table for me. I remember a time when I would have done the same, a time when a hot chocolate and a cake would have been all it took to fill me with pleasure. I'm too unhappy for that now. I know too much, and I gaze at the hot pavement where sparrows squabble over dropped crumbs. Nina will not talk to me, and I feel the pain of it in my belly.

"Can I have it?"

I look up. Anna has jam on her cheek, and I can see where she has pushed a wet finger around the plate to collect every scrap of doughnut. I shrug and push my eclair across.

"Really?" She cannot believe her luck. "Are you going to say you want it back? You can colour in the horse if you like."

I shake my head.

On the way back, we go into the newsagents, where Mum buys cigarettes. Anna spends her pocket money on a comic, and even before we leave the shop, she is ripping the Barbie necklace from the cover and putting it round her neck. I catch her reflection — she is turning her head from one side to the other to judge its appearance. She looks at me with a grin, fingering it and seeking compliments, and I buff her gently across the head.

On the way home, Nina and Scott are coming down the road. My face reddens, and I bite down on my misery. Mum gives me a sharp glance when Nina ignores me, but I am close to tears and can't face her sympathy, so I run up to the stifling heat of the bedroom, where it smells of dust and something sweet. I lie back on the bed and close my eyes and remember how, just a year ago, my life had been so different. I think of Ken, so close, and my stomach shrinks.

Voices drift up, and I get up and go to the window where I see Carol is asking Nina to do something. Nina is scowling, and when Carol is back inside, she slips a packet of cigarettes from her bag and lights one. I feel a rush of longing for her. I have never felt so lonely, and I leap downstairs and into the garden.

She looks up when I close the back door and then turns pointedly away.

"Nina, please," I beg.

"Leave me alone," she snarls.

"Nina." I squeeze through the gap and squat beside her. "I should've believed you. Please, please, don't hate me anymore."

She turns and regards me for a moment, stubbing her cigarette on the ground. "I'm going to give the photos back today."

Relief. She spoke to me. It will be all right. I will do anything to keep our friendship. "When? Have you brought them back from the bunker?"

"No, Ken says he doesn't want them in the house. He's going to come to the bunker later."

"He knows where it is?"

She looks away. "If you're sorry, come with me. I don't like being alone with him, not there."

I feel the sub-layers of undisclosed secrets. "Of course, I'll come."

She turns and looks at me.

"Are we friends again?" I ask.

Nina shrugs. She's wearing a green sleeveless vest and denim skirt. Her slim arms hang at her sides, and she returns the cigarettes and lighter to the heart-shaped bag she got for her birthday. "It's so hot already."

I look up at the sky. It's barely 10 am, but already the cloudless blue shimmers like a fever.

"Let me go home first and tell Mum," I say.

"Heidi," her hand brushes mine, "there's something I need to give you." Our eyes meet, and for an instant the barriers come down, and her despair and fear spill into me like a draught of bitterness. For the first time, I truly see what her life has become, and my own misery shrinks beside it. "I want you to hide it. I'm going to trust you one last time, do you understand?"

I will never let her down again.

She gets up, uncurling like a piece of rope and stands straight backed, looking down at me. We don't exchange words. We don't need to. We both know we've reached the point in time where all the roads that we have travelled up to now have irreversibly led.

2016

DENISE

As they negotiate the drive, Denise concedes that the overgrown gardens appear to confirm that the house is uninhabited.

"Maybe Velker ran out of money. It must cost a fortune to run a place like this," Marion says.

Denise nods, feels a growing disquiet, and fingers the warrant in her pocket. Not that she will need to show it, the place is almost certainly empty.

As they approach, the mansion emerges suddenly, but they have to bring the car to a halt, as the drive is blocked by a fallen tree. Denise gets out, and they begin to walk across the wet grass where frost lies thinly on the undergrowth. The sky is beginning to darken with coming rain.

As Denise nears, the neglect becomes more evident: ivy running riot, missing roof tiles, and broken guttering. Water has forged a green path down the side of the house, and the glass is thick with moss.

"Let's look round the back," Marion suggests. Denise gazes up at the blackened windows and shivers. At the rear, a sapling has fallen against some French windows, smashing the pane of the door.

Taking her jacket off, Marion pushes in the remaining shards, and Denise climbs carefully into the empty kitchen. The smell of mould and rats is a foul breath. Even so, she gazes around at the huge room with awe. On the table is a plate with some remains and a tumbler half stained with whatever the contents had once been.

"Where do you think he's gone?"

Denise shrugs. "No luck with Interpol. He just disappeared."

"The same time as Anna Bevan?"

"Thereabouts, yes."

The silence stretches around them, and Denise catches the anxious shine in Marion's eyes. "Do you think he's the one?"

Denise takes a flashlight from her belt and shines it along the wall, catching the gilt edges of frames. "Who knows. He's certainly top of our suspect board for the girls, and Ken points the finger at him for Anna. Probably best if we do this separately," she says, and Marion heads off to the right.

When she has gone, Denise does not like the way the air settles or the way the corridor stretches before her. She has a feeling, somewhere in the pit of her belly, that she cannot fully explain. Pausing, she opens a door into a large sitting room, but, ahead, a pool of thin light is thrown on to the tiles of the hall and along banisters that curve upwards. Instinct makes her head that way. Somewhere, wind bangs at a door.

As she climbs, she reaches a Palladian window with a view on to the hulk of trees and stretching green. In the distance, a band of rain approaches, and wind begins to tug at the crowns of the oaks. She is suddenly aware of the isolation, of the distance from others; this is a place where anything could happen beyond the eyes of the world.

The first floor is utterly quiet. She can no longer hear Marion downstairs, and, as she begins to explore, the feeling in her nerve endings grows, like another sense, and she does not like what they say.

It's in one of the bedrooms that she sees it, as she shines her flashlight on to the floor. Although someone has tried hard to clean, the bleached areas of wood show traces of something darker, and she summons Marion.

"What d'you think?" she asks.

"It looks like blood to me, and look how big the patch is — this wasn't caused by someone treading on the family hamster."

"We need to call SOCO immediately and set up a cordon." Denise takes some photos and calls it in. She can hear Marion's footfall on the boards behind her.

"Denise!" Marion's voice is cracked with shock. Denise rises from her crouch carefully, easing the ache in her knees. Marion has opened a drawer of one of the dressers and is holding a photograph between the tips of her gloved fingers.

"It's her, isn't it? Anna." Carefully, Denise picks up the photo and, taking it to the window, she uses the last of the light to examine the image. It's been taken in this very house. A young girl. one tooth is missing from the top of her mouth. It's a face that has been inscribed on to the inside of her brain for nearly fifteen years and destined to never fully leave her, not now.

Denise has known, almost from those first days after Nina was killed, that this moment would come, but the reality hits harder than the imagining. She turns from Marion's gaze and takes a deep breath. The first drops patter at the window-panes, bringing a deeper chill. When she lifts her head to answer, Marion is holding out two more photos unbelievingly.

They study the photographs, and when Denise looks up again, they share the moment of realisation and horror. Whatever hope there may have been is finally extinguished. There is no training for such things, and no counselling to replace the bleak sadness such a truth summons.

"This one looks like Holly but who's the third?" Marion asks.

And Denise shakes her head, she doesn't know, but she imagines a family somewhere with an empty room, imagines presents, wrapped and ribboned, and destined never to be opened.

When Denise returns the next morning, the tree has been removed and vans and cars congregate on the drive outside. A light rain spots the ground, and clouds move fast across a heavy sky. She eases herself out of the car, feet crunching on the gravel, and pauses to gaze up at the windows. The house itself is cast in shadow, and she doesn't want to imagine what happened here. She's grateful for the brisk efficiency of the white-suited SOCOs. The officer in charge, Juliet Hussein, catches Denise's eye. She does not smile.

Denise follows her up the crumbling steps, giving her name to the waiting officer, and is handed a disposable suit. Juliet waits until Denise is ready, and then they enter the hall.

It no longer looks as it did yesterday: lights amplify the hanging of wallpaper and the rugs littered with mice and rat droppings. The approach path has been carefully marked, and Denise follows Juliet with a sense of trepidation. They have made so much progress, and she feels the sense of an ending, but satisfaction will be marred with abhorrence of reality.

In the kitchen is the evidence of where she and Marion gained entry.

"Here," Juliet says.

An officer is standing, holding open a wooden door that she hadn't noticed on that first visit. The lock has been forced, and beyond is a flight of narrow steps.

"It's the cellar." Juliet's footsteps echo as they begin to descend, and when Denise arrives at the bottom, she realises that she has emerged, not into one large room, but a maze of them, a catacomb.

"Have you had a chance to fully explore?" she asks.

"It's going to be a nightmare." Juliet has a deep voice with a rough smoker's edge. "The cellars stretch the entire area of the house, we think. But we found this room early on, not very well hidden." Denise can detect the pale tone of something in her voice.

"I think whoever put this stuff here did it in a hurry."

Denise passes a rack where bottles of wine and cognacs gather dust on the bloom of their contents.

There is very little lighting, and she can hear the drip, drip of water from somewhere further away. The aged brick walls and architecture would be beautiful under other circumstances, but Denise is aware of her dread. Juliet takes a spur into a narrower area, her torch forging a pathway ahead.

Apart from the sound of their breathing and the slap of heels, the cellar is smothered in a tense silence. As they round the corner, she can hear the soft murmur of voices that fade to a hush as Denise arrives. Lying against the wall is a hardwood panel and, beside it, the dark mouth of a room.

She doesn't want to go in.

The short-haired policeman that bars the room moves aside, and she steps in, careful not to disturb the evidence. Dust and the odour of staleness spill into the air. There is not much, but enough. Lying on top of a table is a drawstring bag bearing a school logo, and she leans in to read it, her throat tightening. In a corner, a school cardigan lies on the floor collecting dust. There are other items, too, items testifying to other lives.

As Denise leaves, the team are bringing wires from upstairs to connect the lighting.

"What do you think?" Juliet asks.

"It looks right to me. That was Holly Watts' school badge."

Juliet's eyes are sad. "And the other things?"

But Denise shrugs. "God knows. Let's hope we can find out. What about the stain in the bedroom?"

"Definitely blood, but superficial. We've taken samples."

"Have the ground teams arrived yet?" Denise's voice is insubstantial, swallowed by the echoing corridors.

Juliet's radio comes to life, and they hurry through the main house to one of the large rooms at the front, where a rug has been pulled back to reveal a bloodstain, bigger, much bigger than the one upstairs.

Outside, in the pinched sunlight, Denise sucks the clean air into her lungs and removes the protective suit, though the sight of that small cardigan will cling to her psyche for a long while to come.

She almost doesn't want to ask. "Have you found any signs that Anna Bevan was here?"

"Everything we have so far is already bagged up in the van over there."

She bids Juliet goodbye. It's getting colder, and she zips up her coat and wishes she'd remembered gloves.

"May I look?" she asks the officer at the van.

He nods, and she goes through the small pile of evidence bags. It's at the bottom that she finds it: a cloth rabbit, discoloured and with half its stuffing lost to mice. One of the eyes is missing, and its floppy ears have been reduced to a few threads.

"Where was this?" she asks

The officer checks his notes. "It was half hidden under a table in one of the front rooms."

Nodding sadly, she passes a finger over the plastic evidence bag. She does not need to re-read the files. She knows what this is. This is the toy that had been with Anna on the day that she went missing. *Boo*. She remembers the name and bites down on a spasm of heartache.

2001

HEIDI

The riverside is teeming with people, so Nina and I walk past the Canoe Club and the moorings where the big leisure boats pick up passengers for their Thames cruises. One Sunday, Mum had taken us both for a trip, and we had pointed out all the landmarks we knew along the way, eating ice cream and leaning over the rails to gaze into the water. It seems an impossibly long time ago. Now we walk so far that we reach the edge of the countryside, where a small stile takes us into a pasture. Sometimes there are bullocks here, but today it's empty.

We find a quiet spot beneath the shade of a willow and take off our sandals, and, sitting on the very edge of the bank, we dip our feet into the cool water, feeling the tug of the tide. Across the river are houses that belong to rich people with their picture windows and verandas. At the bottom of the gardens, the water is green and sultry.

Once, Nina and I would have speculated about which house we would live in when we grew up and how we would have decorated it inside. But not anymore. A gaggle of ducks and two swans soon congregate at our feet and we throw our bread into the water, listening to their calls and the slapping of their beaks as they attack the crumbs. But there is a silence between us. The past and the future are almost too momentous to tackle with words.

"Is Ken still angry?" I ask.

"Yeah, of course." She frowns at me.

"Are you still scared?"

She gives a dry laugh. "Scared of what, Heidi? Scared they're going to kill me? Or scared of what they'll do if they don't?"

I shrivel inside my skin. She stretches back on the grass with her hands pillowed behind her head and squints at the sky above. When I look at her neat profile, I'm conscious that, somehow, in all of this, we have slipped away from each other, and I long for the unquestioning connection we once had. There's nothing I can do to help her and nothing that I can do to help myself. I reach across and take her hand in mine. When she turns and gazes at me, her face dappled in shadow, her eyes are dead.

"I wish they would kill me," she whispers.

Any hope that I had nurtured of finding Anna alive has been finally extinguished. Visiting Ken confirmed that for me. But the visit had another consequence and later that night, as thoughts of Anna twisted in my head, I remembered the day that Ken had persuaded me into his vehicle all those years ago. This morning, I woke with the memory of his hand on my thigh, his smell, and all I had felt, and I recalled too, the studio and most of that horrifying journey. I wondered if I might still remember the way.

Now, we are in Denise's car with the winter landscape passing outside. Denise glances at me, and a thread of warmth is communicated.

"Could we go back to the crossroads at Hexley? I'm not sure we took the right turning."

Denise steers the car back, swings it on a farm track, and, once again, we approach the landmark in the same direction as Ken had done.

"Have you found Maria yet?"

"No, but we'll keep looking. All this coming to light must have been intimidating. Try not to worry about her."

"And Brandon?" The very name is foul on my lips.

"No, but he's top priority."

"He had her, didn't he? Anna."

"It would seem likely, yes."

Denise slows the car and brings it to a stop at a lay-by. She turns in the seat. Her eyes are pained. "It wasn't your fault, Heidi. You've got to keep telling yourself that."

I open my mouth to say something, but words are not enough, so I shake my head, and Denise indicates and pulls out on to the road once more.

As I stare out at the world, I push back my feelings. The branches of the naked trees are black against the fading sky. When Ken had driven me, it had been green, alive. I remember it all, even though I had gazed frigidly out of the window, holding on to my terror.

"Yes, this is right." I spy a complicated thatched roof with a weathervane on top. "Keep going."

My mouth is dry, and for a brief moment I am cast back, with the heat of the leather seat sweating into my back and breathing the sweetness of his hair cream. We pass a pond, and I know we're close. Anxiety grows. At a pub, I tell Denise to turn again.

"It's down here. There's a track to the left." The car slows, and I remember the horror as Ken's engine stilled to a halt, and how he turned to face me, his eyes lingering with terrifying intimacy. I am so caught up with the recollection that I don't register the slowing of the wheels and the bumpy track. We're on a twisty road, where the rutted surface gathers water and the hedges on either side cast us in shadow.

Denise turns in her seat to look at me. "You okay, Heidi?"

I nod dumbly. The track widens into a field, and the

building itself comes into view, encircled by a high fence. "This is it." My voice is barely a whisper.

The other police cars draw to a halt behind us. "Stay here." Denise gets out of the car and says something into her radio. The place is clearly deserted. I watch as she circles the property, examining the perimeter.

Denise is back within five minutes. "You're sure it's this one?"

I nod. As I wait, I remember the pressure of his fingers at my thigh, the band of his grasp on my arm as he pushed me into the building, and the way he watched as I swallowed the reality of it. And I recall the words I spoke in my head: I would never tell — never, ever, ever.

We drive back silently, and I can't bring myself to speak. As I sit, I am pricked again by the other memory of Nina. As much as I have resisted encouraging it. It has finally been pulled clean, and it fills me with new anxiety. I remember the way Nina's gaze burned into mine and how behind her, a cat jumped from the wall as fluid as treacle and how the sound of an alarm clamoured on the summer's air. I remember what she did next, what she held in her hands. The desperation in her eyes as she passed it to me, entrusting me one final time with something secret. I told her I would keep it safe.

I open my mouth to tell Denise, but the words dry on my lips. I do not want to know where it leads. What I have discovered is burden enough. I twist my fingers inside each other and look down at the scarring of my left hand, the bitten nails. What if I betrayed Nina again? How would I bear it?

We near Riverbridge, and I keep my eyes on the passing view. Ken and others are in custody, but I don't feel safe. I feel watched and sense the drawing nearer of intent.

In spite of the hope I see in all their expressions, I still can't find the memory of the day that Nina was murdered, cannot wrestle it from the gap in my brain. Ken insists neither he nor Brandon killed Nina, but I can't support or deny this. Like Denise and Jason, I want it to be Ken, so the world can descend on him with its righteous fury. But in the dark hours of night, I am aware of doubt. I looked into his eyes; I was there when he protested his innocence, and, as much as I wanted it to be otherwise, I felt its truth.

Denise watches as the door to the Wood Lane property is forced open, and, suited up, she follows the lead of the SOCO's. Inside is one vast room. Wires climb the walls like vines, and she sees the partitions as Heidi had described. As she makes her way through the space, there are areas that have been arranged to give the impression of different sets.

Lingering in the air is the thin scent of cheap perfume. The perfume her teenage niece used to wear far too much of, and she wants to sit down and cry for all the lives that have been destroyed here. The forensic officers talk in loud voices, making notes and taking photographs.

Outside, she leans against the wall, and her hands shake slightly with anger and sadness. For some reason, her mind has never continued the story after the investigation ceased. Nobody was caught. But Nina's death, and the probable deaths of Holly Watts and Anna Bevan, did not represent the end of what happened. They were merely points on a continuing timeline.

The sense of failure is acute. And what have they now,

anyway? Finch and Watson won't talk. Velker is untraceable, and Maria is still evading the police. It seems likely that Velker is the one who pulls all the strings, and they need him desperately. She hopes it is not his blood that they discovered on the floor of his house. They need him alive.

Back at the office, she finds Mike pacing the floor.

"Not here," he says. "Sometimes, I need to breathe different air."

He walks quickly, and Denise has to take large strides to keep pace. After a journey that has her lungs straining, they turn into a small pub on the Recreation Road.

"What is it?"

He takes a deep breath. "We identified a body that washed up in the Kennet yesterday."

"And?"

"She was one on the list of social workers who had dealings with Bayview while Holly was there. Her name was Margery Fordham. We hadn't even got to interview her. It can't be a coincidence."

"Shit," Denise says. "We only received that information a few days ago."

Mike turns and studies the street outside, his expression taut. "Someone on the inside has to be involved. What about your team? Is there anyone you think could be responsible?"

"I trust my team." But Denise can feel doubt spreading like a poison.

"Who else knew about the social worker?"

Denise shakes her head in bewilderment.

"Tell the team that from now on nothing leaves the station or this department. No chatting in the café or to partners. I want any info to be briefed to me only, and make the team aware of what has happened. I'm going to have to take this to Barrett. It's not going to look good. God knows what he will say. Don't repeat any of this to anyone else, and up the security on Heidi and any other remaining witnesses — present or potential."

With a sinking heart, Denise returns to the office where she observes the men and women she has come to trust. She feels a profound chill. Someone here is on the other side or has been forced into betrayal. Pouring a large coffee, she shuts her office door and puts her head in her hands. She is interrupted by a flurry of knocking.

Marion approaches Denise's desk, with a look of triumph. "I've got the property details for Wood Lane. It was really hard to track down, as the company is registered abroad. Anyway, it's in the name of Castle Enterprises, and look here."

Denise glances down. "It's Brandon Velker's name. He bloody owned it."

2016

HEIDI

It's dark, and I look out of the window and on to the rooftops. The house is warm, but I am chilled. The smell of food drifts up from the kitchen where Jason is cooking, but my stomach tightens at the thought of eating. Looking out to the veiled darkness, I feel the memory edge itself out of my mind again, and I suck in my breath. The thought of what I have recalled prickles in my fingertips. As much as I have tried to forget, it keeps returning, nagging for my attention. I lie back on the bed and feel suddenly close to tears. Nina, Anna — my fault. The guilt is like a pistol to my heart. But as I consider, I realise that in resisting the recollection, I may be further betraying Nina. How brave must she have been to steal the photographs, how brave, in contrast to my own cowardice. Because it was not a brave girl who ran through the sheet of rain to post a picture anonymously.

I grit my teeth and let my eyes fall shut and watch it replay — I am on the doorstep. Nina stands in front of me. The sun vibrates in the hot air and a cat pounces to the concrete from the wall opposite. Nina leans forwards, her eyes full of the weight of what she wants to impart and then, in the distance, there is a burst of an alarm. It starts then stops, starts then stops, and I look up — the cat has sauntered to the end of the road and is turning. Nina leans in even closer, her breath warms my cheek.

"If I don't come back, or something happens, give this to someone you can trust."

And she places something into my hands. My scalp itches with sweat and fear, because today is the day we go to the bunker and she returns the photos. Whatever she gives me is inside an A4-sized envelope. It doesn't weigh much.

But most of all, I remember now how I felt. How some prescience of our fates hovered in my knowing, and although it was still early and the sun was burning the concrete, somehow, I knew that this day would change my life forever.

The sound of Jason's voice cuts through the silence of the room, and I stand, ready to go downstairs. Part of me wants to tell someone, but I think of the rabbit and the photograph — the line scrawled on the back: *memories are not for the living.* And where would the package be now? Surely, if I had hidden it, it would have been found. Perhaps it wasn't important at all. I tidy my hair and go downstairs.

Nina spends so long with her eyes closed that I think she must be asleep. From the carrier bag, I take out my last can of Coke, which is disappointingly warm. The sun has shifted, and the fronds of the willow no longer protect me from its rays. Its fierce heat bites into my face and legs.

Across the river, I watch as boats slide to and fro, their inhabitants leaning back, enjoying the pull of the water. I'm draining my can when Nina sits up beside me and flicks a look at her watch. It's gone one o'clock already.

"We better get back."

Suddenly, my stomach is full of flutterings. "Did Ken say when he would be there?"

"About three-ish, I think." She says it casually, but her face is tense. "I want to get there first, so I can take them out. I don't want him knowing my hiding place."

"Are you going to keep some?"

She shakes her head. "No. But I don't want him getting my money."

Reluctantly, I get to my feet and hold out my hand to Nina. For a moment, she pretends that she hasn't seen it, but then I feel her fingers in mine, her palm is cool in my warm one. For a second, our eyes meet, and in them, I can see the fear she is trying so hard to hide.

2016

HEIDI

I don't like the way the memories come, like a letter bomb on the doormat. I don't like the way they are tagged to feelings of grief and rage and self-recrimination. I am never prepared. This one emerges as I fold clothes into the drawer; the overhead light glints on the yellow glass of a dish, and I am whipped back to the bunker with the picture of a cat in a broken frame, the same colour in its crudely painted eyes. I suck in my breath, smell the heat of the sun and terror on my skin.

I reach the bed and lean forward, cupping my head in my hands. Dread is in my throat as I slip between now and then. The memory comes more strongly: a pile of discarded sweet wrappers and a half-filled bottle of Coke on the bunker floor. And I'm not alone. I sense, rather than see, Nina behind me. Turning my head, I regard her as she straightens out the rug. There is a smudge of dirt on her cheek, and her usually sleek hair is out of place. A box of matches rattles in her hand. Close up, she is red-cheeked, and I know that we have been running. She leans across me, lights the candles, and the flames flicker on the walls like the reflection of water, transforming the brick. Far away, a whistle and the bark of a dog, and the bunker no longer feels safe, not anymore. I watch Nina, the set of her mouth and how her eyes have grown hard. There is something I want to say, but whatever it is, I keep inside me. With a finger, I trace my name in the earth. *Heidi*, I write, and beside it, I inscribe a muddy heart. Nina looks up, her teeth caught on her lower lip, and she gives me a half smile, a sad smile, and the sadness in me answers it.

The memory goes adrift, and I'm back in the bedroom with its blue walls and carpet, its clean, uncomplicated lines. It's okay, I tell myself. It's over, and in time, it will pass. I take my hands from my face and place them beside me on the bed. Jason is downstairs with the clatter of pans and a CD playing.

Breathing in shakily, I reassess the room: the yellow of the dish is benign now and the bunker recedes, but not quite. The smell of the grass is in my nose, and I feel the bunker's crouching shadows. Just as I believe it's over, my head grows hotter and hotter, and I am ripped from the safety of now back to the place that sits at the centre of what I have become. I am lying on the ground, where a single candle bears a thumbnail of fire. Pain claws at my head. I try to fight it, but it comes harder, pulling panic into my chest, squeezing my lungs tight, and this time, when the pain comes thundering into my skull, I am paralysed. The earth is cool beneath me, and there is a darkness on my skin. I move my lips, but no words come. Then, a hand, long fingered and sharply knuckled, looms above me, and I see what it holds. Blood and strands of hair are caught on the surface of a brick. I try to raise my arm and push it away, but I am pinned, helpless. As I watch, the brick pauses in its momentum, and then begins its terrifying return towards my head.

When the memory finally passes, I gasp. My heart beats at

terrifying speed, and I lie back on the mattress and wait for the panic to recede. The ceiling above is shades of white and gold. The smell of onion and garlic drift up, and I remind myself that what I experienced is 15 years gone, but the memory burrows deep into long-forgotten passageways, opening doors on its way. And, for an instant, I get a sense of who I was before, knitted into the safety of my family, knitted into my trust of the world about me.

I turn over and bury my head in the pillow and weep. I don't have the strength for what is happening, but when the tears cease, I remember Anna. I cannot bear to think what happened next, but I owe it to her to put them all where they belong. And, as Jason said, I am probably the only living witness. I get up and open the curtains, see the ghost of a fog weave between the branches of trees and lights from the house opposite. I think of Nina and what I now know and feel the pain of my betrayal.

At the front of the house, Nina and I part ways.

"I'll come and see you in a bit," I say. "Before we go." And I watch her retreating figure as she steps into the hall. With a sigh, I enter my own house. Anna is watching a cartoon on the television.

"Danielle has a stomach bug," she says.

"Has she?" I am not in the least interested. "Where's Mum?"

Anna is lying on her belly, her eyes glued to the dancing screen and ears deaf to my question. She is swinging her calves backwards and forwards in the air, her feet neat in their red shoes; her fingers play with the plastic Barbie necklace at her neck. Next to her is Boo. I shrug, feeling a momentary affection. "Here." And I throw her my last packet of sweets.

"Oooooh." Her eyes open wide in excitement, and she gives me a toothy grin. "Thanks Heidi!"

Mum is in the kitchen. "Hi, love, all right? Danielle has a tummy bug."

I lean against the cupboards. "Anna just told me."

"You okay? You look tired."

"I'm fine."

"Give your old mum a hug." I let her take me in her soft arms. Although I stand stock still, unyielding to her, I take comfort in the warmth of her. I long for the time before I knew about Nina, before Ken took me in his car.

"Mum," I moan and flick off the soapy water that she has dripped on to my skirt, but I have a little smile on my face.

"Grrr." She dips her hands into the washing up bowl and comes out with more bubbles, making monster noises.

"Shhhh!" Anna shouts, and Mum raises her eyebrows.

"It's the hottest day so far. I hope you put some sun cream on." She frowns at my arms, which are pink. "Well, put some on, if you're going out again."

"Yes, Mum," I say, and leave the kitchen to go upstairs.

"And don't forget the back of your neck this time."

I sigh as I walk up the narrow stairs and lie on my bed. Heat hangs heavily in the room, and I smell dust and the fabric of the curtains. There is not even the slightest breeze; it is airless. Dread makes each movement feel rehearsed.

Getting up, I look out of the window on to the back garden where the grass is brown and weeds have overgrown the borders. Leaning my elbows on the sill, I gaze out and wish that I were somewhere else, that I was someone else, and wonder how, in the course of just a few months, my life has been twisted into something so terrifying.

2016

HEIDI

As the bus passes through Riverbridge, I am pricked, once again, by the memory of Nina handing me a package, and I recall the urgency of her tone. *"If I don't come back,"* she'd said. But it wasn't just Nina who failed to return. I didn't return either. I must have hidden the envelope, and I begin to burn with the desire to know. She had written a diary naming so many of the men who abused her, perhaps this was even more incriminating.

A quarter of a mile ahead is the industrial estate and the unit that contains what is left of my family's belongings. Is it possible the envelope is somewhere there? I open my phone and consider ringing Denise or Jason, but I am nearly at the bus stop, and, before I know it, I am standing and pressing the stop button.

The world is nearly black outside, and when my feet touch the pavement, I disturb the lightest drifting of snow. Pulling my coat closer around me, I shift my bag to one shoulder and begin to walk along the street. It's silent, and I scan my surroundings, peering into the shadows to see if I am followed. I pass a row of empty buildings and turn into one of the roads that feed the estate. In the distance, the arch of the railway bridge catches the moonlight like the spine of some prehistoric beast.

As I enter the network of buildings, the smell of oil and the nearby Thames hangs in the air. The tarmac has disintegrated, and ice has formed in the rutted hollows. I'm now in a maze of properties: offices, a printing company, the Post Office's parcel depot, a car repair workshop. I follow the pavement and take another turn. Storage Solutions is tucked between a dairy and an area of garages. As I get further from the road, I'm conscious of the sound of my heels.

Most of the buildings are now deserted, and I question the sanity of this impulsive decision. I take out my phone, but there is no signal.

Eventually, I reach a gated area and see the lighted mobile office with relief. The security officer is watching a screen set high on the wall. I knock on the door, and he signs me in and then, after putting on a coat and hat with unhurried boredom, takes me to the unit.

The forecourt is lit by an overhead light, and when I look up, snow is turning in its beam. We wind a path through the buildings, eventually coming to a padlocked door, and I am pointed up a narrow set of metal steps. Wind blows a drift of polystyrene shapes and sawdust across the floor. Cobwebs gather between the struts of the stairway, and our steps echo in the chill. Without a word, he turns, shutting the door with a clang behind him. I climb two floors until I reach number 2041.

Inside, the room is illuminated by a naked bulb, and I gaze round at the familiar objects: chairs and tables are stacked in corners along with the partially dismantled frames of beds. The underside of a sofa has rotted or been nibbled by small creatures, and foam spills out across the floor like spume. On top of the sofa, an ironing board and table lamps rest precariously.

One whole area is piled with books, ornaments, and kitchen items, and there are bags of clothes and bedding. I have been here so many times, trying to make sense of what I see. Today I try to pin something to the memory of the package, but it fails.

Where do I start? I sink into the armchair by the door and close my eyes. The distant scents of childhood are diluted in the air, but I catch them and hold on to them, cling for an instant to the remote sense of belonging they bring.

Across the room, one of the bin bags spews out the sleeve of a jacket that I remember my mother wearing, and when I go over to shove it back in, the hem of a flowered dress that must have been Anna's is just underneath. My brain tries to process a sudden assault of memories. There are too many things here that represent the full stop at the end of my childhood.

I visualise the white envelope Nina gave me, and my eyes drift to where my bedroom wardrobe and dressing table are. It occurs to me that, if I hid anything, it would surely have been in my bedroom. Moving chairs and a rug out of the way, I go through the drawers and shelves thoroughly. Nothing. I begin a systematic search but am constantly distracted by objects that bring back other recollections: a curtain fabric, a wooden box full of buttons, the cover of a fairy tale book.

Finally, I sit with a pile of schoolbooks. My head aches. Perhaps whatever it was, was discovered at the time. Would the police have searched the house, or did my mother find it?

I glance down at my watch with a yawn. It is nearly 9.30, and Jason will be concerned if I don't return soon. As I fling the schoolbooks down, they knock the piano and one of the keys gives a dull toll.

My skin shivers. I cross quickly to the piano, pushing away the boxes that block my path, and I pull at the wooden frontage above the pedals. This is where I first hid the photograph I stole of Maria. I remember now. My fingers tingle with expectation, and I crouch down and work at the side of the panel. The wood is cold to the touch, but it doesn't take much to lever it out. Jammed inside is the envelope.

My heart jars. Outside, I imagine the black Thames and the empty pavements. Anxiety prickles on the back of my neck. I pull out my phone again, but there is still no signal. Turning the envelope over, I decide to open it. It is sealed with Sellotape that has yellowed and come away, leaving a dark band of dried glue across the opening. Inside is a videotape and a slim book. Opening the cover, I see it contains a list of names and addresses.

Is this them? Some of Nina's urgency reaches me across the passage of time, and I think about whoever delivered the rabbit. Is *he* in here?

The cold has found its way deep into my bones, but the thought of leaving and returning to the road fills me with agitation. I'll go to the security guard and ask him to call a taxi. Stuffing the envelope into my bag, I turn out the light and lock the door. My feet ring on the metal treads as I descend. When I push open the doors, I find myself in a changed world. Flakes swirl in the security lights, and the pavement is blanketed in snow.

But when I look down, I see the imprint of someone else's feet. I had not heard anyone enter the building, but perhaps it's the security guard making sure everything is in order. I begin to walk back to the mobile office. As I reach the forecourt, I see, with dismay, that the hut is empty.

I scan the area, but it's silent. Then I hear a sound behind me. I'm about to call out when instinct makes me squeeze between two vans and out of sight. My breath strains against my lungs. My eyes hurt from searching the spaces.

I see a man move into the light, where he seems to be carved out of the backdrop. I know instantly from his build he is not the security guard. When he turns, and I see the balaclava, I freeze. Through the mask, I feel the intensity of his purpose as he looks across the scattered snow. With alarm, I realise that he will be able to see my footprints.

I zigzag through the parked vans until I reach a gravel road that stretches between the buildings and the river. The surface has not been able to hold the snow, and I begin to run along it, hoping I have time before he finds me. Ahead, I see the dark mouth of one of the railway bridges. Before I enter, I turn and see him emerge from the parked vehicles.

I race further into the darkness, my footfalls amplified by the arched roof. There seems no end until, suddenly, I am on the disused railway line where, once again, snow cleaves to the spaces between the rails. There are fields and, beyond that, the river. Everywhere is white.

The hollow sound of him entering the tunnel gets louder. Desperately looking for somewhere to run, I see that, built into the brickwork behind me, is a set of steps and I grab the handrail and rush to the top. From here I can see the strobing of headlights from the main road. I leap awkwardly across the sleepers, towards the line of cars and stop only once to look down.

There is nothing, but then he emerges into the field, his body rotating to take in his surroundings, studying the untouched snow. Just before I turn away, he lifts his head and sees me. For a moment the world stops. I feel the energy strung between us, as tight as a violin string, but I'm too far away for him to catch me now.

When I reach the main road, panting and breathless, there

are more people — late night shoppers, a group of young men on a night out, and people going into the Bingo Hall. I dart in after them and lock myself in a toilet cubicle. Two women chat at the sink. I hear the spritz of a perfume bottle.

Putting my hand into the bag, I feel the edges of the tape through the envelope. I wonder what is on it that wasn't in the photographs.

My heart begins to calm. I take out the phone and call a taxi and send a text to Denise. And then I wait, listening to the sounds of people coming in and out, doors swinging, the flush of toilets and burr of the drier.

When I think the taxi should be near, I leave the bathroom, scanning the hall for someone that could be him. I slip outside to the pavement. The taxi is ahead, and I can't help but run towards it, my heart racing.

Then, out of nowhere, I feel the impact as something slams into me. My arm is wrenched. I hear someone scream as I hit the ground. Winded, I cannot move. Tears start behind my eyes. When the numbing shock has passed, pain filters into the nerves of my arm.

A woman is crouching beside me, her eyes round with concern. "I couldn't stop him. He took your bag."

2001

HEIDI

"Nina." I'm standing in the small bedroom that she shares with Danielle.

"Shhh." She points at the humped form in the bed, dark hair straggling across the pillowcase. Taking my arm, she leads me to the bathroom. Here the heat is trapped, and I feel its damp thickness in my lungs. A fly hums persistently from behind the blinds. Nina pulls the door shut.

"Heidi, Ken doesn't want you at the bunker, so you have to go first. Can you just go now and pretend you weren't expecting to see me up there? When we arrive, say that you went up there to be by yourself."

I want to say no and feel the terrible dread of going alone, but I gather my courage, remembering that it's my actions that brought us here. "Okay. But when are you coming?"

She tugs at the hair on the nape of her neck and gazes at the light in the frosted glass. Her eyes have a greenish tint.

"Soon, stop worrying."

"I'm not," I lie.

"Nina," I hear Danielle's voice from the bedroom.

"Ugh," Nina frowns. "She's got a tummy bug, but I just can't be bothered with her today. Look, see you in a bit." And suddenly, her eyes meet mine for a final time. Something passes between us that surpasses fear — something that is fused in years of friendship. I have an image of her crouched over a pot of mixture we made using Mum's perfume, flour, and blackcurrants from the garden. She has blue stains around her lips. "Let's drink it. It's magic," she says and dips a finger into the mess with something like glee.

A profound tenderness for her bruises my heart, and I put my arms around her, and she leans into me. A momentary softening and something breaks from her throat.

"Wish me luck," she whispers, croakily, so quietly that I hardly hear. Before I can reply, she has gone back to the bedroom, and I walk to the top of the stairs looking down at the hall where the front door has been left open. It is time. And the sunlight beckons me outside.

2016

The air in his flat smells empty. And as he walks to the kitchen, he feels as if he makes no impact on the molecules around him. From a bottle, he pours himself a triple whisky. That is as much as he will have now. Later, he will drink more, otherwise he may not be able to control what happens in his head.

He sits with only the light from the window and looks down at the envelope in his hands. This is what he really wanted all along, this memory in Heidi's head.

Taking a swig from the glass, he tips the contents of the envelope into his lap.

Over the years, The Chief has been careful. There is no question of that. More than careful, orchestrating things like an invisible conductor, allowing only the notes of the orchestra to leave their marks on the score.

Only once did he witness what lay half-hidden in his soul. It had been summer and the day before his fifteenth birthday. He had wound down the windows to let the hot air into the car. The smell of baked earth and sweet crops, the sound of a jazz piano from the radio.

As they travelled though the countryside, the woods at the edge of the road grew darker and the sun set, pooling to shadow. He had felt so privileged to be there in the expensive vehicle with the scent of leather.

The house had emerged at the end of a winding drive, many windowed and immaculate, with pillared steps to a double front door.

"Is this yours, too?" he had asked.

The Chief had laughed. "Not mine. One day, eh?"

He remembers how his feet shifted on the gravel and the sound of the bell in the spaces beyond.

The man who answered was familiar, and he had felt the burn of intense dislike on his skin.

They had passed through the hall and into a huge room, where a football match played out on a television. French doors billowed cool air, and the curtains seemed to dance in the breeze. He had felt suddenly cheap and dirty, glancing down at his trainers to see if he had walked in mud, and wondered whether he should have removed them at the door.

He cannot recall much of the conversation, because he was sent to the kitchen and told to wait. At first, he had sat at the table and lit a cigarette and tried to imagine what it might be like to own such a property. He had examined the sleek cupboards with crystal glassware and looked out to the vast garden.

The sounds of the game drifted backwards, but he had only been half aware. Outside, an owl called, and he went through the back door to stand in the cool air. Silence such as he never experienced at home.

The other noises came out of nowhere, and he had been

suddenly alert, crept to the hall and listened — the roar of the crowd as a goal was scored — but his chest tightened. In the following hush, he heard it again, a cry and a thump, and he stepped out to stand outside the sitting room, where the door was a little open. His heart banged, and he peered through the crack.

The man who owned the house was on the floor in a bloody mess, and The Chief was leaning over, sweat and spittle on his face, a frenzy in his eyes. A hammer swung from one hand. He had moved back, in alarm but continued to watch, transfixed. The thing on the floor was just a body now, no longer a person, but still the mania continued. Something cold had slithered deep into his marrow at each pointless blow.

He had paced back against the wall, which, in spite of the heat, was cool to his neck. Is this why they had come? To kill this man? He looked around at the grand vases and the lip of the white banister that curved away to a staircase.

That was then. Many years ago. A phone call, instructions to clean up, and the smell of sweat and blood in the car.

He had not dared to ask, but he could feel The Chief's satisfaction beside him, and finally he had turned, distracted momentarily by a clot of something on his white collar.

"Why?"

The Chief had said. "If you want to play, you play nice. You play by my rules," he had winked. "Just remember that. But I know *you'd* never betray me." And he had placed one of his tanned hands on his leg and patted.

"Did he betray you?"

The Chief had sighed heavily. "He was too greedy. It wasn't enough. He wanted more, and that's dangerous. Much too dangerous, even for the likes of me."

And he had laid his head upon the seat rest and stared

blackly out of the window, the thump of the hammer replaying in his head.

The contents of the package, which are losing the chill of the outside world, will be exchanged for a renewed sense of security. He can almost see the blue eyes opening into an expression of surprised wonder and love. It is those eyes, that expression, that hold him in place. He is like a man spinning in the seat of a fairground ride, rotating endlessly around the gravity of his benevolence.

He opens the address book and turns it page by page. The names rise up inside him, recalling faces, some long forgotten. There are addresses, too. And at the end, a list of numbers — bank accounts. He recognises the careful writing. It's The Chief's.

What is here would bring The Chief crashing to the ground. He hardly dares to feel the power it holds, and now he understands his hunger to discover Heidi's secrets. Had he known? Or had it been a wild guess?

Perhaps he could save this for a later date, a later time, when he needs something to lean up against. For a moment, he imagines keeping the secret, but knows that it would be impossible. One look into those clear irises and the truth would slip from him like a drop of water clinging to the stem of a leaf.

He puts down the book and takes the tape in his hands, feeling the rattle of the wheels, and wonders what it contains. The Chief would expect it to remain unexamined, as a point of trust, but his attention is propelled across the floor and to the screen of the television.

As he walks silently over the carpet, the terrible audacity of what he is going to do seems to still his blood. Then, back on the chair, he presses play. The blank screen twitches then begins to flicker. The wheels clatter and become a soundless rotation. He leans forward, mouth apart, and the scene shivers to life.

The narrow shoulders beneath the boy's face are rigid, and the camera takes its time. The Chief moves into the screen, returning twice to adjust the angle of the lens. The room is familiar — he can recall the grey walls and white woodwork. He remembers the small splash of paint on the ceiling canopy, executed by a careless hand.

He is transfixed by what he sees. The boy's dark eyes are large and long-lashed. They look bruised against the white skin. His heart clenches with the effort of holding back his responses.

When it is over, the boy lies inert, floppy. The Chief gets up, stretches and turns to the camera with a smile. And slowly, with him out of the scene, the boy's lids open and stare into nothingness, shock rendering them empty. He knows that emptiness. He knows where it comes from. He remembers.

His breath comes out in a rush. The boy's eyes are empty because he had not been there when it happened. He had drifted away, up to the halo of ceiling light, looking down. The boy didn't believe what he was seeing. Much later, with the pain fossilised inside him, no quantity of cuddles and ice cream had helped. At what point had the boy's absence in that moment come to be a perpetual state of being?

He rises from the chair, the edges of his consciousness catching on to new sensations. So this is how it had been done. He understands it now. He recalls the room, but little else of those early episodes. What happened there was smothered, wrapped in strawberry ice cream and presents. But the evidence is here. And for the very first time, he sees it as it really was and recognises the dreadful impact.

What happened under the muted light was an act of devastation, and something was perpetually changed. The thin, sweet taste of ice cream fills his mouth now, and he vomits over his clothes and on to the floor. The recording has ceased, and the black screen rolls across the television.

His mind spasms, and some of the feelings he could not experience as he drifted near the light fitting, looking down on that first assault, come to bury themselves in his gut. At some point, the only power he had left was to turn those brutal acts into something else and become complicit. When had that moment come?

Because he has always believed himself a willing participant, special. But the truth is there on the screen, in the disbelief that renders the boy's eyes so vacant.

He remembers now the terrible helplessness. His hands tremble, and he thinks of him and realises that he has finally been ripped clean from the chain that shackles him. Like a dead weight, he lies on the carpet, his life falling around him — an avalanche of confusion, the smell of vomit and whisky, and rage blistering his thoughts.

There is a squeak and, looking up at the television again, he sees the same room come once more into view. This boy has curly hair and a round face. The walls are now a cream colour, and the curtains that were always drawn are cream, too. Only the silver bedhead remains the same. The same adjustments of the camera, the same leisurely advance, muscles tense. The blonde hair is now silvering, the beautiful face heavier.

This time he cannot watch.

2016

DENISE

Denise looks out on to the town's white roofs. Two policemen are pushing snow from one of the cars, clouds of white breath coming from their mouths. She wraps her hands around the mug of coffee, even though she's warm. The heating in the station has finally been fixed.

The phone rings, and Denise puts down the cup and picks it up. The voice is husky with a hard edge. Grabbing her coat and bag, she pops her head into the investigation room and tells them where she's going.

It's late afternoon, and already the sky is turning pink at the edges. Denise hurries across the pavement and through the café door to where Maria is sitting at the back, her shoulders slightly hunched. She turns with a start when Denise enters. Denise orders a coffee and cake and sits down on the bench opposite Maria, placing her handbag on the seat beside her.

Maria's eyes are slightly bloodshot, and Denise can smell vodka.

"Thank you for agreeing to meet me. It can't have been easy."

"I hate police stations."

Denise remembers Maria's police history — picked up for soliciting at the age of 14, among other things, and she has seen the photos. She is not surprised.

"Heidi said you could be trusted."

"I hope so."

Maria stares off into the distance. "You want to know if I have names, right?"

"Your testimony could help put some of these criminals behind bars. We take sexual exploitation very seriously. I get the feeling that things were different when you were young."

She shrugs her thin shoulders.

"Have you been away somewhere? You took an impromptu holiday after Heidi saw you."

"Yeah, I went away." Maria's eyes slide to hers, and Denise sees a flicker of uneasiness.

"Is there someone you're afraid of?"

She gives a humourless laugh and looks down.

Denise waits, the hum and whirr of the coffee machines breaking the silence. The waitress places the coffee and cake on the table. When she has gone, Maria looks up.

"Heidi said you had reopened the case on Nina."

Denise nods. "We have, and that can't be easy for you either."

Maria traces a finger across the table.

"Did you know Nina well?"

"Kind of. She was there. We would have a fag together."

"Do you know anything about her murder?"

"Heidi told me Ken did it."

"He's in custody now, Maria. He's claiming that he didn't kill her, that Nina was already dead when he found her."

"He would do, wouldn't he?"

"Ken says that it was Brandon Velker who took Anna. Did you know him?"

Maria takes in a breath and nods.

"What was he like?"

"He was powerful." There is a shiver of fear in Maria's eyes.

"Powerful?"

"He kept himself apart, but people were afraid of him."

"How do you mean?"

"He was dead rich. I saw him a few times. He was softly spoken but there was something about him. He scared me. He had money and the others looked up to him, followed his lead. He was protected."

"What do you mean?"

"With the sort of money he had, he could pay anyone off. He boasted about how he was beyond the law, how he had senior officers in his pocket."

"Did he run the organisation?"

She pauses, plays with the edge of her saucer, "No, there was someone they called The Chief. I think he pulled the strings."

"Did you ever hear The Chief's real name?"

She shrugs. "I only saw him once or twice. He kept himself separate."

"Do you know any more about him that might be useful? Could you work with a police sketch artist?"

She gives a thin laugh. "I can't remember now what he looked like, but I always got the impression he was one of you. A copper." She looks at Denise angrily through narrowed lids, and heat floods Denise's face.

"How did you get that impression?"

Maria frowns. "I can't remember now. Maybe it was said, or maybe I just assumed."

Denise nods thoughtfully. The odds are stacking up in favour of it being someone on the inside. "And how did they get to you, Maria?"

Maria's skin reddens now, and she bites down on her lip. "Me and Mum lived with my uncle. He was one of them. He knew them. They find each other," she finishes.

"I'm sorry. Did your mum know?"

"Her? If she did, she turned a blind eye. Who else was going to house and feed us?"

"Where is your uncle now?"

"He met a woman and emigrated. Ten years back or so."

Another one who will be hard to find. "And the day that Nina was murdered, Maria, do you know what happened?"

"No, I don't, and anyway, they're all liars. You can't trust anything they say."

Denise acknowledges that this is probable. "Do you know what happened to Anna after Brandon took her?"

"If he was the one who took her, then you know what happened to her." Denise is taken aback by the sudden savagery of Maria's tone and the anger that glitters in her eyes. "Anna will be long dead by now, and I hope for her sake that it was quick."

"What did they say about Velker?"

She looks away. "Before Anna, there was a rumour." Maria falls silent.

"Go on."

"I don't know. You can't believe rumours."

"Maria. I can promise you that all this is confidential."

She sighs. "There was a rumour that he took another girl."

Denise is chilled. "Do you know what the name was?"

"Holly. Her name was Holly Watts."

Denise clenches her hands tightly. "Was there anything else?"

Maria shakes her head, and her shoulders sink. "They were monsters. All of them. Ken, Watson, my uncle..." She reels off a list of names. "The things they did... Anna is dead." Her hand trembles. "You didn't honestly think that she would be alive, did you?"

"We suspected it was unlikely."

She takes a deep breath. "So you have Ken? What about the others?"

"We have five people in custody at the moment, but we know there are more out there. The other victims? You knew Nina, but did you know any of the other girls or boys?"

"Not really. I knew a lot by sight, but I couldn't tell you who they were."

"So why did you first get friendly with Nina?" she asks curiously.

She gives a sad sigh. "One day, we had this... there was a session, and afterwards Nina gave me a note, just her number on it." She gives a thin laugh. "They would have battered her, if they'd known. We weren't allowed to talk to each other, but Nina was... Nina didn't seem to care."

"And you met up?"

"I went to that den of hers. The one where she was killed."

"What did you talk about?"

Her expression is distant now, recalling that day. "She wanted to talk about Holly Watts. She was in the news, and Nina wanted them to be punished. She had to do something that would stop it."

"Such as?"

"She said we should go to the newspapers."

"Is that what she planned?" She thinks of the photographs, perhaps never intended for the police.

Maria shrugs. "I said I didn't want to know, and anyway the papers would only believe her if she had proof."

"But she had proof," Denise says quietly.

"I know that now." Maria's face grows hard. "But you think I would've let her give them pictures of me?" Her shame falls between them.

"No, I don't think that would have been easy."

"Those pictures of me. Can you, can you get them back? Get them destroyed?" And Denise feels her pain, but that's not how it works. She shakes her head.

"Do you hear about any of them still?"

"No. I got out a long time ago."

"Of course. One thing, after Anna went missing, Brandon also went off the radar, and we still can't trace him. Any idea where he might be?"

"Oh." She's thoughtful now, drains her cup, and then she leans forward. "After Anna went missing, they were all edgy, lots of whispering and stuff. We all knew or guessed it was to do with Nina and Anna. Brandon was always in the background, but I heard him mentioned more than once, and we all thought he was probably the one that took Anna. I even..." she gives a sad smile, "I even hoped that something so big would mean it was too dangerous to continue, and they would leave me alone."

"And did you see him again."

"I'm not 100% sure. But now you mention it, no, I don't think I did."

Denise's phone begins to ring, and she fishes in her bag and mutes it. When she looks up, Maria is studying her with suspicion and doubt.

"I really appreciate you coming today, and what it must have taken."

Maria shrugs.

"Would you be prepared to talk to us again? Help us compile a list of names, look at some face shots? These criminals, they rely on the terror they instil in their victims to keep them from prosecution. They don't deserve to get away with it."

"Yeah, well you'd have to be one of their victims to understand that wouldn't you." Her tone is defensive.

"There is a lot of help out there if you want it. Do you want me to give you some names of people you could talk to?"

"I'm fine just as I am."

"Are you Maria?"

For a moment the mask slips, and Maria is still a child, trapped in a terrifying world. She gets up, fumbling with the buttons on her coat. Under the harsh lights, her skin and hair are painfully dry.

Denise passes her card. "I'm here anytime. Anytime you want to talk."

Maria nods, mumbles something, and begins to walk away, but halfway to the entrance she stops and returns, leans down to meet Denise's face. Denise can see the tiny, burst vessels in her eyes.

"The Chief," she pauses, bites her lip, "the one who ran it, like I said, I know he was a copper. His name was Charlie. But this never came from me, right?" And she turns and makes her way to the exit.

Back at the station, Denise is unable to settle. She gets up and gazes through the window at the darkening sky. Rooks have gathered on the church eaves. Something of Maria still sits inside her, a fold of sadness and impotence. How many other Marias have they failed? A policeman? Charlie? The idea is deeply disturbing.

And Brandon, did he kill Anna, or is the truth still waiting somewhere? There are still no bodies, though there is a forensic team covering the grounds of Brandon's Oxfordshire property.

Running a hand across her mouth where the sugar from the cake feels suddenly too indulgent for such tragedy, the weight of their discoveries rises up in her chest. She thinks of Heidi's guilt, Jason's anger, and now Maria — chipped thin by her experiences.

2016

HEIDI

Sitting up in bed, I rub my skin where a deep bruise is beginning to stain my upper arm. The house is quiet, and I wonder if Jason is up. Last night, there had been a sense of sombre celebration. Scott and Danielle had come round, and although the tape and book had been lost, more arrests were imminent and, somehow, it was as if the monsters were finally being led to their cages and the truth would soon be revealed.

But even through the thin triumph, Nina's unmasked murderer and Anna's disappearance were with us in the room, a dark and angry space that could not be ignored. Everything was minutely discussed, and I was not surprised to hear the vehemence with which they all agreed that Ken was the killer. Nobody trusts his account. I kept quiet about my doubts and wonder if they come from somewhere else — the buried truth. I shiver.

But I can't bear to stay here any longer. When Jason or Danielle talk of Anna, they talk of her as dead, as I do, but somehow, each time, it's like having to relive that pain one more time.

I open the curtains to the morning and imagine layers of black earth and the tangled roots of trees. I imagine Anna, a cluster of undiscovered bones, and experience a fierce jealousy for Nina's grave. Laying the suitcase on the bed, I begin to pack. As much as I have been grateful for Jason's hospitality and his concern, I long again for my own space, for the familiar shabbiness of my own sofa, and the quietness of my flat. My life is full of silences, and I like it that way.

At the bottom of the suitcase, I find the envelope of photocopies I made and give a start. In all of this, I had forgotten them, and just the sight of it takes me back to the crumbling bunker and the expression of desperation on Nina's face. I grimace, put it back, take it out again. I think about the conversation that had taken place the night before, the agony of not knowing, the bewilderment Jason felt when I gave the pictures to Denise and did not let him see them first. What do I do? Do I owe it to Jason to let him see? Or do I owe it to him to keep him from ever seeing? I study the ones of Nina again — the gap where I cut her out.

From my make-up bag, I take my nail scissors and I make the gap bigger, removing Nina further from the scene. I do the same with Maria and the male victims, then I gather what is left and return them to the envelope. Now, only the blurry faces of the men are left. After tidying the room, I look out of the window once again to where a police car pauses outside.

Downstairs, there is a scribbled note from Jason. He won't be back till later. Church bells clamour on the winter air.

I put the envelope on the table and begin writing a letter.

The doorbell rings.

I look up and see that the police car has passed. Perhaps I should pretend nobody is home, but it rings again, more insistently, and I walk to the door and peer through the spyhole.

"Heidi? It's the police," calls a deep voice.

Still, I don't unlock the chain.

"We have pictures of the man we think attacked you last night. We want you to come in and identify him."

"I never saw his face," I say.

"We think he's the one that has been watching you. If we show you some suspects, we are hoping that one of them might be familiar."

"Do I have to do this now?" I look back at the table to my half-finished letter.

"We would be very grateful, Heidi. I'll hold up my badge."

I squint again through the spyhole. He stands back, and I see his clean and handsome features.

"Okay, I'll just get my coat." I collect my things and scribble a PS to Jason about where I am, but hopefully I'll be back before he returns to say a proper goodbye.

The policeman opens the car door for me with well-practised courtesy. He smells of expensive aftershave. "Thank you, Miss Bevan. It's certainly a nippy one." There is just a trace of West Country to his voice.

"Yes." I wrap the scarf around my neck.

In the seat, I turn and take a quick look at his profile. There is something familiar about it, but I can't recall from where.

"Do you think the video and book is what they have been after all this time?"

"I think it's possible."

"Have you found the tape?"

"Unfortunately, no."

"Has there been any more at Velker's property to prove that Anna was there?" I don't say her body, but that is what I am thinking.

"I'm sorry. We're still searching, but we may never find the graves." His voice is full of regret.

Grief. Not now — later, when I am back in my own bed. I hold the pain back like Canute at the edge of the relentless sea. We pass through the town and hit the duel carriageway. My arm throbs.

"Do you work with Denise?"

He swivels in his seat and smiles. His teeth are neat and his blue eyes, which are lined but still clear, crinkle at the corner. "Yes, I certainly do."

It isn't until the car is shooting towards Riverbridge that his face nudges at a memory and the skin along my spine prickles.

"What's your name?" I ask.

"Barrett. Charlie Barrett."

I don't move. Dread floods my veins. I feel his eyes on me, and I turn to look at him. In my head I hear Nina, the foreboding tone of her voice when she spoke of him. And I remember Joan Finch and her remorse — Chuck. Charlie. Charlie Barrett, the one who befriended Ken and who killed the hedgehog — the policeman to whom I posted the photograph, all those years ago. The one who betrayed me.

He smiles at me again. "Good girl. I thought you'd remember."

2016

It is morning when he finally moves — the beep of the special phone somewhere in the background, the white noise of the television, the stillness of the air. He wants to lie on the carpet forever. Never get up. He feels peeled and displaced. The light through the window makes him queasy. Rolling on to his front, he lays his head on the carpet, which is sticky with bile.

He remembers the boy now, the one with curly hair. This was the boy who took his place in *his* heart. That memory tastes of the steak meal he had been bought. Real steak that The Chief had ordered medium rare.

Blood from the meat had puddled thinly on the plate, and he had not been able to eat the chips that had soaked it up and turned pink.

In the car later, with a hand on his knee, *he* had explained that it was best for them both to move on. He recalls the wrenching terror of being suddenly un-anchored, of being left to drift into the open, alone and without guidance. And at home, when everyone was in bed, he had studied himself in the mirror, running a hand over the soft stubble and the thickening jaw line, seen the red spots that pushed through his skin and knew the truth, and that there was nothing he could do about it. His body had betrayed him. Nothing could turn back time. He was too old. As simple as that. He just became too old.

He does not shower but strips off his clothes and changes into a pair of black trousers and shirt. For a moment, he recalls the man he has trusted for most of his life, the man who has handed out small kindnesses and made them feel like gifts from God. The man who adjusted the lens of the camera as he prepared to commit the first in a long of chain of violations against him.

The phone beeps again, persistent. A voicemail from *him*. The Chief will know about this theft by now.

"Well done. Really, well done." The voice is soft, but he can hear the pale shade of uncertainty, too. "Can you drop the items over at my place as soon as possible? I will have to arrange something special as a thank you."

"And one other thing." He says it lightly, but there is something charged in his voice. "You can forget her now. I have all I need." The way it is said is full of intent.

Heidi.

He looks down at his hands, work worn and grimy, and then up again to meet his face in the mirror, truly meet. For the briefest moment, he sees the boy he once was before it all, but the pain of that is unbearable, and he zips it shut. It is better to be lost, to be neither boy nor man.

2001

HEIDI

My scalp is hot and a trickle of sweat runs from my forehead and into my eyes. It hadn't been too bad at first. The playing field was busy, and, as I advanced deeper into the copse, there were children playing and an occasional family eating a picnic or walking dogs. But as I pass the open trees and approach the woods, I become aware of the growing distance of voices, and that I haven't seen anybody for at least ten minutes. Once, I wouldn't have been conscious of my isolation, but it's different now, and I'm uneasy with the emptiness, ever watchful of approaching men. The relentless heat of the sun bleeds through the canopy of leaves, burning my skin.

As I get closer, my dread increases — the bunker has become the dark soul of everything that has poisoned my life, from the brick that swallows the sun to the cool redolent stillness of the earth. No longer is it a place of refuge, and I feel weary with despair. What will Nina do now? I feel caught in her agony and exposed by my impulsive desire to save both her and myself. They know about me now. Will they hunt me down, too?

Finally, I top the hill. Ahead, the white birches are unmoving, and I have the irrational notion that they are not welcoming me but warning me away.

At the bunker, I kick angrily at the brambles, feeling something tear at my ankle. When I look down there is a chain of blood where the thorn has ripped my skin. At least there are cigarettes, and I crawl past the towels and tug the picnic rug away. Bits of glass, from the broken frame Nina threw, glitter in the weave. From the box, I take matches and light one, filling my mouth with smoke. The carrier bag lay at the entrance — I have no interest in the biscuits I bought, and besides, I have nothing to drink and my throat is dry.

"I'm not going to tell Mum."

I start so violently that I nearly smack my head on the brick archway. The cigarette falls from my fingers and lands on my leg, burning into the skin with pain as bright as the sting of a wasp.

"Anna!" She is standing in front of me, hands on her hips, her hair tied to the side with a tartan ribbon. Her face is pink with heat, and freckles stand out over her nose. I flick the cigarette away and extinguish it. Alarm is now added to the tumult of dread and vulnerability, and I scan the woods behind her for Ken and Nina. Nina will be furious.

"Cigarettes will kill you." She sounds cross, but her eyebrows are raised.

"Well don't tell her, okay? Or I will tell on you."

"I haven't done anything."

"You know you shouldn't follow me. Mum has told you loads of time. For goodness sake, Anna."

"Danielle has a tummy bug, and I wanted to play with you."

"Ugh." I look away. The burn on my leg is red and it hurts.

Anna crouches down and looks at my thigh. "See what happens when you smoke cigarettes." She slumps herself beside me with a prim sigh. Beside mine, her legs look so short, and her little toes are impossibly sweet in the red sandals. I soften, comforted by her closeness.

"Can I have sweets?"

"I don't have any."

"You and Nina always have sweets. What about in your box?"

"You're so bloody nosy. No, there are no sweets."

She is crawling deeper into the bunker, "Is this where you have the cigarettes? Can I light the candles?"

"No. And you've got to go away and hide. Nina is coming up here in a bit, and if she sees you, she'll be really angry, okay?"

She gives me a soulful look and passes me matches. "You light them."

"No."

"If you light them, I'll go... please."

Sighing, I flick the match across the rough strip, wait until the head is afire, and then ignite the wicks. Light flickers on the walls, and Anna crouches close, gazing at the little flames with awe.

Then I hear Nina's voice. "Go away..." Even at a distance, I catch the urgency in it.

Shit. My heart starts to thump, and I peer through the brambles. She isn't far, and I see her half running through the woods towards us. There is someone with her, someone with dark hair, but most of him is obscured by the trees. He catches her shirt in his fingers, pulling her back. They are hidden completely now, shouting, and I can't hear what they say. When she runs out from behind the thicket, I see how afraid she is. Who is it? It isn't Ken. It has to be one of them, one of them come to mete out the punishment they promised. And Anna is here.

Anna looks up from the candle, and a shiver of anxiety passes between us. It's too late to seek refuge outside the bunker. Suddenly, I hear a smack and Nina stumbles, her hand against her cheek, her mouth open in shock. Whoever did it is still out of sight.

"Back there," I whisper to Anna, my burn forgotten, and I point to the rear of the bunker where there is a tiny offshoot. We crawl quickly to the back, where I shove Anna in first.

"Quiet," I whisper, but she does not need telling. She feels my terror. Squeezing in beside her, I try to make my body fit in the enclosed space. Brick makes a barrier to sound, and I hear only the banging of my heartbeat in my ears and the huff of my breath. Beside me, Anna's body is pressed to mine, and I smell the lemony scent of her shampoo. I want to cry.

Anna starts beside me, and I hear the noise of their feet.

"I'm not going anywhere till you tell me the truth."

There is silence.

"Who showed you? Did he?" There is hysteria in his tone, and I hear her squeal again. Something nicks at my memory — his voice.

"Stop!"

"Who have you told?" Slap.

"Nobody. Stop. Please stop." Nina's voice is tight with disbelief. "You knew all this time."

"Who showed you?"

"Nobody. I took them." She is sobbing. "And you've done nothing about it happening to me, too." There is a wild desperation in her voice. "We could stop this together."

"Who else knows?"

"No one, I promise."

"I don't believe you." And I hear his groan. He is wailing, and it is a terrible sound.

Anna stiffens beside me, and then there is a dreadful thud and Nina gasps.

From where I am, I hear his breathing, harsh and desperate and then a choke, the sound of something banging to the ground repeatedly, and then nothing but his whimpering cries. I am too shocked to move; terror has frozen me to the walls. The appalling whimpering goes on and on, and, when it finally stops, it's not relief I feel but something worse. There is a quality to the silence that chills me. And Nina, I cannot hear Nina anymore.

It's then that I remember the lighted candles and the bag with the biscuits.

"Who's there?" His breath seems to stretch through the thick stone as he enters the bunker, and, when he drags me from my hiding place and I try to scream, I am brought to a full stop with the crash of a brick against my temple. His eyes are wild with anguish and a sort of mania. Seeing his face stuns me — how could it be him? I sense the looseness of his control, the looseness of his sanity. Desperation leaks from his skin and into mine.

I lurch backwards, but he drags me out by the feet, earth scraping my back. I try to scramble, but he's pulling me to the entrance, and as I twist and turn, I get a glimpse of Nina's still face.

It is happening too quickly. There are so many things left that I need to do, so many things I haven't said. My whole future seems to shrink before me to this one terrible ending that silences all else. It's impossible that this is my last moment. I haven't prepared for it.

I look up and see the brick coming down again with dreadful slowness but am helpless to stop it. Next to me, on my upper arm, I feel something warm and still and realise, with anguish, that it's Nina's lifeless hand. She is dead. As my eyes close, I think of Anna. He doesn't know she's here. Stay hidden, I beg her, stay hidden. I think of Mum. Mum. Too late. All too late.

2016

He cannot move. His body is welded to the seat. He is aware that he is chilled. It is not necessary to close his eyes to replay the tape in his head, but that is what happens, over and over again. At times, whatever is left of him, drifts away from what he sees and seems to watch from a great distance. At other times, part of him shoots into the skin of his young body and remembers.

He knows that he is broken, but he has always known it. Now he understands he can probably never be fixed. It is too late. What is the point in holding on anymore? Rage takes hostage of his flesh like a disease.

The doorbell rings out against the silence and he gets up, movements stiff and somehow difficult to coordinate, and makes his way into the hall.

As soon as he opens the door, he knows that something has changed.

Jason's face is taut with pain. "Why didn't you tell me, Scott?"

Their relationship has never felt real, how could it? He has never been real himself. But he sees now, too late, that with Jason, with his family, it has been possible at times, to pretend.

Jason holds out a sheet of paper. It's a photocopy, blurred and grainy. He recognises the location, the people there. And as he leans into it, there, half hidden by somebody's arm is the distorted face of a boy. It is so indistinct that he nearly misses it altogether. The image is so poor that unless the face belonged to someone you knew well, you would never recognise it. It would take someone like a brother or a mother to do that.

Shame drenches his insides. Shame for what they did to him. Shame that Jason has seen it. The terror of that discovery still holds him so tightly that he opens his mouth to deny it.

"Scott?" Jason's voice breaks on his name, but love is far too late. "Why didn't you say? Jason's face is appalled. He shakes his head as if he wants to dislodge the truth. There are tears in his eyes. "You never said... you never said anything?" But Scott can see that Jason is remembering Nina's own long silence.

Then something else moves into Jason's face. "Was it Ken?"

"Not Ken." He doesn't want to lie any longer.

"Who? Who did this to you?" Jason's voice breaks, and he slumps into a chair and cups his head.

Scott doesn't answer. He feels uprooted from all his previous understanding. The world lies in pieces that can never be put back together.

Scott hardly knows where to begin. "You don't know me."

"Nina. Nina was being abused, too. Did you know? It must have been the same group. These photos prove it. I know this must be hard, but please talk to me, Scott. If you were being abused by them, you have to go to the police. You're a witness."

Jason doesn't understand at all. It's not Ken, *them*, or even *him* that he's protecting. It never has been. It's always been himself — shielding himself from the shame and the terrible thing that came next.

When Jason raises his head, his gaze flicks to the table and the envelope, browned at the edges and the balaclava that Scott has left carelessly beside it.

Comprehension dawns. "What have you done?" Jason's voice is a whisper. "What do they have on you? How can you be on their side? After what they did to you? After what they did to Ni—" Something in Scott's expression makes Jason pause. "No, not you. Tell me it wasn't you."

But somehow, the truth falls between them. And Scott is back there again, back at the bunker where the sweat that ran into his mouth tasted sharp, and the brittle sun was too hot, and he could not control the helplessness in his belly. And Jason knows it, too.

"It was you, wasn't it? You killed her." Quieter than a sigh, the truth, more painful than anything Scott can imagine.

And Scott feels the tearing of the memory inside him — the clammy air, the knowledge in Nina's pupils, the terror of her telling, of someone finding out — and the way his desperation took control of him, as if he was only an onlooker as Nina took her final, laboured breath.

How afterwards, he had run down the hill, tears streaming over his cheeks, across the field crowded with white daisies and into the shade of the trees where suddenly, what had happened became real, and there was blood on his hands and the scent of Nina's cheap perfume, and the horror of it had struck him. Nina. He had killed Nina. Then he had killed Heidi. He had wiped frantically at his hands as he ran through the knotted oaks, but half-way down, he had been struck with another thought. Perhaps they were not dead. Perhaps they were okay, and the relief of that was so immense that he stopped. If they were alive, then he would go to the police. He would tell, because Nina being dead now felt worse than being found out. And so he had turned, running back through the fern and towards the bunker. As he ran, the first drops of rain began to fall, tapping gently and then more insistently on the canopy overhead.

But as he neared, he saw with alarm that Ken was there. Ken, crouching over their bodies. If Nina was still alive, surely, she would stir. He could see the soles of her worn sandals. Blood pooled beside her from Heidi's head, and he felt sick and afraid.

Then he heard a voice, and Brandon stepped into the scene. Brandon was taking out a match and a small canister. He was going to burn it down.

They were talking in voices too low to hear, but then they had both looked up, and Brandon had stepped forward carefully to peer into the bunker.

Scott watched as Brandon crouched to enter. Then a scream had rent the air, and Brandon was standing there, a smile on his face and Anna in his arms. Anna. Ken and Brandon had started to argue, Ken tried to grab Anna's legs Anna kicked wildly, squirming in his grip, her blonde hair falling over his forearm. Brandon had his hand clamped tight over Anna's mouth. The fight grew heated. Ken took the canister and sprinkled it over Nina and Heidi and the entrance of the bunker and set a match.

Scott could not move. A curl of smoke rose into the air, like a smudge. The rain pelted down and spots of dark wetness appeared on the dried mud.

And then they were gone, Anna in the crook of Brandon's arm and Ken following behind, as smoke began to billow from the bunker. Scott continued to stand, his body trembling, unable to move.

When Ken and Brandon were out of sight, he had stepped out of the woods and run to the bunker where smoke snaked into the air, and his heart felt swollen in his chest. One look and he knew the truth. There was no return. He would never be able to take it back. They were dead. He had killed them. And in that moment, whatever was left of his soul died like the last gasp of a match-head flame.

And now, as he watches Jason, some of that hot day when he lost what was left of his life returns and opens up a fissure of feeling he thought he could no longer experience. But it is too much to hold. He will surely break now.

Jason begins to weep, and the sound is so terrible that Scott gets up and paces, trying to ram his own emotions back into place.

"So it was you?" Jason says. "Following Heidi all this time? It was all about getting this envelope back? Who wants it so badly? Is it you or someone else?"

The time for pretence is gone. "Charlie Barrett. Do you remember him?"

"Him? But he was good to you. He was always trying to keep you out of trouble. If it hadn't been for him, you would have ended up with a charge sheet. I thought he was one of the good guys." And realisation is born. "Was he the policeman Nina warned me about, the police involvement?" Jason pales. "Shit. Barrett, where is he now? He's still a policeman, right? Does Barrett know about Heidi?"

For the briefest moment, Scott experiences a strange pride for Charlie's cleverness, his immense success, and that he, Scott, had been special to him. "He's the Assistant Chief Constable. He's been following everything about this. He's way ahead of Denise, way ahead of all of you. He played everyone — Ken, the care homes managers," he pauses, "me. And you have no idea how big it is, how wide it stretches."

And suddenly, through the tumult of emotion, The Chief's last words return to Scott with urgency: *You can forget her now. I have all I need.*

Jason looks at his watch, runs an anxious finger across his chin. "Heidi says she was called into the station. That was ages ago." He takes out his phone and turns it in his hands. "Is she going to be all right?"

Scott doesn't answer.

"Scott?" Jason dials a number, and Scott can hear Denise on the other end. Heidi is not at the station.

But Scott is already out the door.

2016

HEIDI

Charlie is back, and I turn my head to look at him. My neck is pinched with agony. I don't know how long I have lain here, but my body is numb with cold. Through the dark panes I see lights at the windows of his house. As I move to look at him, I'm aware of the sticky patch on my cheek where blood has collected beneath it.

He's watching me with a strange intensity. There is a heater on one of the worktops, and he switches it on. The bars turn from grey to orange, and the space is filled with the dry smell of burning dust. Then, with careful hands, he removes his jacket and trousers, placing them on the back of a chair.

I begin to cry. Once I start, I cannot stop. I cry for Anna, Nina, and for myself, and for what he is about to do. As he unfastens the knot of his tie, he gazes at me with a blank expression. Beneath the shirt, I see the muscular breadth of his shoulders, the grey hair of his chest and begin to scream. The gag masks the sound, but I continue, feeling blood rushing to my face and pressing behind my eyes. I kick out with my legs. "No, no, no," I whimper. He's fully undressed now. Bile rises in my throat. Terror solidifies me until I feel nothing else.

He turns away from me, and I see the soft curve at the base of his spine as he pulls on a white coverall suit. His movements are spare and unhurried. Any relief I experience from the delayed assault is suddenly suffocated by a premonition of something that is worse — much, much worse.

When he's finished dressing, he stands before me, and I can think of no other reason why he might be wearing the suit except that he is going to kill me. The skin of my body cringes with the expectation of pain, and my eyes scurry for a weapon. I pray that it will be quick. Then I recall what Joan Finch had witnessed when Charlie had caught a hedgehog at the back of her garden and what they had done to it. He likes pain. He will not hurry.

Suddenly, he is crouched beside me, and I smell his hair and the plastic suit. I am gazing into eyes that carry no sense of what I understand about the world. There is no pity, no emotion, just some strange otherness — the eyes of animals that hunt at night.

I can hear the pulse of my heart, the hum of the heater, and, beyond that, the terrible silence that is waiting to entomb me. Time warps as I grapple to find something that I can cling to in the emptiness of his gaze.

When he touches my head, his finger seems to sink deep into the tissue and into my skull. He pushes back my hair and traces the scars, and then he rises to his feet and opens the case. I see the curved leather of a sheath and then the lethal sharpness of a blade.

Just as the screams once again begin to fill my throat, the door behind him opens and Scott walks in. Scott, *thank God, thank God.*

But whatever I was expecting does not happen. It's all

wrong, because Charlie is smiling, and Scott barely looks at me. The blade shivers in the light.

"Scott." Charlie's voice is moist and warm.

I stare at Scott, his pale cheeks and the beautiful eyes, so like Nina's.

Charlie smiles again, and his hand falls briefly upon Scott's, and then he looks to me and laughs. "Did you think your knight in shining armour had arrived?"

My mind is too full to understand what I am seeing. Relief turns to dismay as Scott finally looks at me, and my attention is drawn to his hands, which are long fingered and supple. The fifteen years between then and now shrink to nothing. I see that hand raised above me, the brick clutched in its palm. I see the tears that pour down his anguished face. My panic. Nina's lifeless skin on my arm. No.

"Thought Scott had come to save you, Heidi? Scott is your masked pursuer. Tell her, Scott."

He looks to me, but his face tells me nothing.

"Where is the tape, Scott?" There is the smallest edge to Charlie's voice. "Why have you made me wait?"

"Don't worry. I have it."

Charlie nods with satisfaction.

There is something in Scott's gaze that makes Charlie take the smallest step back. He cocks his head to one side. "What is it? Is someone on to you?"

Scott is so still, but I feel the burning concentration of him. I tug desperately at my bindings. The floor grazes my skin.

Charlie has put the knife on the worktop, and he moves towards Scott once more. "What is it?"

Scott reaches into his back pocket and pulls out the video-tape, which he places on the bench. Charlie's blue eyes falter.

"I watched it."

Charlie spreads his hands.

"I remembered you," Scott says, and there is something in the way that he says it that gives me pause.

Charlie laughs now, but with less confidence. "You don't need to remember me, Scott. You *know* me. As I know you." His face is soft and considered, full of charm. I can imagine it pulling me along, luring me to places I do not want to go.

"I remembered me."

As I watch Scott, I sense his unbalance. His fingers twist inside each other.

"What?" A fleck of uncertainty slides into Charlie's voice. "What are you trying to say?"

Scott turns from Charlie and looks at me. "I killed her," he says.

But I know already, and it seems like the saddest thing that I have ever heard.

"You?" Charlie says. "*You* killed Nina?" He begins to laugh, shaking his head in bewilderment. "And here was I, thinking all the credit was owed to me or someone in the group." He reaches out a hand to Scott. "It's okay. I'll make it all right. Don't worry about her." He flicks his head to where I lie.

"But what about me?"

"What about you?" Charlie says.

"How do *I* forget?"

Charlie's lips thin. "This is silly talk, Scott. Come with me. We'll go away somewhere and talk it all through. Everything will be fine. We can go anywhere you want, where nobody can find us."

"I didn't want this. I never wanted this."

"But this is who you are." There is hardness in the blue of Charlie's eyes.

"Who I am? I don't know who I am." Tears begin to form at the edges of his eyes. "I've spent my life running from who I am. I'm empty."

"Scott, please. You're overwrought. We'll find somewhere beautiful, somewhere hot. We can talk it all out. I understand you, don't I? Haven't I always been on your side?"

"My side? *I watched the tape.*" Scott picks up the tape and begins to pull the film from its reels.

His eyes dart to the knife, but Charlie catches that look, too. In an instant, the mood in the workshop has changed. Charlie and Scott lunge for the knife, but Charlie gets there first.

There is a moment when neither of them moves — all the energy in the room is sucked into their orbit until they alone are held by time. The air around them shrinks. I watch, transfixed, and the room is filled only with what is between them, then Charlie smiles sadly and leans in towards Scott. Scott doesn't react — he is still held in Charlie's gravity. But in one slick movement, Charlie slips the blade deep into Scott's gut.

Scott starts to fall, knocking tools from the workbench, one arm flung out, clutching at air. As he falls, he turns his head and fixes his dark eyes upon me. Eyes that are heartbroken. He tries to say something that could be sorry, but he hits the ground.

And then, unbelievingly, there are sirens. Charlie cocks his head and pauses to study Scott as he spasms on the floor. His gaze drifts up. He doesn't seem perturbed, and he pulls out a chair and sits. When Denise and the other officers surge into the room, he is humming quietly to himself. Scott isn't moving anymore. Through the door, I see Jason push his way in, a policeman trying to drag him back, and then his cry of pain as he wrestles out of the policeman's grasp and falls on to his brother's body.

2016

DENISE

As Denise walks towards the small gathering, light is beginning to fade, and mist threads the wood beyond. Once again, the house captures the dusk. She considers Jason, Danielle, and Carol, and the new and dreadful truth that they have to swallow.

Mike Tennant and the pathologist are in conversation, their breath steaming in the air. It is impossible to describe the dread that attends such scenes. Dread, but also a vein of excitement that reverberates just beneath the surface. The mood is sometimes jokey, an air of false joviality, but later, in the stillness of their own spaces, without the warmth of each other's presence, the reality will gape wide like the open grave about which they stand, and all the horror will spill out.

Inside the tent, the lights are harsh. She can see the faces of the SOCOs digging, red-cheeked and damp-haired, and the growing pile of soil to the side. The lamp from above throws the grave into relief. As she approaches, her heart is heavy in her chest. She thinks of the families, of the pain the discovery of these bodies will cause. If they had given up hope, they may think that they have accepted the worst, but the reality of the bones will bring fresh mourning.

"Sir?" Denise says.

Mike glances over. His face is worn. "We've found them — finally. Two bodies at the moment."

"Children?"

He nods.

"Any identification?"

"Not yet." He glances at another space in the ground. It's impossibly small.

"There's more?"

"At least another one here, they think. And the dogs reacted in the woods, too."

Through the smell of cigarette smoke, sweat, and desperation, there is the scent of earth and matter, and she visualises the huddle of small bones, tiny teeth, and shudders. Deaths such as these are against nature and civilisation. She is assailed with a rush of pointless rage. An owl hoots from the woods beyond, a hollow sound, like grief.

"We have a name for the other photograph in the bedroom."

She has his full attention now.

"Hanna van Swieten, a Swedish girl who went missing in 1997." She gazes at the wood and wonders how many lost children there are and whether it will ever be possible to find them.

The ancient trees that stretch into the sky, that have been here long before even the house was built, stand dignified above the scene, and a half moon casts a thin light over the frosted ground. There is a profound stillness. It would be a beautiful place to spend an eternity, except for the absence of a marker, an appropriate farewell.

These girls are long dead, but like Heidi, Lynn, and Wendy

Martin, there will be those who need a grave to mark their loss, who will want the bodies of those they cherished laid somewhere undisturbed, somewhere where flowers can be placed, and a name carved upon stone. An acknowledgement forever of a life once lived.

She senses rather than witnesses the sudden change of mood, and they turn together. The group stand alert beside the two diggers, who have stopped what they are doing, and the evening is pitched to a reverent hush until the SOCO gives a nervous cough and adjusts the lamp. Denise can see her taut face in the light. She and Mike walk to the edge of the hole and peer into the cavity. Whatever is there is barely distinguishable from the thick mud around it, but the officer scrapes away at the surface gently with her fingers, revealing a wad of fabric. Denise feels Mike tense beside her, feels the looping of her insides. The light catches something in its focus and the digger looks up. Nobody speaks. Earth is carefully shifted, revealing a pair of red sandals, one strap destined never to be repaired. Her throat tightens. The SOCO returns to her work, brushing away the remaining soil, with a tenderness that makes her heart ache, and, at last, Denise can see, quite clearly, that it is hair, and beyond that the arc of a small but perfect skull.

ACKNOWLEDGEMENTS

No book is written entirely alone, and this one certainly hasn't been. Many, many thanks to the talented Sam Brace of Agora Books for her editorial vision and for her excellent guidance. She has made the whole editing process enjoyable and easy. I am grateful, too, to Peyton Stableford and all the team at Agora who have worked so hard to bring *Monstrous Souls* to publication. I want to thank Anna Morrison for a cover I fell in love with straight away.

Thank you to my wonderful sister, Julia Kelly, who has encouraged me from the start and been with me every step of the way. I have been blessed too in having the almost daily and mutual book support from my dear friend Anita Sloan — who has helped me to unravel so many plot knots and been generous with her advice and expertise when I needed it. It's been a privilege to share the writing journey so closely with these two talented and most lovely of people.

A very special thanks to Danielle Devlin, who used her professional experience to cast a forensic eye over the book, correcting my mistakes and advising me on procedure. If any errors remain they are my own.

Massive love to all my friends @virtwriting on Twitter: a truly fabulous group of dedicated and talented writers, and my second home. They are there every day with advice, support and an endless supply of diverse conversation and insane and irreverent GIFS.

And not least to the group of friends who read the first version of this book and gave me the confidence to write on: Yvonne Richards, Debbie Clarke (and also for the excellent proof reading), Jill Hendy, Teresa Gordon, Helen Bateman, and Rachael Staines.

LOVE AGORA BOOKS?

JOIN OUR BOOK CLUB

If you sign up today, you'll get:

1. A free novel from Agora Books
2. Exclusive insights into our books and authors, and the chance to get copies in advance of publication, and
3. The chance to win exclusive prizes in regular competitions

Interested? It takes less than a minute to sign up. You can get your novel and your first newsletter by signing up at www.agorabooks.co

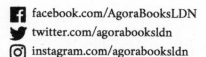

facebook.com/AgoraBooksLDN
twitter.com/agorabooksldn
instagram.com/agorabooksldn